THE
SECRETS
OF
WINTER

ALSO BY NICOLA UPSON

Sorry for the Dead

Nine Lessons

London Rain

The Death of Lucy Kyte

Fear in the Sunlight

Two for Sorrow

Angel with Two Faces

An Expert in Murder

THE SECRETS OF WINTER

A JOSEPHINE TEY MYSTERY

Nicola Upson

CROOKED
LANE

NEW YORK

Copyright © 2020 by Nicola Upson

Published in the United States by Crooked Lane Books, an imprint of The Quick Brown Fox & Company LLC.

Crooked Lane Books and its logo are trademarks of The Quick Brown Fox & Company LLC.

Library of Congress Catalog-in-Publication data available upon request.

ISBN (hardcover): 978-1-64385-634-6
ISBN (ebook): 978-1-64385-635-3

Cover illustration by Mick Wiggins

Printed in the United States

www.crookedlanebooks.com

Crooked Lane Books
34 West 27th St., 10th Floor
New York, NY 10001

First North American Edition: October 2020

10 9 8 7 6 5 4 3 2 1

*For all the readers, librarians and booksellers
who love this series. Happy Christmas.*

MAP OF THE ISLAND

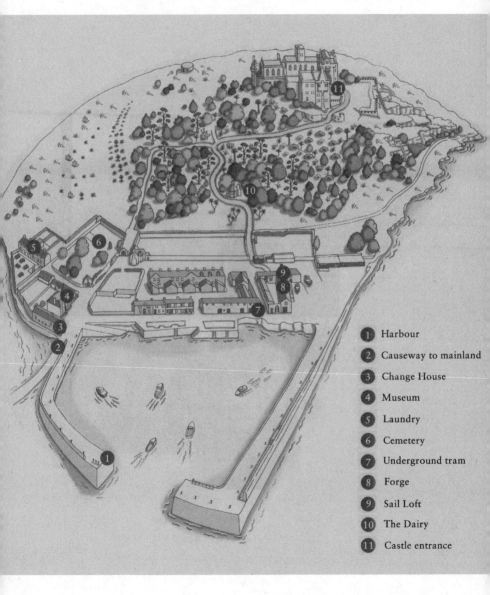

1. Harbour
2. Causeway to mainland
3. Change House
4. Museum
5. Laundry
6. Cemetery
7. Underground tram
8. Forge
9. Sail Loft
10. The Dairy
11. Castle entrance

MAP OF THE CASTLE

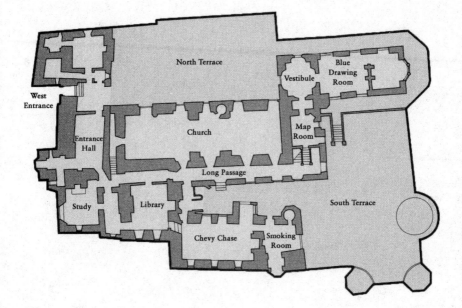

'Will you decide what men shall live, what men shall die?'
Charles Dickens, *A Christmas Carol*

CHRISTMAS DAY, 1920

It was the day that stripped the joy from Christmas, or so he thought afterwards – everything a parody of what it should have been. The snow was dirty and trampled underfoot, the children frightened and cold, and even the robin – perched on a dustbin in the street – refused to sing, complicit in the horror that awaited him inside the house. And then there was her face, of course. For years to come, he would never be able to hear the carol that he was once so fond of without remembering the expression in her eyes, such a stark reminder of how little comfort and joy there really was in the world.

A crowd had already gathered outside by the time he arrived, a young detective sergeant, newly promoted and keen to make his mark. The house was in Notting Dale, a rookery of overcrowded streets and run-down buildings, and although the snow had covered some of the area's shortcomings, it was still a wretched part of the city – one grim, monotonous row after another, untouched by any sort of spirit, seasonal or otherwise. He parked his car at the end of the street where Mollie Naylor and her children had lived, and walked over to the group of neighbours, all silently waiting for something to happen. Pushing his way through the onlookers, he could feel the hostility closing in on him, as cold on his face as the harsh December air. Somewhere over to his left, a man's voice muttered a sarcastic happy Christmas.

A uniformed constable stood by the front door, his face as white as a sheet, and Penrose guessed that he was the local bobby whose misfortune it had been to pass by. 'Who found them?' he asked, after the briefest of introductions.

'The next-door neighbour, sir. His wife heard a bit of shouting last night, but she didn't do anything about it because she was on her own with the baby, and anyway, she didn't want to get involved. Then this morning there was no sign of the children. She couldn't hear a peep out of them through the walls and she thought that was strange, bearing in mind the pandemonium going on in her own house. You know how kids are at Christmas.' He stopped suddenly, as if he had said something inappropriate, and Penrose guessed that the tragedy of what lay upstairs had struck him again, more forcefully than ever. 'Anyway, she sent her husband round to check. The back door was unlocked and he soon found them, although he says he didn't go any further than the first room. I believe him, too. You wouldn't, if you didn't have to.'

'Where is he now?'

'Back at home, sir. Sick as a dog, he looked. Said he wanted to hug his kids. I've told him you'll need a word.'

'And no one else has been in?'

He shook his head. 'No, only me. I thought I was going to have a bit of trouble keeping people out once word got round, but no one's tried anything.'

'That's about the only thing left to them, I suppose – respect.'

'Or fear, sir.' Penrose looked at him sharply, and he shrugged. 'That's what it feels like to me. A woman who could do that to her children . . .'

'It's a bit early to be making assumptions like that, Constable, no matter how likely it looks. Did you know the family?'

'No, sir. Not before today.'

But everyone would know them now, Penrose thought. He thanked the PC and walked past him into the house, closing the door behind him. There was an absolute silence inside, eerie and unsettling, and although he had reproached the constable for saying more than he should have, Penrose knew exactly what he meant. It wasn't respect that he had detected in the people who knew Mollie Naylor, and it wasn't even a familiar antagonism towards the police; it was horror, in its purest form – a superstition of sorts, as if they could be tainted by the grief if they got too close to it, or perhaps simply a reluctant realisation that violence could be dragged from any human heart if the circumstances were bad enough. The stillness was oppressive, and Penrose had to force himself to move further into the room and shake off a feeling of dread. He shivered, knowing that the cold creeping through his bones was something more than the weather and the desperate state of the house had conspired to create.

There was just one room downstairs, a kitchen parlour containing bits of old furniture that had seen better days. The plaster was falling off the ceiling in places, and paper peeled from walls so damp that it was a wonder anyone had bothered to put it up in the first place. A piece of string had been hung from corner to corner to dry the washing, and the floorboards were rotten here and there, where water had repeatedly dripped onto them. Patches of mould gave the house a musty air, mixed with something metallic and sickening that was both out of place here and horribly familiar.

At least the cold was good for something, he thought bitterly; the stench of death in summer would have been intolerable. As it was, the tiny, well-worn clothes still hanging near the hearth were unbearably poignant, and he had to turn away.

The general state of neglect was only to be expected: rents were so low after the war, and housing in such short supply, that landlords had no incentive to carry out even the most basic of repairs. Yet he couldn't help noticing how clean the room was. There was a standing joke among his colleagues that a dark blue uniform would invariably be turned brown by any visit to a slum building, but so far the house was as cared for as the fabric of the building would allow, and this small, defiant hint of pride made the sign above the fireplace – 'God Bless Our Home' – something more than a bad joke.

And then there was the tree – a scrawny, grudging specimen of which Scrooge might have approved, but a tree nonetheless, decorated with love. Penrose walked over to look more closely at the stars and angels fashioned from bits of old material, at the cotton-wool snowman that hung from the top branch, the type of toy that had been so popular when he was a boy. He knelt down to see what was underneath – six presents of varying shapes, all wrapped in newspaper – and couldn't remember ever having seen something so pathetically out of place. What could possibly have happened in just a matter of hours to change this family's fate so dramatically?

There were two envelopes laid neatly on what passed for a kitchen table, perhaps containing the answer to his question, but first he needed to see the tragedy for himself. He climbed the dark, narrow staircase which led directly to the smaller of two bedrooms, and located the first bodies before he had reached the top step. Not even his imagination – fed by the

4

brutality of war and his job – could have anticipated the horror of what he saw. Two little girls – twins, of around seven or eight – were tucked up in bed, their fair hair entangled on the pillow as they lay close together. Penrose could almost have believed they were sleeping quietly in each other's arms were it not for the stain of livid red on their bedclothes. His hand shook as he pulled back the blood-stiffened sheet, but he forced himself to examine the wounds on their throats; the cuts were deep, with the windpipe and jugular veins almost severed in each case. Penrose could only pray that the work had been done too swiftly for the realisation of what was happening to sink in. Anything else was unthinkable. The girls were clothed in matching nightdresses and their likeness made a mirror image of their deaths: pale faces showing the first signs of discolouration, eyes closed to the horror of what had happened. As far as he could see, there were no bruises or other marks on their skin to suggest long-term abuse, and he wondered again what had brought them to this.

Gently he replaced the sheet, noting the chalkboard above the bed on which the days of December had been struck through one by one; what had begun in a flurry of excitement at the approach of Christmas had ended in a mocking countdown to their deaths. Sickened already, he turned to the room next door. It was ridiculous to consider the privacy of a woman's bedroom in a situation like this, but still he hesitated on the threshold, hampered by a reluctance to intrude and a selfish desire simply to turn and run. An infant boy with a shock of blond hair had been thrown across the bed, his throat also slashed through, and a woman lay dead with her head resting on her son's body. In the corner of the room, a drawer on the floor functioned as a crib, and Penrose could just make out a tiny hand amid the grey blanket. The air was tainted with the smell of blood, the grief in the room just as palpable, as he stepped carefully across the floor, avoiding the blotches on the boards. The blade of a white-handled knife was still deeply embedded in the right-hand side of Mollie Naylor's neck. Her eyes were open, glazed over now, with brownish triangles starting to appear on either side of the pupils. Penrose searched them for an explanation, but found nothing more than his own assumptions, worn-out clichés of how her life might have brought about her death. Outside, in the narrow alleyway that ran between this terrace and the next, someone oblivious to the misery was whistling 'God Rest Ye Merry, Gentlemen', and Penrose was struck by how suddenly the normal, uplifting conventions of the day had become the aberration; there was no possibility of rest here, and he wished with all his heart that he had never come.

He couldn't face the crib. Down below, he heard someone else enter the house and brushed the tears from his face before going downstairs. His superior was looking through the envelopes on the table, and a police photographer stood by the front door, waiting to go up. Penrose nodded to him, then joined Inspector Cornish on the other side of the room. 'Looks like she planned it,' Cornish said.

'Did she leave a note?'

'No, but she'd made sure her affairs were in order, such as they are. Give the woman her due – she didn't want to die in debt.' He handed the envelopes over, meeting Penrose's eye for the first time. 'It's obviously as bad as they said, then. You look bloody awful.'

'I've never seen anything like it, sir.'

'And there's nothing to suggest anyone else was involved?'

'Not as far as I can see.'

The first envelope was labelled 'Mr Taylor's rent' and contained a modest amount of money. The second was addressed to the Railway Benevolent Fund, and Penrose read the brief note inside: '*Dear Sir, please accept this letter as confirmation that I do not require any more help from this institution.*' The handwriting was neat and fluent, something which Penrose found as surprising as the sentiment. 'Do we know anything about her circumstances?' he asked.

'She was a widow, according to one of the neighbours. Her husband died a few months before the youngest child was born – killed in a railway accident, hence the help she'd been getting. They say she kept herself to herself, but she loved her kids. If I had a shilling for every time I've heard that . . .'

There was a cynical note in his voice, but Penrose looked again at the parcels under the tree. 'How many children did she have?' he asked.

Cornish shrugged. 'How many are up there?'

'Four, but there are six presents, so there might be a child missing. Two if she didn't buy anything for herself.'

The inspector nodded, chafing his hands against the cold. 'Good thinking, Penrose. Go and find out, and get a statement from the bloke next door. I'd better have a look upstairs.'

The crowd outside was growing steadily, and there were bound to be one or two news reporters sniffing round by now, so Penrose decided to use the back entrance. Each house had its own small yard and the snow here was deep and untouched, a refreshing contrast to the compacted mess of slush and dirt to which the street had been reduced. If they *had* been looking for signs of an intruder, another heavy snowfall in the early hours would have foiled them; as it was,

Penrose was grateful to step out into something clean and invigorating, into something natural. He stood in the middle of the yard, hoping that the shock of the cold might dull his other senses, but the memory of what he had seen continued to haunt him in vivid detail, and the more he tried to blot out the images, the more relentless they became. Further down the road, the bells of St Clement's church began to ring.

Afterwards, he could never quite be sure why he paused as he opened the back gate, whether it was a noise that made him turn and walk over to the brick-built coal bunker, or simply an instinct that the missing children – if there *were* missing children – wouldn't stray far from home. He brushed the snow from the top and lifted the wooden cover, and two dirty, tear-streaked faces stared back at him – a boy of about fourteen and a girl, younger, but not by much – who gripped her brother's hand. 'I'm sorry,' the boy said, entirely unprompted, and just for a second Penrose thought that he was making a confession. 'Ma was so angry. I was too late to save the others.'

EIGHTEEN CHRISTMASES LATER

I

The older she got, the more it seemed to Josephine that the only possible way to enjoy Christmas was to avoid it altogether. Every January, she promised herself that she would do things differently the following year – fewer presents, cards sent only to the people she actually liked, food that at least one person in the house might eat – but by the time December arrived, the pressure of expectation had begun its slow tyranny. The pile of winter books that for some reason she thought she would have time to read sat untouched by the fire, ready to be returned to the shelf; the hall table was covered in lists, a perpetual reminder of everything she still had to do before she went away. The Christmas-loving Germans had a lot to answer for, she thought as she picked up her gloves, and that was before anyone even mentioned the war.

It was easier to appreciate the festive spirit outside in the streets, where the responsibility for creating it wasn't hers. The landscape around Inverness always looked beautiful at this time of year, but a prolonged spell of seasonal weather had given the town a timeless magic which would have graced any greetings card, and she took a circuitous route from Crown Cottage to enjoy it. The air was exhilarating, and she pulled her fur tighter around her as she walked slowly down the hill. There was no preamble to a Scottish winter, she thought; the cold began fiercely and bitterly, just as it meant to go on, scarring the landscape and leaving everything bleak and exposed. South of the border, the seasons changed gradually, almost apologetically, but here she couldn't remember a single December that hadn't announced itself with a flourish.

Christmas was less than a week away and the shops in Queensgate were busy, but the atmosphere was one of unhurried contentment, and she browsed for a while before heading for the post office. There was a long queue at the counter, and she cursed the friend in Suffolk whose card she had forgotten until an envelope with an Ipswich postmark landed smugly on the mat that morning. She took her place in line, and soon found herself standing awkwardly between the woman who ran her local paper shop and one of her father's Castle Street tenants, whose name she couldn't remember. 'Are you at home for Christmas, Miss Tey?' the newsagent asked, when there was nothing more to say about the weather.

If there were half a dozen words more likely to stir guilt in the human heart, Josephine had yet to hear them. 'Not this year,' she said, conscious that the same answer would have applied to last Christmas and the Christmas before that. 'I'm going to stay with a friend in Cornwall.'

'My, that's a long way to travel! You don't do things by halves, do you? Would that be the same friend you went to America with last year?'

'No, a different friend. I have more than one.'

'Of course you do. You must bring them all home to meet us one of these days. So your father . . .'

'Will be staying here, yes. My sisters are both coming up for the holidays.' Josephine looked at her watch, surprised by how long she had been out. 'In fact, Moire should be here by now. We thought it would be nice to spend a few days together before I have to leave.' A summons from the counter saved her from any further conversation, and she bought her stamps and headed for home. Her brother-in-law's car was standing in the driveway, its back seat piled with parcels, and she opened the front door onto a hallway which was scarcely recognisable as the one she had left an hour earlier. Rather than take her cases up to her room, Moire had begun to unpack at the bottom of the stairs, much to the frustration of the daily woman. The floor was littered with clothes, shoes and cosmetics. 'Have the January sales started early?' Josephine asked wryly. 'This could give the ground floor of Benzie's a run for its money.'

Moire laughed and got up to give her older sister a hug. 'You've run out of sherry,' she said by way of greeting. 'We bought you a bottle but I wrapped it in one of Donald's pullovers to stop it getting broken, and now I can't remember which bag it was in.'

'There's more sherry in the cupboard under the stairs. They delivered a case this morning but I haven't had time to unpack it yet.' She glanced round at the chaos and raised an eyebrow. 'I put it in there so it wouldn't make the place look untidy.'

'Ha! Here it is.' Moire waved the Tío Pepe triumphantly and began to shove everything else haphazardly back into the suitcases. 'The house looks wonderful,' she said, 'but I wish you were staying for Christmas. We come home and you leave three days later. I could take that personally, you know. It's been ages since we spent any decent time together.'

She was right, but before Josephine could say anything her father popped his head round the sitting room door. 'Ah, you're back – good. Chief Inspector Penrose telephoned while you were out.'

It amused Josephine that her father held the authority of Scotland Yard in such high regard that he could never quite bring himself to use a first name, even though she and Archie had been friends for more than twenty years. 'Did he leave a message?' she asked.

'It's about the arrangements for Christmas. He said he'd be at his desk for another half an hour, so you should just catch him if you ring now.'

They left her to it, and she picked up the receiver to call Archie. She watched her family through the sitting room door while she waited to be connected, noticing how happy and animated her father seemed. They rattled around contentedly enough in a house that was far too big for two people, but there was no doubt that Crown Cottage had come to life the minute that Moire and Donald walked through the door. She felt a sudden pang of regret that she wouldn't be part of it for longer. Her father wasn't getting any younger, and with war more inevitable by the day and her middle sister now married to a naval officer, the opportunities for a family Christmas in the future might be few and far between. Moire's words hadn't been meant as a reproach, but the two of them had always been close; she, too, was sorry that their lives kept them apart except for snatched lunches in London, where Moire worked for the Gas Board, or the briefest of stays in Inverness.

'Josephine, thanks for phoning so quickly.' Archie's voice cut into her thoughts before regret could turn to guilt, and the warmth in his tone reminded her of how much she was looking forward to seeing him. 'I'm afraid there's been a change of plan for the holidays.'

'Why? Has something come up at work?'

'Not exactly. How do you fancy spending Christmas in a castle?'

They had arranged to stay on his family's Cornish estate, and the question took her by surprise. 'I suppose that depends on whether or not it's got central heating,' she said. 'Where is it?'

'On St Michael's Mount, so we'd only be going a few miles further down the road. Have you got today's *Times*?'

'Yes, I think so. Hang on.' She put the phone down and went to the dining room, where her father had been reading the paper over breakfast. 'All right, I've got it. What am I supposed to be looking for? Are you in the headlines again?'

She heard him laugh, still embarrassed by the publicity surrounding a recent case that he had solved, bringing to justice a man who had brutally murdered his wife and three children. 'You're never going to let me live that down, are you?'

'Probably not. You're the only person I know who's been in a newsreel.'

'Well, that's all over and done with now, thank God. Look at the main story on page six.'

She did as he asked, finding the clue to what he meant in an article headed 'Ingenious fundraising idea boosts Refugee appeal', and Archie waited patiently while she read the whole piece:

A recent Times *advertisement has met with an unprecedented response, taking the total of The Lord Baldwin Fund for Refugees to £155,730. In Saturday's newspaper, the Hon. Hilaria St Aubyn announced that she will be opening her family home at St Michael's*

Mount in Cornwall to a limited number of guests
for Christmas in order to raise money for this urgent
and important cause. The Mount, which lies off the
coast near Penzance and is accessed at low tide by a
narrow causeway, is crowned by a medieval church and
castle, rich in both history and legend, and the unique
opportunity to spend Christmas in such a romantic
setting has met with an extremely generous response.
One reader alone – whose identity shall remain a secret
for now – has pledged ten thousand pounds to the Fund,
which was established by the former Prime Minister to
bring thousands of Jewish children out of Nazi Germany
and care for them in hostels and private homes. Miss St
Aubyn, who is widely known for her charitable work,
is said to be delighted by the success of the scheme and
promises her guests a Christmas they will never forget.

'It's a marvellous idea,' Josephine said, putting the newspaper down, 'but isn't it a bit out of our league? I can't compete
with ten thousand pounds, no matter how good the cause.'

'You don't have to. Hilaria's an old friend of mine. We
grew up together, and you've met her at a couple of parties
in London.'

'I thought I recognised the name. It's not one that you
forget in a hurry.' Josephine tried to bring Hilaria St Aubyn
to mind, and vaguely recalled a tall, graceful woman in her
mid-forties who had talked about travel and music. 'She's a
brave lady, opening up her home to the highest bidder. You
never know who you might find at the other end of a cracker.'

'Well, that's rather the point,' Archie said. 'She telephoned
last night to ask if I'd come for Christmas and bring some of

what she called my "glamorous friends". Apparently, it's all been much more successful than she thought, and there's one guest in particular whom she doesn't want to disappoint.'

'The one paying ten thousand pounds, presumably.'

'Exactly. She never expected to have a donation from a celebrity, and now she's worried that all the other guests will be dull by comparison. Rich, but dull. She was very excited when I suggested you and Marta.'

'I suppose we should be flattered. Who *is* the celebrity?'

Archie paused, and she found his reticence as annoying as the newspaper's sly teasing. 'I don't want to spoil the surprise, but trust me – you won't be disappointed. And Hilaria has asked me to stress that you'd be doing her an enormous favour and there's no obligation to make a pledge – although I'm sure she won't turn down a modest contribution. God knows this situation is only going to get worse. So how about it? Would you like to go?'

Josephine hesitated. She had been looking forward to seeing the Loe Estate in winter, and the idea of a house full of strangers all striving to impress each other didn't seem like much of a holiday, but Archie was obviously committed and she knew that Marta would love the prospect of something more adventurous. 'All right, then,' she agreed. 'It sounds lovely. I'll tell Marta that we're expected to be at our sparkling best.'

'Good. Hilaria will be thrilled, and it will be nice to spend some time there again. I haven't been for years.'

'Are we still going down on Christmas Eve?'

'That's the other thing I wanted to tell you. I've got to travel separately now to chaperone the celebrity.'

'Is she really *that* famous? I'm assuming it's a she. You've got that tone in your voice.'

17

'Nonsense. But yes, Christmas Eve is fine. There'll be a car to meet you at Marazion – or a boat, depending on when you arrive. The causeway's only open for a few hours at a time.'

'Cut off from the world at Christmas. Right now, that might actually be worth ten thousand pounds.' She recalled the intriguing silhouette of St Michael's Mount that she had seen from the train, never imagining that she might stay there, and began to share a little of Archie's excitement.

'I'm glad you're pleased,' he said. 'How are things in Inverness? Your father sounded well when I spoke to him.'

'Yes, he is, and the baby of the family's just arrived, so that's made his day.' As if on cue, Moire hovered awkwardly in the doorway with two glasses of sherry, and Josephine waved her through. 'Are you busy at work?'

'*Too* busy. It's the usual season of peace and goodwill to all men. A woman's just cut her husband's throat in Ealing. Three little girls have been taken into care, covered in bruises and half starved. We dragged a man out of the Thames last night because he couldn't pay his debts and he didn't want to go home to his family without a present for them.' His voice sounded bitter, and Josephine wondered for the thousandth time how he coped with the relentless sadness of his job. 'I was thinking just now, before you rang – I can't remember a Christmas that wasn't more steeped in misery than the rest of the year. It drives people to do the most terrible things to each other, this pressure to be happy. And on that note . . . I'll see you in Cornwall. Give my love to Marta.'

'I will.'

She put the phone down, and Moire smiled at her. 'I didn't want to interrupt,' she said coyly.

'You weren't.'

'How is your policeman?' Josephine didn't dignify the question with a response, but Moire carried on undeterred. 'I really don't know why the two of you have to keep dancing round each other. You've been so close for years, and neither of you is getting any younger. He's a nice man, you say, and you could do a lot worse. Why don't you just throw your lot in with him, Josephine? We'll sort something out for Dad.'

There were a hundred and one reasons why, but Josephine wasn't about to explain them to her sister. 'We're friends,' she said, and nodded to the small, gift-wrapped box in Moire's hand to change the subject. 'What did you get her this year?'

'A brooch. And you?'

'A ring. I found it in a market in London. She would have loved it.' Josephine watched while her sister put the present under the tree at the bottom of the stairs. It was a ritual that had begun the Christmas after her mother's death and continued ever since, a personal act of remembrance that was special to the two of them and jealously guarded. Funny, she thought, that only Christmas could bring out this uncharacteristic streak of sentimentality, when her mother – like many Scottish women of her generation – had never made much fuss of the day. Whenever Josephine thought of her, it was always summer, and she was striding across the sands at Nairn or playing with her daughters in Daviot, the village they all loved. Winter had never really suited her, and yet here they were, she and Moire, buying her presents and crying into their sherry.

'I can't believe she's been gone fifteen years,' Moire said.

'No, neither can I.' She squeezed her sister's hand and raised her glass. 'Happy Christmas.'

2

Hilaria St Aubyn sat at the window in her father's study, going through the final preparations for Christmas before discussing the arrangements with her housekeeper. It was contrary of her in a home this size to gravitate so often to one of the smallest rooms, but she loved everything about it: the oak-panelled walls and family portraits that acknowledged her long connection with the Mount; the old partner's desk, from which she ran the estate business, taking over new duties each year as her father grew older and more frail; the chair where she sat most evenings, watching the sun setting over the sea and loving the sense of peace and satisfaction from another day safely navigated.

The habitual winter traditions seemed more poignant than ever this year, coloured by the knowledge that this might be her last Christmas here. Her father was in his eighties now, and the grief of losing two much-loved wives in the space of a few years had damaged his health; when he died, his title and the island would pass to Hilaria's cousin, and she would be forced to leave the life that had been hers since she was a girl. There was little point in resenting the laws of inheritance, still less in being sentimental about a home she had loved from the moment she arrived, but she couldn't help the fear that came with knowing that her sense of purpose would be lost along with the right to be here. Like her parents, she felt responsible for those who lived and worked on the Mount;

hers wasn't the only family to have been here for generations, and she loved and respected the islanders for their loyalty and pride; she had hoped to see them through the difficult years ahead, but it was unlikely that she would see out another war here. As her inevitable departure from the Mount grew closer, she found herself increasingly sensitive to the changing seasons and the markers of an island year, acutely aware that it might be the last time she would oversee the daffodil harvest or bathe off the rocks at Cromwell's Passage; the last time she would come home and feel that overwhelming flood of love as the castle came into view. And now, perhaps, the last Christmas, its joy half stifled by uncertainty. This must, she thought, be exactly how it felt to know you were dying.

There was a knock at the door, just as the grandfather clock in the corner prepared to strike the hour, and she smiled at Nora Pendean, glad to be saved from her thoughts. 'The drawing room looks magnificent,' she said, gesturing for the housekeeper to sit down at the other side of the desk. 'Every year I think the tree can't get any better, and every year you prove me wrong.'

'I'm glad you're happy, Miss,' Nora said. 'Everyone's looking forward to tomorrow. The children are starting to get excited now.'

'Good. Actually, I think we *all* deserve a bit of excitement with everything that's going on in the world. Who knows where we'll be this time next year?' The housekeeper nodded and they talked through the arrangements for the islanders' Christmas party, which would be held the following day. It was an annual tradition, going back as long as Hilaria could remember – presents for the children in the afternoon, followed by an early supper at the castle and a concert with music and carols down in the village – and, if she was honest, she enjoyed it more than the more formal celebrations on Christmas Day. 'As you know, we're doing things differently this year,' she said. 'There'll be twelve guests for the Christmas weekend, including a photographer from *The Times*, and they should all be here by teatime on Christmas Eve. Most of them are strangers to the Mount, so it's important that we put them at their ease from the moment they arrive, whilst offering them every possible luxury. None of them will be bringing staff, so here's a list of the ladies who'll need looking after.' She pushed the piece of paper across the desk, waiting for the surprise to register on the housekeeper's face when she read the name at the top, but her reaction was not the one that Hilaria had anticipated. 'Is there a problem, Mrs Pendean?'

'Not at all, Miss. I'll make sure they've got everything they need.'

'Of course you will, but I thought you might show a little more enthusiasm for the task? It's not every day we have a film star for dinner.' She waited, determined to have an explanation for the housekeeper's apparent disapproval. 'Well? What's wrong?'

'I don't want to speak out of turn, Miss.'

'Please, Mrs Pendean, just say what you feel.'

'All right, then. It's nothing to do with her being a film star, Miss, it's where she comes from. You said it yourself – with everything that's going on in the world, I'm not sure the staff will take too kindly to waiting on a German.'

Her boldness surprised Hilaria even more than the sentiment, but it was a common reaction and she wondered in hindsight why she had never considered it. 'Can I remind you,

Mrs Pendean, that the poor children we're raising money for are also Germans? There are plenty of people in that country who are just as horrified by what's going on there as we are – more so, perhaps, because it's their homeland. I hope I can rely on you all to treat every guest in this house with courtesy and respect, no matter where he or she comes from?'

'Of course, Miss.'

'Good. Now tell Mrs White that I need her menus for the whole weekend by midday. That will be all.'

The dismissal was uncharacteristically brusque, and she regretted it before the housekeeper was halfway across the room. 'Oh, Mrs Pendean,' she added, calling her back. 'I noticed when I was in church on Sunday that one of the figures in the nativity is damaged. Will you take it down to Mrs Soper and ask her to make sure it's mended by Christmas Eve? The church always looks spectacular at this time of year, thanks to you, and our guests will love it. It's what Christmas is about, after all.'

The housekeeper nodded, but the praise for the church – always her pride and joy – wasn't met with the usual warm response, and Hilaria realised how much Nora Pendean must be missing her daughter, especially at Christmas. 'How is Jenna?' she asked, more gently this time. 'I can't believe she's been gone from us for nearly a year.'

'She's all right, thank you, Miss,' Nora said. 'At least I suppose she must be. We're only allowed one letter a month, and lately we haven't always had that.'

'She must be getting ready to take her final vows.'

'That's right. In February.'

'She's a credit to the island, Mrs Pendean, and to you and your husband. You must both be very proud of her.'

For the briefest of moments the housekeeper forgot herself, and the expression on her face hovered somewhere between scorn and resentment. There was something else there, too, something like pity, and Hilaria felt the accusation as surely as if the words had been spoken aloud: that she would never know the power of a mother's love for her child, nor its grief. She said nothing more, and it was left to Mrs Pendean to restore the natural order between them. 'I'd best get on, if there's nothing else?'

She left the room, and Hilaria went back to the window, unsettled by their brief conversation. It was high tide and the waves were crashing against the rocks below, hitting the foundations of the castle with the hollow sound that she had always found strangely comforting; there was something reassuring, something safe, about the hours when the sea covered the causeway and the island was less accessible – like being at sea without the danger – but today it only stirred up the doubts she was beginning to have about her plans, and she found herself craving the familiar. Christmas was the time to hold tight to everything you loved, not to bring in strangers. She began to wish heartily that she hadn't allowed her good intentions to get the better of her, but it was far too late to change her mind now. They would just have to make the best of it.

3

Nora Pendean crossed the south terrace to the tiny medieval church that sat at the highest point of the island, the spiritual heart around which the rest of the castle was built. The nativity stood in its customary place just inside the north door – the same solid wooden statues, carved by a forgotten Victorian hand, that had been there when she was a child. Their features were as familiar to her as some of her friends and she soon identified the damaged figure, one of the three kings whose painted crown was chipped and split, revealing the bare wood beneath. She removed the carving from its place, then paused to look at Mary by her makeshift crib in the centre of the scene, just an ordinary woman with her child. Had she felt cheated at the end, she wondered? Had she looked back on those years of love and questioned what it had all been for?

The weather was turning when she left the church, and by the time she reached the handful of buildings at the foot of the Mount, rain was drifting in waves like the sea, sweeping across the backdrop of woodland and darkening the castle's stone. She pulled her coat closer around her, cursing the heavy figure that slowed her progress, and headed for the small museum at the side of the harbour. Her husband was busy on the pier, overseeing a delivery of coal and logs, and she changed direction to speak to him. He waved when he saw her coming, but made a point of continuing with his work, as if that could deter her from what he knew she was going to ask. 'Has the post boat been yet?' she called.

'Yes, half an hour ago.'

'And?'

'There was nothing from Jenna, love. I'd have brought it up straight away.' It was what she had been expecting, but still she couldn't hide her disappointment and Tom put his hand on her arm. 'There's still a few days before Christmas. Don't give up hope.' He meant well, but she shook him off, trying to ignore the hurt in his eyes. Changing the subject, he nodded to the figure in her arms. 'What are you doing with that?'

'Getting it mended. Everything's got to be perfect, apparently. God knows why we're doing all this extra work for a load of strangers with more money than sense.'

'It's for a good cause, Nora. I can't think what it must be like to leave your home at that age.'

She shrugged, hardly in the mood to be charitable about parents who were losing their children, even if they were refugees; her hardness was out of character, and Tom looked at her impatiently. 'It's what she wanted, love. Jenna is happy, even if we find that hard to understand.'

'You're sounding just like her now,' Nora said bitterly, gesturing back to the castle. 'I'm sick of people telling me what's for the best and how blessed I should feel. I just want to know that all those years *meant* something, that she's missing us like we're missing her, even if it's only for a moment. Why can't you support me in that?'

He walked off, refusing to have the argument again. She watched him stride round to the other side of the harbour and begin to load the first pile of coal into the tram which transported goods and luggage up to the castle. No matter how much she loved him and how hard she tried, she couldn't let him comfort her. She knew that he longed to be enough for her, just as she was for him, but she couldn't pretend, even to be kind. As the reality of this bleak, empty Christmas opened up before her, she wondered how she would ever find the strength to get through it.

4

The late-night tram ground its way defiantly across Blackfriars Bridge, an oblong of warm yellow light moving slowly towards the city as the snow fell thickly around it. Alex Fielding waited for it to pass, then checked the settings on the camera for the final shots of the session. It was a photographer's job to see the most familiar things as if for the first time, but not even a lifetime's devotion to this melancholy streak through the city's heart could exhaust its possibilities. The Thames was always at its finest at dusk, Fielding thought, watching as the oily expanse of water defied the snow's attempts to settle; somehow, darkness made more sense of the muddled rooftops, chimneys and spires, simplifying the outline of the city in a way which was reassuring, and for a few, comforting hours it was almost possible to believe that life was as easily sorted.

A police boat chugged under the bridge, dispelling the illusion, and in the glow of the navigation lights, Fielding could just make out two figures hunched in the stern; the engine was cut off suddenly and the boat drifted silently for a moment, then there was a splash as the drag hit the water, seeking some lost soul for whom the season had proved too much. An instinct for news should have rooted any decent journalist to the spot, but it wasn't the time of year for other people's tragedies and Fielding turned to go back to the office, leaving the river police to carry out their sober work in private. In the distance, the chimes from Big Ben struck the hour.

The air was raw now, even away from the water, but the brightly lit windows on the north side of the street helped to temper the bleakness which had crept up on Fielding like an early morning mist. *The Times* headquarters – a plain, red-brick building opposite Blackfriars underground station – stood aloof from the pack of press in Fleet Street, as if keen to claim superiority. The latest fall of snow had deadened the city's familiar evening sounds, and the photographer crossed the road to deliver a good day's work, glad that the thrill of the job was still as fresh and unspoilt as the whited streets and pavements.

The fug of cigarette smoke in the third-floor offices was less opaque than usual, a sure sign that things were winding down for Christmas. Fielding knocked at the editor's door and received the customary curt admittance. Dick Robertson was standing by the window, laying down the law to a junior reporter who fled the room gratefully at the first sign of a reprieve. Tuesday's paper lay open on the desk, already dissected and annotated as old news gave way to the stories that had arrived too late, and Fielding wondered if Robertson even had a home; no matter what the shift, he was invariably somewhere on the premises. 'You asked to see me, sir?'

'Yes, but that was hours ago. Where the hell have you been?'

'Down by the river, gathering shots for the piece in tomorrow's—'

'Yes, yes, yes,' Robertson interrupted, holding up his hand in exasperation. 'Sometimes I wonder why I do this job. We've got all hell breaking out in Europe, and still the only thing that anyone wants to read about is the weather. What's wrong with people? Why can't they just look out of their bloody windows?'

'It *is* Christmas. I suppose they're making plans for the holidays.'

'Yes, well, so is Hitler.' Robertson gestured to the open newspaper, where a picture of starving refugees arriving in Shanghai sat incongruously next to Fielding's own photograph of the skating in Hyde Park. 'Anyway, Christmas was what I wanted to talk to you about. Are you all set for Cornwall?'

'Raring to go. Any final instructions?'

Robertson looked his senior photographer up and down, taking in the shapeless trousers and the overcoat with its missing buttons. 'Smarten up for a start, and try to look a little more . . . well, respectable. You know what the aristocracy's like, and you *are* representing this newspaper while you're there.'

Fielding winked. 'I won't let you down, sir. Best bib and tucker already packed. They'll think I was born to it.'

'That's what I like to hear. You wanted the story and God knows we've paid enough for the privilege of sending you there.'

'Well, it's not every day you get the chance to sit down to dinner with a Hollywood star. I don't think I've taken a decent picture of that woman in five years of trying.'

'So make sure you get more than a good meal out of this trip and don't ruffle any feathers. I know what you're like.' He glanced down into the street where the snow was deepening, stealthily undoing the hours of work that had gone into clearing it. 'Mind you, it'll be a miracle if you get there at all at this rate – you or any of the other guests. It would have to be at the other end of the bloody country, wouldn't it?'

'Don't worry – I'll get there, come hell or high water.' The words came out more passionately than intended, and Robertson raised an eyebrow. 'It's such a good story,' Fielding added, worried that too much enthusiasm might betray a more personal motive for wanting to be part of the Christmas gathering at St Michael's Mount. 'People are really getting behind Baldwin and this refugee fund, and the more closely we associate ourselves with that, the better the publicity we'll get out of it. Throw in a glamorous film star with a point to make . . .'

There was no need to preach to the converted. Robertson sat down at his desk and took a bottle of whisky from the top drawer; he poured two glasses, never seeming to remember that Fielding hated the drink. 'There's something else I want you to keep an eye on while you're down there,' he said.

'Oh yes?'

'I've been having a word with a friend of mine who runs one of the Cornish papers. Rumours are that Hitler's got his eye on Cornwall, and the Mount in particular.'

'What?'

'Von Ribbentrop spent a lot of time there when he was the British Ambassador, and apparently he's been promised St Michael's Mount. Alf was in the room when he announced it, at some do with the Lord Lieutenant. Spitting nails, he was, after two hours in that idiot's company.'

'Now that I *can* believe.' The Nazi Foreign Minister was a figure of ridicule in the press for the gaffes he made on a regular basis. 'So why hasn't Alf printed the story?'

Robertson scoffed. 'He can't, can he? Not while the official line is still appeasement – but that won't last for ever, so get plenty of shots of the castle while you're there. You never know when they might come in handy.'

'The Lord Lieutenant's coming for Christmas, isn't he?'

'That's right, with his daughter – and she's been *very* friendly with Von Ribbentrop's aide, if you know what I mean, but for God's sake don't mention that at the dinner table. Now, I've got a final list of guests for you somewhere.' Fielding waited while the editor rummaged through a full in-tray, eventually pulling out two lists of names and discarding the older one in an overflowing wastepaper basket. 'Here it is. We've got a vicar, a policeman, two writers . . .'

'Sounds like a game of Happy Families,' Fielding said. 'With Angel the Actress at the top of the pack.'

There was a knock at the open door, and the office cleaner stuck his head round. 'Sorry, guv, I didn't know you were busy. Do you want me to come back later?'

Robertson shook his head. 'I'll be busy all night, Jack, so you might as well get it done now while we're finishing up here. Don't go overboard, though.'

Jack grinned at Fielding as he emptied the ashtray and gave it a polish. 'Looking forward to your Cornish trip? All right for some.'

Fielding ignored him and stood up to go. 'If that's it, sir, I'll be off. I'll check in with you again before I leave on Friday.'

'No you won't, because you're leaving on Thursday. Who knows what this weather will be doing by the end of the week, and I can't risk any mistakes. I've cleared it with your hosts.' Robertson slid an envelope across the desk. 'Here's your train ticket, so get yourself there in good time and make sure you've got a feel for the place. Detective Chief Inspector Penrose of Scotland Yard is escorting our Hollywood star down on Christmas Eve, and we'll need plenty of shots of her arriving at the Mount. Penrose is a good friend of Miss St Aubyn and he's from that part of the world, so keep on the right side of him.' He smiled at Jack, who had stopped what he was doing at the mention of Hollywood. 'Yes, I'm sure you're dying to know who we're talking about, but you'll have to wait until Saturday.'

'She must be someone important if she needs a police escort.' The cleaner looked curiously at Fielding as he gathered up the rubbish from the waste basket. 'Are you sure you don't need someone to carry your bags for the weekend?' he offered. 'I've got nothing special planned for Christmas.'

'Thanks, Jack, but I've got this one covered.'

'I'm glad to hear it,' Robertson said. 'Seriously, Alex, I've stuck my neck out to persuade the boss that this story is worth a generous donation to the Appeal. Don't let me down. I want you right there on the spot every time she so much as sneezes.'

'I won't let her out of my sight,' Fielding promised. 'By the time this is over, I'll know her better than she knows herself.'

5

The tearoom was even busier than usual, but for once everyone seemed happy to wait and the season of goodwill lived up to its name. The morning flew by in a flurry of Christmas shoppers, and an assortment of bags and boxes from every store in town spilled out from under the tables, taking up precious floor space. Violet glanced at the clock and was surprised to see that it was already a quarter to twelve – time to brace herself for the lunchtime rush and a different clientele. The shop girls and office clerks were never as patient as the housewives, but at least she'd have room to move without causing an avalanche.

She collected the tip from a table by the door – more silver than copper at this time of year – and re-laid it quickly for a party of four young men in naval uniforms. They were in high spirits, full of their plans for Christmas and the girls they were going to spend it with, and she dealt with their flirting as efficiently as she handled their order. It came naturally to her to be nice, and she always smiled when she remembered the manageress telling her at her interview that a pleasant personality was more important than good looks. She had taken the back-handed compliment in the spirit it was meant, and it turned out to be true: she hadn't been short of offers, although she'd vowed never to do anything as predictable as falling for one of her customers. It wasn't the first time she'd been wrong.

A queue built steadily at the door, and she was far too busy running to and from the kitchen to see Johnny arrive. By the time she noticed him, he was already seated at a table next to the Christmas tree which had had a reserved sign on it all morning. He grinned when he caught her eye, pleased to have surprised her, and she thought how nice he looked – smarter than usual in the better of his two suits, with a tie that she hadn't seen before and diligently polished shoes. Instinctively, she straightened her cap, glad that she'd found a minute to comb her hair between orders. 'Got time to join me?' he asked, when his turn to be served finally came.

'Are you mad? It's the busiest part of the day. I'll be flat out for the next hour and a half.'

'It's all right, Violet – you can take your lunch break early today. The girls will cover for you.'

Violet turned round and looked at her manageress in surprise. 'I'm sorry, Mrs Ridley, I didn't know he was coming . . .'

Her apologies were waved away. 'Go on. Don't keep the poor man waiting. I can't spare you all afternoon.'

'Of course not. Thank you, Mrs Ridley.'

'You can fetch your own lunch, though. I'm not made of festive spirit.'

Violet nodded and turned back to the table, but not before she'd noticed her colleagues nudging each other. 'Johnny Soper, what the hell are you playing at?' she whispered. 'You'll get me the sack, and a fine bloody Christmas present that'll be.'

'You won't get the sack. You're entitled to a lunch hour, just like the rest of us.'

35

He smiled again, and Violet wondered what he was up to; it was out of character for him to break any sort of rule. 'All right then, but I can't be long. What do you want?'

He knew the menu by heart and didn't even bother to open it. 'Sausage and mash, and I'll have a coffee nut sundae, too. Let's put the boat out, my treat. It *is* Christmas.'

When she came back with a pot of tea, she noticed a present on the table – a small box, carefully wrapped. 'What *is* all this about?' she asked guardedly, taking off her apron and sliding into the seat opposite him. 'Why are you smiling at me like that?'

'Can't you guess? I was going to wait until we'd finished eating, but I don't think I can stand the suspense. Go on – open it now.'

She did as he asked, surprised by how badly she wanted the present to be what she thought it was. Here, next to the tree, the sweet scent of pine held its own against the stronger aromas of coffee and bacon, and she felt suddenly like a child on Christmas morning. The ring was beautiful: an amethyst – her birthstone – surrounded by eight tiny pearls and set in yellow gold. When she looked up, he was already out of his seat, and she noticed that the other diners were beginning to stare over at their table. 'Johnny, you're not going down on one knee . . .'

'Of course I am. I want to do this properly. Violet Carter, will you marry me?'

It wasn't the first proposal the tearoom had seen, and Violet had always felt sorry for the woman put so publicly on the spot, but now she found she didn't mind. She threw her arms around him, and a cheer went up from her colleagues. 'Of course I will, you daft bugger. Who else would have you?'

36

She pulled him back to his seat as the customers began to applaud. 'You arranged all this behind my back? And they were all in on it? Mrs Ridley as well?' He nodded. 'You were taking a risk! What if I'd said no?'

'You wouldn't do that to me.'

'No, you're right – I wouldn't.' She was going to tell him how much she loved him, how happy his love had made her, but she knew it would embarrass him; in spite of the grand gesture, he wasn't one for too many words. 'What on earth will my mum and dad say? That'll teach them to have five girls. They've only just finished paying off Julie's wedding, and now mine's on the horizon.'

'Not too far on the horizon, I hope. And your dad couldn't have been more pleased when I went to see him.'

'I don't expect he could. He worships the ground you walk on.'

'Which is a damned sight more than my own father did.' He smiled to take the edge off his words, sorry to have spoilt the moment. 'I shouldn't have said that. This is our day, and I want it to be special.'

'It is special, but you're bound to be thinking about your dad,' she said, reluctant to let him change the subject so easily. 'Christmas does that to all of us, and he hasn't even been gone a year yet.'

'I just wish I'd said more to him. Done more to make him proud of me . . . but it's too late now.'

'Don't take all the blame yourself. It takes two people not to get on.'

'Stupid thing is, I don't even know why we didn't. But I shouldn't have left like that, if only for my mum's sake.'

Violet took his hand, wondering how many sons and

daughters were tangled up like this in the emotions of the season; regrets were always so much greater at this time of year. 'Do you want to go home for Christmas?' she asked, feeling suddenly selfish for the relative happiness of her own family.

He shook his head. 'No, we've said we'll spend it with your parents. They're expecting us.'

To his credit, he said it without resentment, but perhaps she had assumed too readily that Christmas would be spent at her family table rather than his, and not just because it was so much closer. 'We can change our minds, if it means that much to you.'

'But you hate my mother.'

She burst out laughing at his directness, and that brought a smile from him, too. 'Of course I don't hate your mother! I've only met her twice, and one of those was at your dad's funeral. I just wish she'd stop treating you like a younger version of your father.' She remembered how alien she had found those visits to his island home in Cornwall, and hoped with all her heart that he would never want to move back; no matter how much she loved him, she knew she couldn't be happy there, and just for a moment she feared what their marriage might mean. 'I'll never be the sort of wife that your mother was – or my mother, come to that,' she said firmly, as much to herself as to him. 'We've got our own lives, you and me, and we'll do things our way, but I don't want you to cut yourself off from your family. Write to her now and tell her we're coming.'

He looked at her doubtfully. 'Are you sure?'

'Of course I'm sure. I wouldn't have suggested it if I wasn't.'

'All right, but I won't let her know in advance,' he said, and Violet wondered if he thought she would change her mind. 'We'll go over and surprise her.'

She shrugged. 'Whatever you think's best. We've got a lot to celebrate this Christmas, you and I. At least we might have if you ever get round to putting this ring on my finger.'

6

Archie hesitated outside the Brook Street entrance to Claridge's. The hotel's glamour didn't usually intimidate him, whether he visited for work or for pleasure, but a rendezvous with a Hollywood star was hardly in the line of duty and he had been jittery about it all day, much to the amusement of his colleagues. He pushed through the revolving doors and stood for a moment in the entrance hall, where a chequered marble floor and gracefully sweeping staircase made the space look much bigger than it actually was. Claridge's gilt mirrors and grand Art Deco arches made it easy to forget that the ground on which he stood had once been the turning circle of a carriage drive, serving nothing but a modest guest house. The foyer was a palace of glass and sparkling lights, and only the fireplace offered some welcome respite from the glacial crispness of the décor.

There was an enormous Christmas tree at the foot of the stairs, decorated to within an inch of its life, and Archie walked past it to announce himself at the reception desk. 'I'm here to see Miss Dietrich,' he added. 'She's expecting me.'

'You're a nice change from her usual visitors, I must say.' The comment came out before it could be stopped, but it was in such stark contrast to the hotel's customary discretion that Archie heard a sharp intake of breath from the couple checking in beside him. The clerk flushed as his colleague glared at him, then smiled apologetically. 'I'm sorry, sir. I'll let

Miss Dietrich know that you're here. Just one moment.' He went to the telephone and dialled a room number, returning after the briefest of conversations. 'She'll see you now, sir. Her other guests are just leaving. I'll call someone to take you up to her suite.'

'There's really no need. I'm sure I can find it myself.'

The receptionist seemed to have learned his lesson. 'It's no trouble at all,' he insisted, sticking politely but firmly to convention. 'We won't keep you a moment.'

Archie waited impatiently, his tetchiness made worse by the final throes of a cold. A bell boy appeared in due course, understandably eager to show someone to the star's rooms. The lift purred quietly to the fourth floor and he followed his guide down plushly carpeted hallways, noticing that – for all its fashionable elegance – there was something sedate and restrained about this particular hotel which encouraged a reverence more appropriate to a church. The bell boy turned a corner and gestured to the door at the far end of the corridor, which led to an outer lobby. Two men stood guard there, one on either side, and Archie stopped in his tracks, understanding now what the receptionist had meant. Their dark uniforms struck a jarring note in the hotel, the silver eagles and swastikas giving the lie to an otherwise convincing illusion that the world was a place of peaceful civility; in spite of a life that had seen more than its fair share of war, Archie was shaken by their presence. 'You can leave me here,' he said, dismissing his chaperone. 'Thank you.'

The bell boy took his tip and hurried back to the lift. Archie headed for the suite, and as he approached the inner door opened, giving him his first glimpse of Dietrich. She was dressed entirely in white, and the contrast with her

41

visitors – whether coincidental or carefully staged – could not have been more dramatic. The Nazi she was showing out was taller than his colleagues and his face looked vaguely familiar from the newspapers; he snapped his heels together and kissed the hand that she held out to him, a movement that was simultaneously chivalrous and threatening. Then, after a clipped 'Heil Hitler' which met with no response, he strode from the room. His henchmen fell into step, as if joined by an invisible thread, and Archie stood aside to let them pass.

Marlene looked at him and smiled. 'Christmas greetings from the Führer,' she said. 'They have been waiting downstairs for hours. I only saw them because my daughter said no one should be left in the lobby at Christmas time, not even a Nazi.' Her smile faded, and she looked intently at Archie. 'She has no idea how much I hate them.'

'What did they want?'

'The same thing they always want. My triumphant return to the homeland. Sadly, you arrived before I could give them my answer. Sadly for them, but not for me.' The smile came again, but this time it was more genuine. 'Come in, Mr Penrose. I've been looking forward to meeting you.'

A butler appeared from a side room to take his coat, and Archie followed his host through to the main suite. The sitting room smelt of cigarette smoke and perfume, something heavy and floral, and was spacious enough to contain everything that a guest could need with several extravagances that most would never use: a grand piano stood over by the windows, and a self-contained recess was dominated by a carved oak desk, whose size most boardroom executives would struggle to justify. French doors led out to a balcony, and the Mayfair rooftops were softly silhouetted in the dusk. In the corner of the room there was a Christmas tree, simply decorated like those of his own childhood; the snowman perched on top brought back a memory that he couldn't quite place. Perhaps it was the company, but the apartment had the feel of a stage set, reminding Archie that luxury on such a scale was always a theatre of sorts, and he wondered why one of the richest women in the world would want to trade this in for a draughty Cornish castle.

'My visitors are just one of the reasons I'll be glad to get away,' Marlene said, answering his unspoken question. 'Please, Mr Penrose – take a seat.' She gestured to a sofa and Archie sat down, surprised to find it more comfortable than it looked. The actress pressed a service bell in the wall and the butler returned immediately. 'Pour us some champagne, darling, would you?' She turned to Archie. 'Unless you'd prefer something else? Whisky? A martini?'

Her voice was so familiar from the screen that he had to remind himself he was no longer a passive observer in the conversation. 'Whisky would be lovely,' he said, trying in vain to suppress a sneeze. 'Thank you.'

'You are not well?'

'I'm fine. It's just the end of a cold.'

'William, bring Mr Penrose some of the chicken soup that Maria liked so much when she was here.'

'No, really,' Archie protested. 'There's no need.'

'Nonsense, I insist. You will feel better before you know it. Go now, William. Leave the drinks to me.'

The butler was ushered from the room, and Marlene busied herself at the bar. She ignored the Dom Pérignon that sat on ice and poured two large whiskies instead, talking all

43

the time about her daughter and what a fuss the hotel had made of her. Archie was struck by how English her accent was. Without asking, she added lemon to his drink and disappeared into another room, returning seconds later with a jar of honey. 'Do you have children, Mr Penrose?'

'Yes, a daughter. She's twenty-one now.'

'Ah, they grow up so fast. I bet you can scarcely fathom where your little girl went.'

Before he could explain that he hadn't been part of Phyllis's childhood, the butler returned with a bowl of steaming soup and some bread. Archie stood to take the tray while the actress fussed round him, plumping the cushions on the sofa; her attentions were so unexpected that he began to think he must be running a fever which threatened his grip on reality. When she was satisfied that he was comfortable and had sat down next to him, he noticed that the lighting in the room had been carefully arranged to emphasise her beauty as it was seen on the screen – the hollow cheeks, the full lips and thinly pencilled eyebrows. 'It was so good of you to offer to be my escort for Christmas.'

Archie couldn't help but smile. 'It really doesn't feel like a favour,' he said, 'but I can't imagine your visitors would be very pleased by your plans for the holiday? Donating so generously to a charity for Jewish refugees is a courageous thing to do when the Gestapo are standing outside your door.'

'By courageous you mean foolhardy.'

'In my experience, they're often hard to tell apart.'

'They will not criticise me while they still think they have a chance of persuading me to return. Anyway, they are always keen to assure me that there is no anti-Semitism in Germany.'

'What happened last month makes that a very hard position to maintain.'

'You would think so, wouldn't you, and yet Hitler made a speech the following day without mentioning it once.'

Her voice was understandably bitter. The events were still recent, but Archie knew that he would never forget the shocking newspaper accounts of the way in which synagogues and Jewish businesses throughout Nazi Germany had been ransacked and destroyed in the course of a single night, dubbed 'Kristallnacht' after the shards of broken glass that littered the streets. Nearly a hundred Jews had been murdered and thousands more taken away, sparking outrage around the world. 'It must sadden you to know what's happening in your country,' he said.

The actress shrugged, deflecting the observation, and Archie realised what an understatement it had been. 'Helping people is the decent thing to do, and it is the time of year for goodwill. I love Christmas, don't you? We always start it early because Maria's birthday is in December. She's just fourteen. What do you think of our tree? We decorated it together when she was here with me last week. We went shopping. There's nowhere quite like London for shopping. Maria had such a happy time. Is the soup good?'

Despite his earlier protestations, a hot meal was just what Archie needed and he nodded. 'Yes, very good. You're not taking Maria to Cornwall with you?' he asked, intrigued by this woman who could stand up to the Nazis one minute, then fuss like a mother hen around a policeman she had only just met.

'No, she's spending the rest of the holidays with her father in Paris. She left this morning.'

45

'You'll miss her.'

'Of course, but she will be safer there, away from me.'

He looked more closely at her, and saw for the first time the tiredness that make-up disguised so well. 'Are you worried that the Nazis will use her to get to you?'

'Not the Nazis, no – they wouldn't risk it. As I said, we are playing a game of cat and mouse. They want me too badly but I cannot afford to upset them. I need my German papers to be in order if I'm to get my American citizenship. As long as I behave, they wouldn't dare touch Maria. But others, perhaps; others who always seem to know where I am.' She hesitated, and Archie waited to see if she would confide in him. 'I get so many letters, but some of them lately have been a little . . . well, obsessive.'

'Anonymous, I presume?' She nodded. 'Can I see them?'

'I always destroy them. I didn't want Maria to find them and be frightened, not after last time.'

'What do you mean?'

'There were some kidnap threats a few years ago, when we were in California. It was just after the Lindbergh baby had been taken. You remember how hysterical everyone was?'

And with good reason, Archie thought. The son of the famous aviator had been abducted from his home in New Jersey, and although his parents had paid a huge ransom demand, the toddler's body was found by a truck driver a couple of months later, dumped near the side of a road. 'I don't remember any publicity surrounding your daughter,' he said.

'We kept it quiet and nothing came of it. One day the letters just stopped.'

'No one was ever caught?'

'No. These are different, though. The others were just about money.'

'And these are targeted at you, not your daughter? And sent to you here?'

'That's right.'

'Have you told the police?'

'No. There's nothing actually threatening about them. It's hard to put my finger on it, but something isn't right. He knows too much about me.'

'Or she.'

'Where I'm concerned, it's usually a "he".' She finished her drink and lit a cigarette. 'I'm probably being too sensitive. It's no secret that I'm here, so why shouldn't I get letters?' That was true, Archie thought, although he had a feeling that she was keeping something back; someone in her position would know the difference by now between an over-zealous fan and a real threat, and she was clearly unsettled. She shrugged again, and smiled. 'So you can understand why a castle surrounded by the sea has its attractions, and Miss St Aubyn strikes me as a very gracious host. She said in her letter that you know St Michael's Mount?'

'I grew up nearby, yes.'

'You must tell me all about it on the way. What time will your car be here in the morning?'

He looked at her stupidly. 'My car?'

'Yes, your car. How else will we get all the way to Cornwall?'

'But we're not going by car. There's a sleeper booked on Friday's overnight train. That's why I'm here – to go through the arrangements—'

'No, no, no,' she interrupted him. 'Friday is too late. I've spoken to my astrologer, and he tells me we must leave sooner. My luggage will be sent on, of course, so shall I expect you here straight after breakfast?'

'Driving down really isn't sensible in this weather. It's such a long way, and we'd have to break the journey.'

She raised an eyebrow. 'There are no hotels outside London?'

'Of course there are, but—'

'Then that is what we will do. Go home and pack, Mr Penrose. I'm not in the mood to be sensible, and being a long way away is exactly the point.'

7

Richard Hartley put his head round the living room door to make sure that his wife was still dozing by the fire, then went quietly upstairs. He shut himself in their bedroom and set about repacking the suitcases that Angela had so carefully prepared the night before, removing the summer things that should have been stowed away at the end of the season; the outmoded dress that she hadn't worn for years but was still sentimental about; the ill-matching ties and socks. There was far too much luggage for three nights, so he put everything back where it belonged as quickly as he could, then set one suitcase aside to return to the box room. He had only just finished choosing clothes more suitable for the weekend when he heard footsteps on the stairs and her voice at the door.

'Is everything all right, Richard?'

Angela looked anxiously at the freshly packed cases, and he saw the familiar uncertainty in her eyes, the lack of confidence in her ability to do the simplest of tasks which never failed to break his heart. 'Perfectly all right, my dear,' he said reassuringly, hating the brightness in his tone which seemed so necessary and yet so false; they had never spoken to each other like this when she was well. 'I was just making sure I'd got my tippet, but you've already packed it. As usual, you're one step ahead of me.'

She smiled, like a child who had been praised by the adult she most wanted to please, and he prayed that only he was aware of how much their marriage had changed. He remembered so clearly the first indication that something was wrong – five years ago now, when they were still living in London. It had been such an ordinary day – he at home in his study, working on his sermon for the weekend, while Angela went to a committee meeting for one of the charities to which she gave so much energy. At five o'clock, just when he was beginning to worry about her, the telephone rang and he heard her anxious voice at the end of the line, tearful because she couldn't find her way home. It was a route she had taken for years, little more than a mile through a handful of streets that she knew like the back of her hand – and yet she had been walking for hours, too ashamed at first to admit that she couldn't remember where she lived. In the end, he had gone out to find her, and their silent walk home through the fog of a November evening had seemed such a cruel metaphor for what lay ahead.

Angela took the black silk tippet out and refolded it, carefully aligning the ends. 'It was nice of Hilaria to ask you to take the Christmas Day service again,' she said. 'Have you decided what your theme will be?'

'Love,' he said, without hesitation. 'What else is Christmas about?'

'And not just Christmas.' She sat down next to him on the bed and took his hand. 'We've been happy, haven't we?'

'Yes, and we still are.'

'Even here?'

'Here, or anywhere else, as long as we have each other.' He wondered why the sincerest of words invariably sounded so trite, and put his arm around her to give them substance. They had come back to Cornwall in the spring, having spent most of their married life in the city, and he had tried – successfully, for the most part – to make the move without resentment. He was used to a busy parish and his work in London was by no means finished, but he had given it up for something less demanding, knowing that if he didn't spend more time with his wife now, while it mattered and while she still had a sense of who he was, he would bitterly regret it later. The parish he had taken in Marazion was even quieter than he feared, the community too self-sufficient to need him for much between birth and death, but it made sense: Angela had a sister nearby to whom she had always been close, and he knew that he would need help with her care eventually. 'Let's get these cases ready to go,' he said, before the mood could take hold of them both. 'Now we've packed everything, we can just look forward to the day.'

'Oh, I *am* looking forward to it,' she said with feeling. 'It will do us good to meet some new people, and Hilaria is such a wonderful hostess. I dare say my mother will be furious that we're not spending Christmas with her this year, but we'll just have to make it up to her.'

He fumbled over fastening the suitcase. Angela's mother had died shortly after the war, but he knew better than to contradict her; these sharp reminders of a reality that now ebbed and flowed only made her anxious and less self-assured than ever, and more often than not he colluded in keeping them at bay. 'I'm sure she'll forgive us,' he said. 'Now, let me bring these downstairs while you go and make us some tea.'

'And we'll have some of Mrs Curtis's Christmas cake,' Angela said. 'We might as well cut it now, as we're going to be away.'

'Perfect. I'll be down in a minute.' She left him to it, and Richard noticed the sudden emptiness that he had felt more acutely of late whenever she left the room – and, occasionally, even when she was at his side. As the older of the two, he had always assumed that he would be the first to go and he had worried about how she would cope without him; now, he faced a different sort of loneliness, and he wondered again if he had the strength. The air in the room was chilly, and he got up to close the curtains against the draught. Already, the waves were high up the beach, and he never ceased to marvel at how quickly the water covered the causeway once the tide had turned. He waited until the last glimpse of the cobbles had disappeared, transforming the Mount once more into an island, familiar but unreachable, then went downstairs to be with his wife.

CHRISTMAS EVE

'Happy Christmas.'

The station platform was so tightly packed with Christmas Eve travellers that Josephine hadn't seen Marta fighting her way through the crowds. She turned and gave her lover a hug, shivering as the snow on Marta's coat and hair touched her face. 'Happy Christmas. I was beginning to think you'd had a better offer.'

Marta waited to catch her breath. 'It's bedlam out there. Nothing's moving. I'm only here now because the taxi driver ditched his cab on Craven Road and helped me with my bags.'

'I hope you tipped him.'

'The fare cost more than the hotel room, but it was worth it.' She smiled, and squeezed Josephine's hand in the crush. 'Typical. You're on the sleeper from Inverness and I'm five minutes round the corner, and still I've kept you waiting.'

'It doesn't matter. As you can see, no one's going anywhere in a hurry.' She looked round as the crowds continued to spill into Paddington, some taking the crush in good heart as part of the holiday mood, others frustrated by the threat to their plans. The Cornish Riviera Express had laid on three extra trains to cope with the pressures of Christmas Eve, made worse by the heavy snowfalls of the previous week which had forced many travellers to delay their journey or choose the train over a perilous drive out of London. Now, an air of suppressed panic had begun to take hold as people imagined the empty places around the dinner table and the presents left unopened, and Josephine was glad that their reservations were for the first scheduled train, before the chaos had a chance to build. 'We could just stay here,' she suggested, watching as an angry couple stopped an already overburdened porter and added more luggage to his trolley. 'I fancy a quiet Christmas, with just the two of us. No house parties, no strangers, no awkward parlour games.' She smiled at Marta and shrugged. 'After all, if the trains aren't running, there's really nothing we can do.'

'But the trains *are* running, and Archie would never forgive us. He's promised we'll be there, and then there's his big surprise . . .' The shrill sound of a whistle cut through the noise and Josephine's fate was sealed as the passengers for the Cornwall train were encouraged to start boarding. 'Anyway, it's not just Archie who's made plans,' Marta called back over her shoulder as they forced their way to their carriage. 'I've had your present sent on ahead.'

'That was uncharacteristically organised of you.'

'Perhaps I'm turning over a new leaf.'

'Not too new, I hope.'

The train settled down quickly and Josephine glanced round the carriage, pleased that fate had seated them with other couples who seemed content to keep themselves to themselves. 'I suppose some of our fellow guests might be on here somewhere,' she said.

'How many people are going?'

'About a dozen, I think, including us. I've got the details here somewhere, and a copy for you, too.' She searched through her bag for the letter from Hilaria which had arrived by special delivery before she left Inverness, a short note of welcome accompanied by a brief history of St Michael's Mount and a list of those coming for Christmas. 'Right – Detective Chief Inspector Archie Penrose and guest.' She rolled her eyes, and Marta laughed. 'I really don't know why they're stringing the suspense out like this. It's going to be very embarrassing when the big reveal comes and none of us have ever heard of her.'

'We can but hope,' Marta said, reading quickly through her letter. 'I see what Archie meant by the company being dull, though. The Reverend Richard and Mrs Angela Hartley, Colonel Arthur Penhaligon and Miss Barbara Penhaligon . . .'

'Daughter, presumably.'

'Or sister. Either way, God and the military round the dinner table doesn't sound like my idea of fun.'

'No, nor mine.' Josephine scanned the list, trying to find some common ground in the names. 'Mr and Mrs Gerald Lancaster—'

'I've never liked *anyone* called Gerald,' Marta interrupted, 'but there's an Alex Fielding from *The Times*. He might be interesting.'

'Yes, if a little intrusive. I'm not sure I like the idea of a journalist hovering round all weekend.'

'I wouldn't worry. He won't be remotely interested in us once Archie arrives with his "guest". Have we missed anyone?'

'Only Mrs Carmichael. No other information supplied.'

Marta smiled. 'Thirteen at dinner, then, if you include our hostess. That bodes well. I hope nobody's superstitious.' She took off her coat as the train pulled slowly out of the station, glad to be warm at last. 'You say Archie's a friend of the family?'

'That's right. He and Hilaria are roughly of an age, so they were children together at the same dull, grown-up parties, and they've kept in touch ever since. She's often in London.'

'Which is how you know her.'

'I wouldn't say I know her. Archie had to remind me that we'd met, but I do remember finding her interesting. I think you'll like her.'

'The paper said she was connected to a lot of charities. Just how much of a do-gooder is she?'

Josephine laughed at the horror on Marta's face. 'I don't think we'll be forced onto too many committees, if that's what you mean. It's going to take more than a well-intentioned coffee morning to solve this particular problem.' The early edition of *The Times* did nothing to curb her pessimism. She flicked through the first few pages, stopping at a photograph of Hitler leaving for Christmas at Berchtesgaden, having just had dinner with the seven thousand workmen building the new Reich Chancellery. 'Money will decide who wins the war,' she said with a sigh. 'I just hope we're up to it.'

She put the paper down and looked out of the window, tired of news which grew more inevitable and depressing every day. The country seemed divided between frenzy and apathy, between those who argued passionately for or against another war, and those who were resigned to trouble but too weary to do anything about it. She veered unreliably between the two. Today, though, she was happy to join with the rest of the country in using Christmas as an excuse to put her fears to one side, and there was something soothing about letting the countryside slip past as they moved further away from the capital. She watched, entranced, as dense evergreen forests gave way to more typically English stretches of woodland: thickets of silver birch, their distinctive feature now lost against the snow, and ancient oak trees whose gnarled branches drew stark, charcoal shapes in the air. The train entered a long cutting, then the banks cut away without warning, revealing a vast, sloping landscape of white, leaving the carriages feeling suddenly exposed.

'Oh my God.' Josephine looked at Marta, who had picked up the discarded *Times*. 'No wonder Archie was so smug. Just look at this.' She passed the newspaper back, open at the article that had caught her interest. 'Christmas with Marlene. That really *is* a coup. Why on earth didn't I pack something more daring?'

Josephine laughed. 'I love the idea that we could even begin to compete.' She scanned the news story in disbelief, feeling both excited and intimidated at the prospect of meeting one of the most famous women in the world. The headline – 'Hollywood's "Angel" lives up to her name' – sat next to a familiar photograph, a still from the film *Morocco* in which Dietrich wore a man's tuxedo and top hat, brazenly modelling the androgynous image that had made her so popular with men and women alike. There was a cigarette poised provocatively at her lips, her eyes a mixture of defiance and devilish charm; Josephine looked admiringly at the high cheekbones, sculpted so carefully by the light, and wondered what it would be like to sit across from that face at the dinner table.

Marta seemed to share her thoughts. 'It's silly, isn't it? You and I know lots of actors and actresses. We're both familiar with that world and really shouldn't be star-struck, but I'm already panicking about what I might find to say to her.'

'At least we can be honest about her last film,' Josephine said wryly. 'It was the first time she seemed human.'

'And it's given *The Times* a good headline.' Marta took the paper up again, but it was impossible now to settle to the rest of the news. 'I bet Archie will have some tales to tell by the time he gets to Cornwall,' she said. 'I can't wait to get him on his own.'

2

The church was quiet in the early morning, although the wind was rising again outside, finding a rhythm with the waves on the rocks below until it was difficult to separate one sound from another. Nora Pendean hesitated by the north entrance, taking in the familiar stillness, the faint smell of incense and polish, and the soft rattle of the organ loft door as the draught from the terrace caught it. She had known this church all her life, through good times and bad. People had worshipped here for eight hundred years, and – despite the hand of a more modern restorer – these old stone walls still carried echoes of the monks for whom they had originally been built. Sometimes, if she was here at night, she imagined she could hear their prayers in the wind that came off the sea, their footsteps climbing the narrow staircase to the top of the tower, lighting the beacon to guide fishing boats home under a star-bright sky. Here, the past was never far away.

She closed the door behind her and walked down the central aisle, where a shaft of light through the east rose window threw a kaleidoscope of colour onto the flagstones to dance in patterns at her feet. The winter sun was grudging, but still it reached the statue of the saint who gave St Michael's Mount its name, bringing out the fire in the bronze and giving the winged figure a dramatic intensity, appropriate to the struggle of good over evil. The combination of zeal and mercy on the saint's face never failed to move her, although she couldn't help but feel that it was she who was judged these days, and not the figure of Lucifer who lay at his feet. She shivered as the initial relief of coming in from the cold subsided, and turned to set about her work, struck by how beautiful the church was, and by how much she hated it. Its magic, once so compelling, was dead to her.

Two crates of holly and other greenery had been left ready for her, freshly cut and brought over from the mainland. She rinsed all the vases in the tiny vestry and began to make up the arrangements for the service the following day, wincing whenever the holly caught her skin. There was more than enough to dress the altar, so she filled each window ledge with garlands of ivy and mistletoe, the berries stark against the green like tiny moons on a winter's night. The wood around the altar needed polishing and she did it with care – not out of love now, but because it was her job – then hung the last of the greenery at the end of the family pews, fighting back tears as the familiar rituals of the season emphasised the passing of time.

The pews hid a narrow staircase leading down to an underground chamber, once a hermit's cell and used these days as a storeroom. Nora took the uneven steps carefully, glad of the daylight that followed her down, and braced herself against the mustiness of the small, enclosed space. She rummaged around in some boxes and soon found the last of the decorations, together with one or two pieces of silver which were used for the most important services of the year. When the altar was complete, she unwound the chain which lowered a heavy gilt chandelier down from its place above the nave; changing the candles was a laborious task and she was glad that they were lit only at Christmas, but

Jenna had always loved helping her, demanding to be lifted up in her mother's arms until the year that she was finally tall enough to reach the highest crown of fixtures on her own. Nora paused, feeling for a moment the warmth of her little girl's body, remembering the laughter that had seemed to fill so much of those eighteen treasured years. She had been so proud of the young woman who replaced the child, and even now, when there was no option but to accept it, she could scarcely believe that she would never see her daughter again. Perhaps, in time, her memories would be a comfort to her; at the moment, with her grief still so raw, it was as much as she could do to get out of bed in the morning.

The sun had moved round while she worked, a reminder that the day was slipping away and she still had plenty to do. She had forgotten to collect the missing nativity figure from the museum, which meant an extra trip down to the village that she really could have done without, and hurried across the terrace and back through the house. The doors to the guest rooms were wide open, and she could hear the crisp snap of sheets being shaken as she passed, accompanied by expectant chatter amongst the housemaids. She had been wrong to assume that Marlene Dietrich's birthplace would be more important than her celebrity; most of the staff had been thrilled by the prospect of looking after a Hollywood star, and only the older members of the household had shared her reservations, most notably those who remembered the last war. She looked at the clock: the first train was due soon, and from then on there would be a steady stream of arrivals, taking advantage of low tide to cross with their luggage by car rather than boat. She told the maids to get a move on, then left the castle and took the Pilgrims' Steps down to the harbour.

The brightness of the morning lingered, but it was combined now with the peculiar, metallic intensity of a sky which threatened snow, so rare in this part of the world that she could only remember two or three winters when the familiar landmarks of the Mount had stood strange and silent, transformed by an invisible hand. She shivered, chafing her hands as she walked through the lodge gate and past the island's tiny graveyard, where the wind rustled through the leaves of the palm trees, hissing like the serpent in the statue above the lych-gate until she could almost believe that it had escaped St Michael's spear. The museum stood opposite, housing a miscellaneous record of the Mount's history to entertain the scores of visitors who came over from the mainland in the summer. It was usually closed at this time of year, with its more fragile exhibits shrouded in dust sheets, but Emily Soper – who lived and worked on the premises – had obviously been instructed to put on a good show for the Christmas guests; the lamps were all lit, and Nora could see Emily inside, rearranging one of the displays. She opened the door, glad to be out of the cold, and smiled at her friend. 'I'm doing the church up for tomorrow,' she said, 'and we seem to be short of a wise man.'

'It wouldn't be the first time, and I doubt it'll be the last.' They both laughed, and Nora was grateful for a moment's easy company. The two women had always been close, growing up together on the island, and she realised now how important the friendship had been to her recently. 'Have you got time for a cup of tea?' Emily asked. 'The kettle's just boiled.'

Nora shook her head reluctantly. 'I'd love one, but I'd better not. It's pandemonium up there today.'

'Well, if you will mix with the stars . . .'

'It wouldn't be my choice.'

'Ah, get away with you. I won't be moving far from this window until I've seen her arrive, and you're not telling me you won't find an excuse to pop up to her room later.'

Nora smiled. 'I wouldn't be doing my job if I didn't make sure she was comfortable. Is the figure ready?'

'Good as new. I'll go and fetch him for you.'

She went through to the back room and Nora slipped off her coat and hung it on a chair by the fire to warm while she was waiting. The museum seemed more crammed than ever, a motley selection of stuffed birds and fossils, carefully arranged cigarette cards immortalising the legends of giants and kings, paintings of the Mount over the centuries and obscure weapons from its military past. A recently opened Christmas card lay on the counter, and Nora recognised the handwriting on the envelope; she picked the card up and read the greeting, Christmas wishes for a mother from her son, sent with fondest love.

'Have you heard from Jenna?'

Nora shook her head and pushed the card to one side. 'Sorry. I didn't mean to pry.'

'I know, and you weren't.' Emily put the figure down and squeezed her friend's hand. 'The first Christmas without her is bound to be hard,' she said quietly. 'I know how I felt when Jonathan moved away, but you'll get through it.'

She meant it kindly, but Nora wasn't in the mood for sympathy. 'At least Jonathan might come back one day,' she said.

'He might, but I doubt it. He's happy up in Plymouth, and he and Violet will be married soon. They'll put down roots of their own, and that's as it should be, but it doesn't make it any easier for me.' She sighed, tracing the image on the card with her fingers, as if it could compensate for his absence. 'I hoped at one time that Jonathan and Jenna might end up together, but children have their own ideas, don't they? Still, they were close. Do you remember that Christmas they hid in the church after the morning service and tried to ring the bells? Thank God it was Miss Hilaria who heard them and not His Lordship. She's always been good to the children.' Nora tried to block out Emily's voice as her friend recalled one memory after another, playing out scenes from Jenna's childhood like her very own Ghost of Christmas Past. 'She always *loved* being in that church with you, right from when she was a toddler. Such bright eyes, she had – I'll never forget how happy she looked. I suppose we should have seen it coming.'

Emily's observations seemed to put into words the resentment that Nora felt more strongly every day. She had been so happy when Jenna began to share her joy in the beauty of the church and all it stood for, but now it was as if she had been the victim of a cruel joke, tricked like a fairytale mother into offering the most precious thing in her life to the wolf in sheep's clothing. It broke her heart whenever she thought back to the day that she and Tom had been invited to visit the convent where Jenna would spend the rest of her life, that square, featureless building with its ordinary gardens and drab décor. The hardship of the order had shocked her, and she couldn't bear the thought of her daughter in those poor, simple cells, with their bare walls and comfortless beds, where any tiny personal touches seemed tawdry and desperate. The woman who would sleep every night beneath that crucifix was a stranger to her – and she had been such a carefree, normal child.

Nora dragged her thoughts back to the present, suddenly aware that Emily had asked her a question. 'Sorry, what were you saying?'

'I just wondered if she'd be coming home again before she takes her vows?'

Nora shook her head. 'No, and it's probably for the best.'

'You don't mean that, surely?'

'I do. It was awful last time she came. She didn't want to be here, I could see that. We got on her nerves, and everything about the island bored her. It was like she had sawdust in her mouth.' Even the church that Jenna had loved seemed shabby and ordinary through the eyes of her new faith; her daughter chose a different sort of worship now, in a world of which her family knew nothing, and when she had asked Jenna to explain it to her, all she had said was that her faith was like a stained glass window: only beautiful from the inside. In that moment, God forgive her, she had despised her daughter. Jenna had chosen a spiritual life, and yet it seemed to Nora that all the spirit had been knocked out of her, with her folded hands and her downcast eyes; at times, she had longed to strike her simply to get a reaction, to catch a glimpse of the defiant little girl who feared nothing and had always known her own mind. 'I'm relieved I don't have to go through that again, Emily,' she admitted. 'It's the only thing I've got now, the knowledge that we made her happy once. I don't want that spoilt.'

'Nothing can take that away. You couldn't have given her any more love, you *or* Tom. If anything, you gave her the courage to go her own way.'

The thought didn't comfort Nora. 'It's just not what I ever imagined for her,' she said. 'For her, or for us.'

'I know.'

Nora sighed, conscious of time slipping away. 'I'd better get back to the castle,' she said. 'Moaning won't change anything.' She picked up the nativity figure and turned to go, but now that she had begun to talk about her feelings, it was hard to stop. She and Tom avoided the subject these days, too numb to risk another of the fights that had shaken their marriage to its core, and the simple understanding coming from one mother to another was seductive. 'I keep thinking about all the things I'll never have,' she admitted. 'I know it's selfish, and I know that any sacrifices I've had to make are so insignificant compared to what Jenna is giving up, but still I can't help it.'

'Why should you? It's hard to be selfless about sacrifices that other people make on your behalf, no matter how much you love them.'

'I know, but I don't want to be that person. Just now, when you were talking about Jonathan getting married, I was so jealous I could have screamed.' Nora smiled apologetically. 'I thought I'd see *her* married, Em – properly married, not that mockery of a wedding we had to go through at the convent.' She thought back to the scene and how picturesque it had all been, how deceptively gentle – a procession of nuns holding lighted tapers with the new novices in the middle, dressed as brides. She had watched while her daughter knelt before the priest at the altar and asked for God's mercy; watched as the young women were led away to have their hair cut, with tears pouring down her cheeks as Jenna's long, blonde hair fell to the floor like a light extinguished. The mother superior had dressed her in a girdle and veil, and all Nora could think about, stupidly, was how hot the habit would be in the summer and whether or not the veil would protect her daughter's pale skin from the sun – ordinary, motherly things that she really had no right to consider any more, because now someone else was Jenna's mother. 'They even had a wedding cake in the refectory afterwards,' she said, trying to laugh, but the words came out in a strangled sob as she thought about all the things she had taken for granted. 'I thought *I'd* be planning her wedding, *I'd* be the one by her side when she was having last-minute doubts or trying on her dress. And now I can't even call her by the name I gave her at birth. She's Sister Mary Theresa, but I have no idea who that is.' It was the first time she had used the name, and it broke her. 'Why, Emily?' she demanded through her tears. 'Why did she have to be that way? Why couldn't it be someone else's daughter?'

'I can't answer that, Nora. No one can except Jenna and God. I suppose it's what He wanted for her.'

'And what about what *I* wanted for her?' Afterwards, Nora couldn't remember if she had screamed the words aloud or said them only in her head. She swung round, lashing out at her friend, and the next thing she knew, Emily was lying on the floor with blood seeping from a wound in her head. She was horribly still.

Nora looked at the figure in her hands as if it had nothing to do with her, but the stain of red on the newly painted wood brought her back to her senses and she let it fall to the floor as if it had burnt her. She rushed to the door to lock it, terrified that someone might come in before she had decided what to do. Emily was partially obscured by the counter where she had been standing, and Nora knelt down to check her pulse, trying not to recoil from the blood that had begun to matt her hair and stain the collar of her blouse. There was nothing, and Nora began to cry again, shaking her friend's shoulders and begging her to wake up, but the only response was a noise from the floor above, a soft thud like the closing of a door. To her horror, Nora realised that she had no idea if anyone else was on the premises; Emily had lived alone since her husband died, but she was popular with the villagers, and as she had said only a few minutes ago, the kettle was invariably on, waiting for visitors.

She took one of the dust sheets from a pile of boxes behind the counter and covered Emily's body with it, then dragged the boxes across the floor to cut off any prying glances from the window at the side of the building. Her heart was pounding as the shock of what she had done threatened to overwhelm her, and she tried to calm her breathing before climbing the stairs, which came out onto a narrow landing. Emily's sitting room was straight ahead and she began to panic when she saw a coat draped over the arm of a chair, but relaxed when she recognised it as Emily's own mackintosh. 'Hello?' she called out, trying to keep her voice as normal as possible. 'Hello?' The silence gave her courage, and she was relieved to find the room empty except for a black-and-white cat sitting by a pile of books that had toppled over onto the floor, staring at Nora as if to say that the accident had nothing to do with him. That must have been the noise she had heard, but the explanation didn't comfort her, and as the cat began to rub round her legs, oblivious to what she had done, Nora's guilt hit her with all the force of a blow.

She hurried back downstairs, conscious that she would soon be missed at the castle, but still at a loss to know what to do. For a moment, she considered fetching Tom, but the harbour was always busy at this time of day; it would be impossible to bring him here without attracting somebody's attention. In any case, she realised sadly, she couldn't rely on him to save her. Emily was like family to them both, and he was a good man with a strong sense of right and wrong. He would make her go to the police and explain that what she had done was an accident, putting his faith in a justice which he never questioned – but she knew different. There was no justice in the world, the last few months had taught her that, and she didn't want to die for what her grief had made her do.

The urge to survive was sudden and primitive, and its strength took her by surprise; for months she had believed that there was no point in going on, but now, faced with the prospect of giving her own life for the one she had taken, she wanted nothing more than to live. Possibilities raced through her mind, some more plausible than others. The causeway was open at the moment and anyone could access the island. If she took some of the more valuable objects from the displays when she left, people would think that Emily had disturbed a burglar, a stranger to the Mount whose guilt would shame no one. She had read somewhere that crime always went up at Christmas as people struggled to pay their debts, and why should that be any different here?

There was no time to think more logically. She picked the nativity figure up from the floor and took it through to Emily's workroom to wash it in the tiny sink, but a noise from the floor stopped her in her tracks, a terrible, hollow gurgling that came from Emily's throat. She looked back and stared in horror as the dust sheet – now stained with blood – stirred almost imperceptibly, as if her friend was trying to lift her arm. 'No, please God, no,' she whispered, but the movement came again, stronger this time, and Nora began to whimper like an animal, torn between a longing for her friend to live and the possibility of escape which she had so briefly glimpsed. She looked round, desperate for an answer, and saw the statue of St Michael through the museum window, standing above the lych-gate with his spear raised ready to strike; there was a judgement to be made, between good and evil, between life and death, and in that moment she knew that she was damned whatever she did.

She pulled the sheet back to see if she could help, forcing herself to look at Emily's face. The wound was still pouring with blood, so Nora scrunched the material up and tried to stem the flow, begging all the time for her friend's forgiveness, for a second chance for them both. Emily's eyes and mouth were open, her lips moving in agitation, but no words came out, only a dreadful wheezing that grew more shallow and laboured by the second. Nora knew in her heart that there was no hope, but still she kept talking, praying for a miracle until the rise and fall of her friend's chest – already barely perceptible – stopped altogether. There was a final, forlorn groan, so difficult to separate from her own despair that Nora half wondered if she had uttered it herself, then silence – a bleak, wretched silence that was the very opposite of peace.

She knelt by her friend for a long time, waiting for the nausea to pass, then shakily stood up and went through to the back to wash off the blood, scrubbing persistently at her hands and face and then at the figure. When she was sure that the painted king held no lingering evidence of her guilt, she dried it with a towel, ready to carry to the church, and took her coat from the chair by the fire, hoping that it would cover her uniform while she went home to change. There was a display of jewellery in the glass case nearest to her; she put a handful in her pocket, then blew out the lamps and left the museum as calmly as she could, waving back over her shoulder as if nothing had happened, and leaving her friend's body lying on the floor for someone else to find.

3

The drifts were deeper than ever as the train moved on into Devon – great swathes of white beneath a leaden sky that threatened worse to come. All across the moors, ponies stood huddled against bleak stone walls, and Josephine pitied them; the snow that had seemed so radiant and magical amid the comforts of a London winter was shown up here for what it was – harsh, unforgiving and relentless. She was glad when they reached the milder climate of Cornwall and the snow began to dwindle.

'It's a big county, isn't it?' Marta said, fidgeting in her seat. 'I always forget we're not there just because we've crossed the Tamar.'

She was right. The train's progress grew more laboured as it neared the end of the line, stopping at a series of towns filled with dark, stone buildings that reminded Josephine of Scotland. 'It'll be worth the wait,' she said. 'It's not far now.'

A number of the remaining passengers left the train at St Erth, ready to make the connection to the north coast. Josephine sat forward in her seat, eager for the first glimpse of St Michael's Mount, and it didn't disappoint. The island moved in and out of view between the tall reeds lining the track, and somehow the movement of the train served to emphasise the castle's solidity, standing majestic and forbidding over the crescent-shaped bay. 'God, it's stunning,' Marta said. 'The photograph doesn't do it justice.'

'Isn't it magnificent? I've only seen it once before, but I've never forgotten it.' That had been on an early summer's day, when the Mount seemed more like a fairytale castle, glistening and insubstantial in the sunlight; today, it had a completely different atmosphere, dark and brooding under a bruised sky, with a handful of buildings clustered round its foot. The tide was out, leaving the causeway clear to cross, but a choppy sea licked at the rocks around the island and white horses flecked the surface as far as they could see. As they watched, a shaft of sunlight broke through the purple underbelly of cloud, changing the character of the day yet again, and Josephine couldn't help but feel that the scene in front of them would easily upstage any film set that Marlene had stepped onto.

The train came to a halt and a guard announced their destination. Marazion was a tiny station, consisting of nothing more than a modest station house sandwiched between the sea and a stretch of marshland, a small goods yard and a row of stationary railway carriages – apparently used as accommodation – with curtains drawn across their windows. At the far end of the platform, crates piled high with fruit and vegetables were being loaded onto the back of a horse-drawn cart, changing places with several braces of pheasant that were destined for the train. There was a smart black car parked next to the cart, and Josephine noticed that it carried a coat of arms. 'That must be our transport,' she said, raising her voice above the starlings that swirled over the reed beds, their cries woven into a long, rambling song.

'I'm rather relieved it's not a boat,' Marta admitted, looking round for a porter. 'Do you think she's here yet?'

75

'Who?'

'Marlene, of course.'

'I've no idea, but I hope you're not going to spend all weekend in a state of high alert. You're making me nervous.' It amused Josephine that Marta – who rarely gave a damn what anyone thought – could occasionally fall victim to the same bouts of shyness that dogged her on a daily basis. 'I doubt she'll be travelling in a horse and cart, though, so we're probably safe to go over.'

The car was unattended, although a man in a chauffeur's uniform seemed to be giving instructions to the station master, presumably making arrangements for the guests arriving later. A young couple stood next to the car, and as she and Marta walked over to join them, Josephine noticed how nervous they both seemed: the man was tapping his hand repeatedly against his thigh and looking anxiously at the car, as if it might somehow move off without him, and the woman at his side – slightly taller than her husband, and attractive in a pale, delicate sort of way – was tying and retying her scarf in the reflection of the rear window. 'The Lancasters, do you think?' she said to Marta.

'Must be. He certainly doesn't look like a vicar or a colonel.'

The couple brightened as they approached, apparently relieved to have company. 'Christmas at the Mount?' the man asked, and then, when they nodded, offered his hand. 'Gerald Lancaster, and this is my wife, Rachel.'

Mrs Lancaster smiled, and shook hands a little too vigorously. 'Very pleased to meet you,' she said.

Josephine and Marta introduced themselves, and Josephine was about to ask how far they'd come when Lancaster interrupted her. 'Thirty-nine across!' he said, looking at her triumphantly. 'I'm right, aren't I?'

'I beg your pardon?'

'Thirty-nine across in today's *Times* crossword.' He poked the newspaper that Marta had tucked under her arm. 'It was a crime and detection special. You must have seen it?' Josephine nodded, still confused by the turn in the conversation. They had resorted to the puzzle during a long wait in Exeter, but Marta didn't read much crime fiction and there were too many clues about Dorothy L. Sayers for Josephine's liking, so they hadn't got as far as looking for a pen. '"Her victim had to wait his turn, nine and three",' Lancaster continued. 'That's obviously a reference to your first novel, *The Man in the Queue*, so *you* must be the answer.'

'Gerry knows everything there is to know about detective fiction,' his wife added, and it was hard to tell if her tone was nervous or simply weary. 'He has all your books.'

'That's very kind,' Josephine said, smiling as her heart sank. 'I hope you enjoyed them.'

'I did, very much, but there's something I must ask you about *A Shilling for Candles*. Do you *really* think that Inspector Grant would have allowed Tisdall to give him the slip like that? I mean, he seems a perfectly competent policeman in most other respects, but that was a classic schoolboy error, and I wondered why you showed him up like that?'

Josephine was saved from having to justify the premise that most of her plot had been built around by the return of the chauffeur, who gave his name as Trannack and apologised for keeping them waiting. 'Your luggage will follow on,' he said, 'so if you're ready, I'll take you across to the Mount. Is this your first time on the island?'

Marta and Josephine nodded, but Lancaster shook his head. 'I came here as a child. We used to holiday in Cornwall with my grandmother.'

His wife looked at him curiously, as if his childhood memories were new to her. 'Are we the first to arrive?' Marta asked casually, not quite brazen enough to enquire specifically about Marlene.

'No, the Reverend Hartley and his wife came over this morning, and Mr Fielding has been with us since yesterday. Everyone else is arriving later this afternoon.' So Archie was still on the road, Josephine thought, and would no doubt be taking his time; there was little point in travelling with a Hollywood star unless you planned to make an entrance. 'It's just as well you're staying for a couple of days,' Trannack added. 'There's rough weather coming in later, and you won't get on or off the island until it's passed.'

'Even at low tide?' Mrs Lancaster asked, looking anxiously across to the cobbled pathway, which seemed so safe and inviting.

The chauffeur smiled, apparently accustomed to her scepticism. 'It changes quicker than you'd think. You get a southerly gale and a swell building, and the causeway's covered for days at a time.' He went into a detailed explanation of neap tides, wind direction and the cycle of the moon, which Josephine tried in vain to follow. 'In an emergency, three or four of us might get across at low tide if we roped ourselves together, but thankfully we don't have many emergencies on the island.'

'Well, if we're here for the duration, it doesn't bother me,' Lancaster said. 'It just gives us all a chance to get to know each other better.'

He beamed round at them, and Josephine could already see by the look on Marta's face that she was unlikely to change her mind about people called Gerald. Trannack opened the rear door and Lancaster stood aside to let the three women get into the back seat, but his wife hesitated. 'Can we walk across the causeway?' she asked, looking appealingly at her husband, and Josephine got the impression that she was trying to delay her arrival at the house for as long as possible. 'Some air might be nice after the journey.'

The chauffeur hesitated, wrong-footed by the request, but Lancaster saved him the trouble of replying. 'Don't be ridiculous, darling. How long do you think that would take? Get in.'

She did as she was told, and Marta glanced at Josephine, who rolled her eyes. She hated the way that Lancaster had so publicly dismissed his wife's suggestion, even if it was impractical: Marazion Station was set apart from the town, where the causeway began, and to access the Mount on foot would first have involved a lengthy walk across the sand and pebble beach, which stretched for miles in front of them. The car took them out into a narrow country lane, parallel with the railway track, and they travelled back the way they had come until they reached Marazion. Josephine looked with interest at the little market town, which seemed to be organised around one winding street with houses straggling up the hill on the left-hand side. Its ancient buildings and curiously named alleyways intrigued her, suggesting a rich past independent of its connections to the Mount, and she hoped for a chance to explore it more thoroughly before they left Cornwall.

Trannack turned right and drove down onto the beach,

heading towards an impressive mass of rock which marked the beginning of the causeway. 'That's Chapel Rock,' he said, slipping effortlessly into the role of guide. 'The pilgrims used to wait there for the tide to go out, but they pulled the chapel down during the Civil War.'

'Which side were you on?'

'The right one, of course,' he replied, without missing a beat, then added: 'We held out for the King as long as we could. The Prince of Wales stayed at the Mount on his way out of the country. There's a little room off the south terrace where they hid him – you'll see it later on, no doubt. Mind you, the current Lord's ancestor was for Parliament, but we don't hold a grudge down here.'

He smiled at her in the rear-view mirror, and Josephine remembered how welcome she had felt the last time she was in Cornwall, staying with Archie's family. 'Do you live on the island?' she asked, already fascinated by its history.

'Yes, in the village. My family's been there since the seventeen hundreds, but that's not unusual. Most of us go back a few generations, usually doing the jobs our fathers did. There's not as many of us as there used to be, mind, and even fewer since the war, so you have to be able to turn your hand to most things now.'

The car took the causeway slowly, its tyres bumping over the cobbles as they left the mainland behind. On either side, flocks of oyster catchers searched for food along the shoreline, plunging their bills deeply into sand left bare by the fallen tide, and the smell of seaweed was rich and pungent. Up ahead, the path's halfway point was marked by a square stone embedded with a cross, another reminder of the island's holy origins; the image was already stark, silhouetted against an increasingly angry sky, but a carrion crow perched on the upright post gave the scene a still more ominous appearance. 'Not exactly robins and festive cheer so far, is it?' Marta whispered. 'I hope they've lit the fires.'

Rachel Lancaster took a handkerchief from her bag to wipe some condensation from the window, and as the sleeve of her coat fell back, Josephine noticed a faint bruise on her arm. She would have thought nothing of it had it not been for the brusque exchange she had just witnessed, but now she wondered if the careful arranging of the scarf was down to something more disturbing than nerves. 'Have you come far?' she asked, conscious that the couple hadn't spoken a word since getting into the car.

'From London,' Rachel said. 'We live in Somers Town, near Gerald's work, but we came down yesterday and broke the journey overnight. It's our wedding anniversary today. This trip is Gerald's present to me.'

'You were married on Christmas Eve?' Marta said. 'That was brave, with so much to organise already at this time of year.'

'I suppose it was, but neither of us has particularly happy memories of Christmas from when we were children, so we thought we'd make up for it, didn't we, Gerry?' She leaned forward to squeeze her husband's shoulder and he nodded, but his eyes remained fixed firmly on the Mount. 'And it's not as if we have big families to juggle, so most of the time we can just please ourselves.'

The silhouette of the castle grew more defined as they neared the end of the causeway. It had obviously been built to accommodate its unique position, rising steeply from dramatic areas of exposed rock, and its features sharpened gradually into a blend of the sacred, the military and the domestic: fortress walls, softening at intervals into more picturesque turrets, parapets and terraces, with a church rising up from the centre, its tower marking the highest point of the island. It was a strange mixture to find in such close proximity, and yet there was a harmony about it, Josephine thought, a simple honesty about the relationship between God and war over the centuries.

The causeway joined the island to the left of its compact harbour, and the car drew up by the first cluster of buildings. Modest, traditional stone cottages rubbed shoulders with a solid Victorian lodge and a handsome white house in the Regency style. A museum and gift shop stood on one corner, opposite the lych-gate to a tiny cemetery. To the right, a wider, cobbled road ran past an attractive row of cottages that fronted the harbour, their lamps already lit against the early gloom. The village seemed self-contained and detached from the castle's grandeur, Josephine thought, but she guessed that the lives of each set of inhabitants must be closely connected.

'Have we missed Twelfth Night?' Marta asked ironically, pointing to an area of lawn where two men with ropes were laying a huge Christmas tree on its side.

'They're taking it down before the storm does it for them,' Trannack said. 'If you don't mind waiting a moment, I'll call in at the Change House and get someone from the castle to come down and meet you. I won't be long, but feel free to stretch your legs and look round if you'd like to.'

'Can't you just drive us straight up there?' Lancaster asked impatiently.

'I'm afraid it's not as simple as that, sir. Cars don't go much further than this.'

Lancaster glanced doubtfully at the steep ascent to the summit. 'So what about our luggage?'

'Ah, there's a service tram that runs up to the castle, so no need to worry about that. Your cases will be taken to your rooms as soon as they get here.'

'But we've got to walk?'

'There is another option, sir. The pilgrims used to crawl up on their knees, but we don't insist on that nowadays.'

His remark came with a charm that cancelled out its insolence, and Josephine hid a smile as Trannack walked off to make his call, heading for the building nearest the causeway which presumably functioned as a reception point for the island. The cart laden with provisions and luggage was making swift progress across from the mainland and the driver touched his cap as he passed, then continued along the harbour, stopping outside a single-storey granite shed to unload. Elsewhere, vast amounts of logs and coal were being hauled off boats, and there was a strong sense of the islanders stocking up and hunkering down against the weather, rather like an old-style military siege. Rising to the challenge, the first flakes of white began to fall – hardly the blizzard that Trannack had forecast, but enough to soften the Mount's predominant greys and hint at how enchantingly the island might be transformed if the snow had a chance to settle.

The silence in the car grew more awkward as they waited, and Josephine was casting round for something harmless to say when Rachel Lancaster beat her to it. 'I don't want to stay here,' she announced from nowhere, and Marta and Josephine looked at her in surprise. 'Gerry, please – let's leave now, while we still can. This was a mistake.'

Lancaster turned round, and Josephine felt his wife flinch in the seat next to her. He must have caught her expression because he seemed to check himself, responding more kindly than he had intended. 'You're just tired, darling. It's been a long day,' he said, but there was a cajoling note in his voice which was almost as unpleasant as his temper. 'You'll feel better once we've settled in.' Rachel stared out of the window, refusing to meet his eye, and he looked at Josephine instead. 'Perhaps you could give us a moment in private?'

'Yes, of course.' Marta got out and Josephine followed, glad to feel the air on her face after the stuffiness of the car.

'Well, that wasn't very comfortable, was it?' Marta said as they walked over to the quayside, putting a discreet distance between themselves and the argument. 'I hope we're not seated next to those two at dinner – if they're staying for dinner, that is.'

'The very thought of it fills me with horror,' Josephine admitted. 'I think I might come down with something infectious and have a tray in my room.' She glanced back to the car, where the Lancasters seemed to be in animated conversation. 'Did you see the bruise on her arm? I shouldn't jump to conclusions, but . . .'

'Bastard. If I see him lay a finger on her . . .'

'Sssh, it will only make things worse if they know we're talking about them.' She looked over to the Change House, hoping that Trannack would soon be back to dilute the tension, but the only person on that side of the harbour was a solitary figure, dressed in black, who had just come out of the cemetery; for no apparent reason, the man turned at the head of the causeway and stared back in their direction, looking at the car for a long time before moving on. He strode out towards the mainland with his head bowed against the stiff Atlantic breeze – exposed and vulnerable, and yet somehow threatening. Unsettled by the image, Josephine shivered.

'Let's have a look at that museum,' Marta suggested. 'We'll catch our deaths if we just stand here.'

There was no light coming from inside the building, although the sign on the door said it was open. The window display featured various local curiosities – cannon balls fired during the Civil War, a spider crab with four claws – and a handwritten notice promised many more inside. 'At least we'll be out of the cold,' Marta said, 'and I've always wanted to know more about tin mining.'

She pushed at the door and a bell rang as it opened, but a voice from behind distracted her. 'Excuse me! Hello!'

A woman was hurrying down one of the paths from the castle, waving frantically to get their attention, and Josephine smiled at Marta. 'Looks like your education will have to wait. This must be our welcoming party.'

Sure enough, the woman introduced herself as Nora Pendean, the castle's housekeeper. 'Welcome to St Michael's Mount,' she said when Josephine and Marta had given their names, 'and a very happy Christmas to you both.' She paused to get her breath back, and Josephine wondered if her agitation was down to the general workload of a house party or the arrival of one guest in particular. 'I hope you'll be comfortable with us,' she continued, 'and please don't hesitate to ask if there's anything you need – anything at all. I'll take you up to the castle now and show you to your rooms, and Miss St Aubyn would be delighted if you would join her for drinks in the library at six. All our guests should have arrived by then. In the meantime, we'll bring you some tea.'

She glanced behind them at the open museum door, and Josephine felt obliged to explain. 'We thought we'd have a look round while we were waiting,' she said. 'You've obviously got a fascinating collection.'

'Oh yes, there are one or two things here that you won't find anywhere else, but I'm very sorry – it's closed now until after Christmas.' She reached inside to turn the sign round and shut the door firmly behind her. 'Family commitments. This shouldn't have been left open today, but I'm sure there'll be time for you to have a look round before you leave. Now – shall we go up and settle you in?'

Trannack had returned and was by the car with the Lancasters; other than an embarrassed glance towards Marta and Josephine, they made no reference to the earlier conversation, and when Mrs Pendean began the steep climb to the castle, they followed her without another word.

4

The temptation to call in at his uncle's house and introduce his travelling companion to his family was almost too much for Archie, but their progress through Devon had been hampered by icy roads and snowbound villages, and he wanted to reach Marazion before the causeway closed. In spite of sending luggage on separately as she had promised, Marlene could never be described as someone who travelled light, and the idea of transferring everything she had brought from his car to a boat was a mountain which he would prefer not to face at the end of a long journey.

Contrary to his expectations, the hours spent together on the road had been relaxed and enjoyable, and Marlene was excellent company – gracious and undemanding, and appreciative of everything that was arranged for her. Knowing that nothing he booked could compete with the hotels she was used to, Archie had chosen simple country inns to break their journey, full of English charm but suitably anonymous, and he would never forget the look on a Wiltshire landlady's face when the actress marched into her kitchens to demand the recipe for a venison and chestnut casserole. They talked constantly while they drove, and yet – while Marlene had quizzed him expertly on everything from his job to his favourite foods, teasing him gently at times and flirting when the mood took her – Archie would have been hard pressed to say that he knew her any better now than he did when they left Claridge's; only once, when she had talked again about the letters that were causing her so much concern, did he glimpse someone more vulnerable beneath the natural self-assurance.

'You are lucky to come from such a beautiful place,' she said, as they drove across the wild, treeless moorland between Launceston and Bodmin. The landscape was dotted with granite boulders and thickets of rough furze, devoid of human markers except for the occasional isolated farmhouse, and it interested Archie that she should find its starkness beautiful. 'Why did you leave it?' she asked.

'College first, and then the war.'

'You must have been young to fight.'

'That's kind of you, but not really. I was twenty when I signed up, and there was nothing particularly young about that, even in those early days. I suppose you were still at school?'

Marlene nodded. 'They made us knit for the soldiers – mittens and scarves, sweaters if you were older. I'm sure they only did it to make us feel useful.' She stared out of the window at a dark mass of rock on the summit of a hill, silhouetted against a pale sky like the ruins of a castle. 'The wool was so rough, and I could never keep it from tangling. They called it field grey, which puzzled me. I'd never seen a field that was grey, but I suppose the battlefields were.'

'Brown and grey, yes – like a never-ending winter. I remember coming back to England on leave, and all those summer greens seemed so artificial.'

She lit a cigarette for each of them and looked curiously at Archie. 'Why are you smiling? You surely don't have fond memories of that time.'

'No, not at all. I was just trying to reconcile the little girl and her tangled knitting with the woman I saw showing the Nazis out of her hotel suite.'

'The little girl was defiant too.'

'Yes, I'm sure she was.'

'I was thrown out of school for it,' she said, a hint of pride in her voice. 'There was a French POW camp near my home and we weren't supposed to go anywhere near it, but I loved France, even then. On Bastille Day I took the soldiers white roses and pushed them through the barbed wire fence. Someone saw me doing it and the mothers demanded my blood.'

Archie smiled again, picturing the scene. 'How did your family fare during the war?' he asked, realising how little he knew of Marlene's life outside her films. 'Did your father fight?'

She shook her head. 'No. My father was a lieutenant in the Royal Prussian police, but he died when I was six and I never really got to know my stepfather. He was killed in the middle of the war. Most of my cousins, too. By the time it was over, we were a family of women, all in black.' She had spoken vehemently against the Nazis throughout the journey, expressing opinions very similar to his own, and it was easy to forget that he and her family had fought on opposite sides. 'It seemed to go on for so long,' she said. 'My cousin Hans said that your men pitied ours towards the end. They threw cans of food over whenever the gunfire stopped. He loved your corned beef.' There was a weariness in her voice, which spoke for both sides. 'It's good to know that people can think for themselves when it really matters, isn't it? It gives me hope.'

89

Large, uneven flakes of snow began to fall onto the car and Archie looked anxiously at the sky, hoping that the weather wasn't about to take a turn for the worse, but the flurry was nothing more than that and the last few miles passed quickly. Marlene's delight on seeing the castle for the first time was a distraction from his own more complex feelings; with his parents and many of his friends now dead, coming home for Christmas was invariably a tangle of comfort and loss, much harder than staying away. He had seen St Michael's Mount at midnight under a harvest moon and shimmering in the midday sun, ghostly through a sea mist or defiant against a raging storm, but it always transported him back to his childhood. 'We're here in time,' he said, before his emotions could get the better of him. 'The tide looks like it's only just turned, so we can cross by car.'

'That's probably just as well. I have never been a very good swimmer.'

Archie announced their arrival at the estate office on the mainland, and by the time he had driven across the causeway, Hilaria was waiting on the quayside, flanked by two footmen and a man with a camera. 'I feel as if I'm about to be presented at court,' Marlene said.

'I suppose you are, in a manner of speaking. They're used to royalty here.'

He drew up by the museum and opened the door for Marlene, noticing how many of the islanders had suddenly found a reason to be out and about or sitting at their windows. 'Miss Dietrich, how lovely to meet you,' Hilaria said. 'Thank you for coming. Your support is so valuable to us.'

'I'm glad to help with such a good cause. It's very good of you to open your home for Christmas – and what a magnificent home it is.'

Archie waited while Hilaria talked briefly about the island and its history. She seemed completely at ease, and – not for the first time – he envied the English aristocracy their self-confidence, then reminded himself that in this particular case it stemmed from more than generations of entitlement. Hilaria was a remarkable woman in her own right, an adventurous, inquisitive traveller who had flown across the equator and sailed around the world, showing as little regard for safety in later life as she had when they played together as children. She and Marlene were bound to hit it off, he thought; they had so much in common.

The photographer hovered awkwardly on the sidelines, a guest whose presence was tolerated rather than welcomed, and Archie felt sorry for him. He had expected someone older, a version of the pushy, world-weary journalists he had often had to deal with in his work, but Alex Fielding was around thirty, dressed impeccably in a dark blue suit which was new enough to have been bought especially for the weekend; he looked incapable of intruding on anyone's privacy, let alone a Hollywood star's. 'You must be from *The Times*,' Archie said, holding out his hand. 'I'm—'

'Detective Chief Inspector Penrose – yes, I recognised you. From the newspaper,' he added, seeing the look of surprise on Archie's face. 'You've been splashed across our pages several times in the last few months.'

Hilaria waved them over before Archie had a chance to respond. 'Miss Dietrich, allow me to introduce Alex Fielding from *The Times*. Mr Fielding was just telling me how often he's photographed you in the past, so he'll probably be familiar to you.'

Marlene looked at him and Archie could see that she had no recollection of him at all from the sea of photographers who must greet her at every turn, but her graciousness was impressive. 'Yes, of course,' she said. 'How nice to see you again, Mr Fielding.'

'And you.' He took her hand, then seemed to remember why he was there. 'Perhaps I might get some shots of your arrival at the Mount? Now, while we've still got the light?'

'By all means.' She put a hand on Archie's arm and said under her breath: 'You see? Why do they always think they know me?'

He smiled and watched her walk a few yards round the harbour, admiring her instinct for the best vantage point. Fielding turned to him. 'You too, Chief Inspector.'

'You want me in the photograph?'

'Why not? Our readers will want to know that Miss Dietrich is in safe hands.'

It seemed an odd thing to say, and Archie noticed Hilaria glance sharply at Fielding. He stood by Marlene, waiting while the photographer fumbled nervously with the camera, then moved to one side to allow him to take some pictures of the film star on her own.

'I'm so glad you're here,' Hilaria said, giving him a hug while the others were preoccupied. 'I was beginning to wish I'd never started this.'

He laughed. 'You've really got nothing to worry about. She's nowhere near as difficult as you might expect.'

'That's not quite what I meant, but I'm glad to hear it.'

'There's an awful lot of luggage in the car, though,' he added quietly, 'and very little of it is mine.'

He had meant it as a joke, but Hilaria didn't smile as she beckoned the footman over. 'Take Mr Penrose's car round to the tram, will you, Mason?'

Archie thanked him and handed over his keys. 'Have Josephine and Marta arrived?' he asked.

'Yes, about half an hour ago. I haven't had a chance to call in on them yet, but we're gathering for drinks at six.'

'I'll go and say hello when we've finished here.'

'Do, but can I speak to you first? In private?'

'Yes, of course.'

She looked concerned, but before Archie could ask her what was wrong, they were distracted by another car driving quickly across the causeway, a large Mercedes-Benz with whitewall tyres. 'Ah, good – that's the colonel and his daughter,' Hilaria said, as the chauffeur pulled up outside the Change House. 'Excellent timing. We can all go up to the castle together.'

But the man who got out of the back seat was certainly nothing to do with the British army, retired or otherwise. Barbara Penhaligon's chaperone was a handsome young blond man in a dark uniform, and Hilaria stared in horror at the swastika on his arm. 'I don't understand,' she faltered. 'Where is Arthur? What is that man doing here?'

'I was about to ask the very same thing,' Marlene said, and her voice was suddenly like cut glass.

Barbara Penhaligon waved and made her way over, and it seemed to Archie that she was perfectly aware of her host's discomfort; not only that, but she appeared to be enjoying it. 'My father isn't well,' she announced, kissing Hilaria on both

93

cheeks. 'He's so disappointed not to be here, but he's gone down with a terrible cold and he wasn't fit to travel.' She looked round at everyone, waiting for the introduction that was hardly necessary. 'He sends his apologies, but you really wouldn't thank him for passing it on, I'm sure.'

'I'm very sorry to hear that,' Hilaria said, just as her lack of response was verging on rudeness. 'We were looking forward to seeing you both, but you shouldn't feel obliged to stay if you'd rather be at home with him. Christmas isn't a time to be on your own.'

The attempt to avert a social disaster was both clumsy and transparent. Barbara smiled to show that she'd seen through it, but played along with the game. 'That's thoughtful of you, but he really was most insistent that we don't both let you down, and Max was kind enough to bring me across. You remember him from last summer, when he was here with the British Ambassador? It would have been at the Godolphin garden party.'

'I was away in Egypt last summer, so I'm afraid I haven't had the pleasure until now.' She shook hands with the German, and out of solidarity Archie did the same, resisting the urge to wipe his palm on his trousers afterwards.

'Delighted to meet you all,' Max said in flawless English, 'and particularly you, Miss Dietrich. We are great admirers of your work back in Germany, as I'm sure you know.'

He held out his hand to Marlene, and Archie glanced at Fielding and the ever-present camera, but the actress was one step ahead of him: under no circumstances was she willing to be photographed shaking hands with a Nazi, and she simply nodded, her face expressionless.

'Aren't you going to invite Max to stay?' Barbara asked,

looking provocatively at her host, as if daring her to choose which guest to offend.

Archie felt sorry for Hilaria, put so publicly on the spot, but ironically it was the German who saved her. 'Thank you, that is very kind, but I have business to attend to over Christmas. The compliments of the season to you all.' He gave a curt nod and spoke quickly in German to Barbara, then strode round the harbour to the waiting car. Hilaria sent the second footman after him to collect the luggage.

'What did he say to her?' Archie asked Marlene under his breath.

'He told her to telephone at once if she needs anything. He said he will be waiting just across the water.' They watched as the Mercedes turned and drove back along the causeway, which was now partially covered by the incoming tide. The actress turned to Hilaria. 'Perhaps you would be kind enough to show me to my room.'

It wasn't a request, even if her hostess had been inclined to suggest an alternative. Fielding stayed behind in the village to take more photographs, and Hilaria set off up the steep path to the east door. In the entrance hall – with a certain amount of relief, Archie thought – she handed Marlene and Barbara over to the care of two waiting housemaids. 'Could that have been more awkward?' she asked, when she and Archie were finally on their own.

'Not really. I hope you haven't put them in adjacent rooms.'

'Mercifully no, but there are still plenty of opportunities for them to clash at meal times. Poor Arthur. As if that girl hasn't caused him enough worry already. Thank God her mother's not alive to see it.'

'At least her friend didn't stay, and any animosity between Barbara and Marlene will be diluted in a larger group. We'll do our best to keep them apart, and if all else fails, just think of the money you're raising.'

She sighed. 'Even that isn't turning out quite as I expected. The Lancasters' cheque was returned to me in the post this morning, so what do I do about that? I can hardly throw them off the island now they're here.'

'Have you said anything to them?'

'No. They were on the same train as your friends, so I haven't even met them. I've been hoping for the right moment, but, as you can imagine, it hasn't arisen yet. And now we've the German question. Thank God for Richard and Angela, although she's hardly herself, poor woman. And you, of course. Thank you for coming, Archie. More than ever now.'

'Why? What's happened?' he asked, concerned to see her so anxious. 'What did you want to talk to me about?'

'It's best if I show you. Come with me.'

Intrigued, he followed her up a spiral granite staircase and along a series of passages which led away from the east wing and into the main body of the house. The castle's geography was confusing, built as it was on different levels and linked by numerous corridors that twisted this way and that, doubling back on themselves until he lost all sense of direction. There were steps up and down where they were least expected, and he stumbled a couple of times in the fading light as he tried to keep up with his guide. Eventually, they reached the Long Passage that ran parallel with the church, its walls lined with portraits of the St Aubyn family. He was struck by a magnificent oil painting of Hilaria's stepmother, who had died earlier that year. 'How is Lord St Levan?' he asked. 'I'm sorry he won't be with us for Christmas.'

'Yes, so am I, but it's much more sensible for him to spend winters on the mainland now. It can be bitterly cold here, as you know, and he's very frail. Julia's death hit him so hard. He's been blessed with two happy marriages, but to lose them both – well, it takes its toll. That, and the state of the world. It's a terrible thing to say, but I half wish he could be spared what we're heading for.'

'Yes, I can understand that. It will mean big changes for you, though.'

Hilaria stopped to straighten one of the pictures, conveniently not meeting his eye. 'You're right, it will. I'm trying not to think about that, though. Not until I have to.'

They were in the Victorian part of the house now, and Archie followed her down the kitchen stairs to the staff quarters. The door swung heavily shut behind them, marking the point where the tapestries and richly coloured rugs gave way to bare stone floors and walls painted an anaemic shade of green. It was draughty in the bowels of the house, and the passage – which was actually more like a tunnel – echoed with the footsteps of staff going purposefully about their work. Archie wondered why they were there.

'Do you remember Henry Lee?' Hilaria asked, stopping outside the door to the pantry. 'He's been here for nearly fifty years now. He was a footman when you and I were growing up.'

She knocked and went in, and although the name had only rung the faintest of bells, Archie recognised the elderly butler instantly. The room was spacious, with a high ceiling, good natural light and a cosy fire in the grate, and two footmen sat at a long table, polishing silver. Their stools scraped back noisily on the wooden floor as they stood to greet the lady of the house, and Hilaria nodded to them. 'You'll be pleased to see Archie Penrose, Lee. He often came over from the Loe Estate when we first arrived here. He and I used to get up to no end of tricks, and I seem to recall you colluding in most of them.'

'Yes, of course, Miss.' Lee smiled and bowed his head. 'Very good to see you again, sir – and happy Christmas.'

'And to you, Lee. It's nice to be back.'

'We've just had a message from Trannack, Miss. Mrs Carmichael wasn't on the scheduled train, and there isn't another service now until this evening. I've made arrangements with the Godolphin Hotel for her to stay there overnight if she arrives late. Depending on the weather, we can try and bring her over tomorrow.'

Hilaria sighed. 'Very well, Lee. I don't see what else we can do. Perhaps she'll telephone to let us know. In the meantime, is that item still in the flower room?'

'Yes, Miss. Locked, as you instructed. I'll take you there now.'

'Thank you.' She turned to leave, but paused to admire a work in progress on one of the wide shelves that lined the room's longest wall – a beautifully scaled model of the castle, made entirely from champagne corks and meticulous in its detail. 'This is coming along well, Lee. We'll do our best to give you plenty of raw materials to work with over Christmas.' She cast a wry glance at Archie. 'Heaven knows, we'll need a drink. You could probably have it finished by Boxing Day.'

The butler led the way further into the staff quarters, past the kitchens and servants' hall and up a short flight of steps to a room on the castle's cold outer wall. As he unlocked the door and stood aside to let them pass, Archie was taken aback by the overpowering scent of exotic flowers. Three dramatic centrepieces took pride of place on the table – arrangements of holly, red carnations and white lilies in various combinations – and more holly stood soaking in buckets on the flagstone floor. A bench ran the length of the room, littered with scissors, string and vases, and the next candidates for display – roses and chrysanthemums in shades of gold and burnt orange – were waiting in the sink. Two crates with a Scilly Isles stamp stood by the door, and the simple, tightly budded daffodils – their yellow-green heads promising the first sign of spring – came as something of a relief.

'Shall I get it down for you, Miss?' the butler asked.

'Yes please, Lee.' He moved the floral displays carefully to one end of the table, then took down a long gift box from the top shelf. 'This arrived yesterday for Miss Dietrich,' Hilaria explained, seeing the look of confusion on Archie's face. 'I'll let you open it.' He took the lid off and looked down at the perfect red roses. 'There are thirteen,' she said, as he began to count them. 'Look at the card.'

He picked it up and read the message. '*Mein Engel, mit wärmsten Wünschen für Weihnachten – und mit Bewunderung – Adolf Hitler.*'

'I was hoping you might reassure me that this couldn't possibly be genuine,' Hilaria said.

'I'm afraid it probably is.' He told her about the visitors to Marlene's hotel suite. 'Ironically, she came here to get away.'

'We'll have to tell her, won't we?' Hilaria said reluctantly. 'We should at least give her the option to leave if she feels she's being threatened – and sooner rather than later. There are blizzards coming in tonight, and a boat won't get to the mainland once they start.'

'I'll talk to her, but I doubt she'll want to go anywhere. She strikes me as someone who likes to face up to things rather than run from them.' Archie read the card again. 'Now I understand why you were so sensitive when Fielding made that comment about Marlene being in safe hands.'

'Yes, it was unfortunate under the circumstances, but I'm hoping it was just a turn of phrase on his part. The last thing we want is this in the newspaper – although he seemed just as impressed by your celebrity as he was by hers.'

Archie smiled. 'You say these arrived yesterday?'

'That's right. About four o'clock, wasn't it, Lee?'

'Yes, Miss.'

'Before it was announced in the paper that she'd be here. Did the guests know in advance?'

'Only you and Fielding, but he was sworn to secrecy by his editor.'

'I didn't think Barbara Penhaligon looked in the least bit surprised to bump into Marlene.'

'No, but I assumed she'd seen it in the paper this morning.'

'Perhaps, but I still find it strange that a German officer bothered to bring her here when she's got a perfectly good chauffeur. It was almost as if he was checking that Marlene had arrived.'

'You think Barbara is involved in this?'

Archie shrugged. 'There must be several people at Claridge's who know where Marlene is. She said the Nazis had been camped out there for days, so they could easily have twisted someone's arm for a forwarding address. And presumably you told the staff in advance that Marlene was one of the guests?'

He felt rather than heard the butler's indignation, and Hilaria seemed to share Lee's resentment. 'Oh no, Archie, I won't have that. There's no way that any of my staff would be involved in something like this. It's simply not possible.'

'Of course not. I'm sorry.' He was about to suggest that they went upstairs to break the news to Marlene when he heard voices outside in the passage, one of the housemaids talking loudly to her colleague.

'She only wants the thorns cut off the bloody roses! And she's told me what to do with the fruit bowl – all except the apples.' The door burst open and the girl came in, carrying a beautiful vase of red roses which had presumably been exiled from Marlene's room. Luckily, she was too aghast when she saw Hilaria to take any notice of the box on the table, and Lee quickly ushered her out of the room, following her down the corridor to deliver what Archie could only assume would be the scolding of a lifetime. He picked up one of Hitler's roses and ran his finger along the smooth, perfect stem. 'Perhaps now isn't quite the right moment to deliver these,' he said, 'but at least the Führer knows how she likes them.'

5

Josephine thought that finding Marta would be a simple matter of retracing her footsteps, but the castle's myriad corridors and staircases defied her recollection of the route they had taken when the housemaid showed them to their rooms. She lost her bearings at each and every turn, and was just beginning to understand why so many country house murder mysteries opened with a helpful map when she recognised the magnificent Samurai suit of armour that stood rather threateningly at the head of a passageway; Marta's room was just beyond it.

'Who is it?' Marta called when she knocked at the door.

'It's only me. Can I come in?'

'No, you can't. Give me a minute. I won't be long.' Intrigued, Josephine heard the rustling of paper from inside the room, followed by a thud or two, as if things were being hurriedly packed away, then Marta appeared in the doorway. 'All right, it's safe now. I was just wrapping your final Christmas present.'

'So I can see. You've got glitter all over your face.'

'Have I?' She brushed her cheek and stood aside to let Josephine in. 'Isn't this wonderful? Come and look at the view.'

The room was further round to the south than Josephine's, and faced the open sea. She followed Marta over to the window, and the sheer drop to the rocks and gardens below

– just visible in the fading light – took her breath away. The gardens were formal in style, cleverly designed to appeal to a crow's-eye view and arranged on several levels. The wildness of the sea beyond – pounding at the rocks on the fringes of the island – was exhilarating. 'I'm not sure I'd want to be one of the gardeners,' Josephine said, looking doubtfully at the more inaccessible lawns and borders. 'It must be perilous, climbing round there whenever a hedge needs trimming. And look at the battering those bushes are getting from the wind. It's a wonder anything survives at all with so much salt in the air.'

'Yes, but think of the sun it must get in summer. I bet they grow some amazing things. Perhaps we'll get a chance to explore if the weather improves.' She smiled and gave Josephine a kiss. 'How's your room?'

'Magnificent. Big enough to sleep six, with lofty ceilings and the most beautiful tiling round the window. Everything you'd hope for from a castle, from the four-poster bed to the draughts.' She looked round, and added wryly: 'It's less chaotic than this one, though. I see you've made yourself well and truly at home.'

Marta wasn't by nature the tidiest of people and she always took over a room, no matter how brief her stay in it. Josephine recognised the same welcoming touches that had greeted her in her own room – a beautiful arrangement of holly, spruce and ivy, a Christmas card from Hilaria with a box of Prestat chocolates, a luxurious fruit bowl and a decanter of sherry – but Marta had personalised the welcome with some hospitality of her own. There was brandy and red wine, and a collection of elegantly wrapped presents had been arranged by the winter greenery, which now functioned as a miniature Christmas tree. Most touchingly of all, Marta had smuggled in a collection of decorations that Josephine put up each year at the house she owned in Suffolk. The cottage had become something of a haven for them both in recent months, as the wider world grew darker and more dangerous, and they retreated there whenever they could. 'I can't believe you thought of this,' she said. 'You've brought Christmas with you.'

'I dug them out of the cupboard when you weren't looking. They're special to us, so I thought they should travel.'

Josephine picked up the snow globe, which was one of the first things that she and Marta had bought together, and something in its fragility touched her. Continually in the back of her mind now was the knowledge that another war would threaten her independence and all the aspects of her life that were most precious. There were bound to be travel restrictions, which would confine her to Scotland and separate her from Marta for long periods at a time, and she knew in her heart that if hostilities broke out, Marta wasn't the kind of woman who would sit on the sidelines and wait for them to end; she would do something brave and glorious, or leave England altogether and find her freedom elsewhere. As selfish as it seemed, the loneliness of another war frightened Josephine far more than any loss of life. 'Are you all right?' Marta asked gently. 'You don't usually get this emotional about Christmas decorations. That's my territory. You'll be crying at films next.'

Josephine laughed and wiped her eyes. 'I'm fine – more than fine, actually. It's just all this – you getting excited about Christmas, and being able to spend it together again. It matters, this year more than ever, especially now you have to go away.'

'I'm not going for long, but I know what you mean. All the more reason to make the most of this.' Marta pulled a small sofa closer to the fire and put another log on. 'I was thinking about it on the train coming down. The last couple of years are the first time in my life that I've ever spent Christmas with the person I love. Why wouldn't I be excited?'

'I am, too.' She took Marta's hand and snuggled up to her, enjoying the peace and wondering if anyone would miss them if they stayed in front of the fire for the whole weekend. 'I'm glad we're here. Everything feels so gloomy and depressing at the moment. It's nice to be cut off from it all for a few days. I don't want to see another newspaper or hear another political speech until at least halfway through January.'

'You and the rest of the country. We could all do with a bit of sparkle.'

'Speaking of which – I've got a view of the harbour from my room. I think I saw Archie's car arrive.'

'Did you . . .'

'No, not a glimpse. I can just about see the end of the causeway if I crane my neck, but I lost sight of him before he parked. At least we know they're here, though. The star has arrived.'

'I think the real star's just outside the window. Look.'

Josephine turned and saw the snow – not the brief, half-hearted flurry that had greeted them, but a silent storm of white, steady and relentless, peppering the glass and filling the indigo sky beyond with its mournful, radiant beauty. Marta put out the lamps and they lay quietly in each other's arms, watching it fall and listening to the crackle of the fire until a grandfather clock on the landing outside struck five.

'I suppose we'd better get ready for drinks,' Marta said reluctantly.

'Yes, and you'll need to tidy up before the housemaid comes in to lay your clothes out. It never occurred to me that we'd be waited on to that extent.'

'Oh, I told her not to bother. What a bloody nightmare that would be. Surely you did, too?'

'No, I didn't. It felt rude when it's obviously what they do here. I wish I had now.'

'Well, just make sure you stand her down for the night shift. You've already got someone to help you *un*dress.' Marta smiled. 'I'll come and collect you in half an hour. That'll give us time to call in on Archie as we go down.'

'And give him the third degree on Marlene, you mean.'

'Something like that, yes, so make sure you're ready.'

Josephine found her way back to her room, hoping she'd have time to wash and change before the maid came in to do whatever maids did. She cursed herself again for being too timid to refuse help, as Marta had done; it was ridiculous, but the most daunting aspect of the house party so far was how to behave with the servants. The strain of doing things correctly with a butler or housekeeper at her shoulder completely eclipsed any nerves she might have had at meeting Marlene; she was used to actresses, but Mrs Pendean and her effortless courtesy already put the fear of God into her.

She took the towels that had been laid out for her on the bed, and washed quickly in the nearest bathroom. Shivering, she hurried back to dress in front of the fire, but as she turned the corner, she saw the housekeeper coming out of the room two doors down from her own. To her relief, Mrs Pendean turned in the opposite direction and headed for the staircase, but an elderly man wearing a dog collar – presumably the Reverend Hartley – came out of his room after her and called her back. They began what looked like an earnest conversation on the landing, and Josephine made a beeline for her door, hoping to slip into her room unnoticed, but the housekeeper was too sharp for her and she knew it was only a matter of time before she received a visit. Sure enough, a few minutes later there was a polite knock at the door.

'Come in,' Josephine called, struggling with the zip which had caught halfway up in her haste to get the dress on before she was disturbed. She smiled at the housekeeper. 'Good evening, Mrs Pendean.'

'Good evening, madam. Now that you're back, is there anything I can help you with?'

Perhaps Josephine was imagining the implied criticism that she had been absent without leave from her room, disrupting the smooth routines of the house, but she resisted the temptation to explain herself. 'This dress isn't being very co-operative, I'm afraid.'

'Let me see.'

The defiant zip was dealt with in a second, and Josephine thanked her. She sat down at the dressing table to redo her make-up, hoping that Mrs Pendean would take charge of any other rituals that were expected of her, and watched in the mirror as the housekeeper picked up the day clothes that she had hurriedly discarded on the chair as she changed. Mrs Pendean shook the dress out and put it on a hanger, where it instantly fell straight and smooth, the cuffs flat against the skirt, with no errant sleeves sticking out and certainly no sign of the day's long journey; the garment was tidied away in the wardrobe, and Josephine knew that it would emerge creaseless and as good as new whenever it was next required. 'Thank you,' she said again, but the comment met with no response, and she wondered if gratitude was somehow inappropriate. She found the silence awkward as Mrs Pendean walked over to turn down the bed, and decided just to be herself; there was little point in pretending she was used to this, particularly when she probably had far more in common with some of the servants than she did with the family who owned the house. 'I imagine the island will look spectacular in the morning,' she said, as she powdered her face. 'Do you often get snow like this at Christmas?'

'It's unusual, madam. I've only known it once or twice in my lifetime, and not since my daughter was a little girl.'

'We're very lucky then.'

There was no answer, and Josephine assumed that the etiquette was to say only what needed to be said, but when she looked at the woman's reflection in the mirror, she was astonished to find her on the verge of tears. Her instinct was to ask what was wrong, but she put her mascara on in silence and combed her hair, knowing that any further conversation would be unwelcome. Mrs Pendean went quietly about her business, taking advantage of the routine to steady her emotions, and when she spoke again, her voice was perfectly controlled. 'What will you be wearing tomorrow, madam?'

'The blue suit, I think,' Josephine said.

'Very well.' The suit and two pairs of shoes were collected from the wardrobe, and Josephine realised that they were going to be pressed and polished. Briefly, she wished she'd brought some mending that badly needed doing; her own daily wasn't especially handy with a needle. 'And what time would you like to be called in the morning?'

'Oh, I hadn't thought. What time does the family usually go down?'

'We always serve breakfast after the morning service on Christmas Day. That starts at nine o'clock, but I can arrange for you to have something beforehand in your room if you'd prefer?'

Josephine hesitated, tempted by the idea of a quiet start to the day, but her sense of obligation won out. 'No, please don't go to any trouble. After the service will be fine, and perhaps you could call me at eight?'

'Of course, madam.'

She left the room, almost bumping into Archie on her way out, and Josephine stood to give him a hug. 'Happy Christmas! Thank God you're here. Now you can explain how all this works.'

He smiled. 'I'm no expert, but what would you like to know?'

'What do we do about tips, and why does the weather make the housekeeper cry?'

'What?'

'She was upset – something to do with her daughter, I think. It was all a bit awkward and I didn't like to ask.'

'Well, I can't help you with that one, but as far as tips are concerned, it's best to opt for a discreet thank you on your last morning.' He stood back to admire her dress. 'You look lovely.'

'So do you, even more so than usual.' It was true, she thought: Archie could carry black tie off better than anyone else she knew, but tonight he seemed particularly relaxed, and she remembered thinking the very same thing when they had last been in Cornwall together. 'Is there anything you'd like to tell me after two days alone with Marlene?' she asked coyly.

'No, not in the way you mean.'

'How very disappointing. I should warn you that Marta has a list of questions as long as her arm, though, and most of them are far more salacious than mine.'

'Marlene has a few for her, too. She was fascinated when I told her that Marta wrote scripts for Hitchcock. She's a great admirer of his.'

'You probably shouldn't mention that. Marta's jumpy enough about her as it is.'

'When does Marta leave for America?'

'Just after New Year. She'll be there for a couple of months, sorting things out for the Hitchcocks before they make the big move.'

'And how do you feel about that?'

Josephine shrugged, but she knew that any show of nonchalance wouldn't fool Archie and she was glad to talk to him about it. Marta's work for the Hitchcocks was important to her, and although she had refused the offer of a permanent move to Hollywood with them, they valued her enough to let her come and go. Still, Josephine could never entirely rid herself of the fear that one day Marta might not come back. 'I'll miss her. I daren't admit this to her, but I wonder if there'll come a time when she has to make a choice, especially with war on the horizon.'

'But surely you know she'd choose you. She always has.'

'Yes, I know. Keep reminding me of that, would you?'

He smiled. 'Of course I will.'

'Anyway, she'll be here in a minute. You've saved us the trouble of coming to find you. Sherry?'

'Lovely.' She poured three glasses and passed his across. 'Did you have a good journey down?' Archie asked.

'Yes and no. The train was fine – spectacular, actually, with all the snow – but the first guests we met were a nightmare.' She told him about the Lancasters and their bickering. 'What's even worse is that he's a fan of my books. I just know I'll be stuck with him all weekend unless I'm very rude. You too, probably, once he finds out you're from Scotland Yard.'

Archie grimaced. 'I can trump that.' Josephine listened in disbelief as he told her about Barbara Penhaligon's Nazi chaperone. 'Marlene was livid. Everything she's come here to avoid seems to have followed her. I felt so sorry for Hilaria.'

'It makes you wonder why we all look forward to Christmas, doesn't it? Still, I suppose if we drink enough . . .'

He raised his glass. 'And it's only a couple of days. What can possibly go wrong?'

6

Rachel Lancaster waited until their hostess had left the room, then turned on her husband. 'For God's sake, Gerry! That was so humiliating. I don't know how you could have put us in that position. Now we've got to be here all weekend, sitting at their table, drinking their wine, and knowing we owe them money that we really can't afford.'

'It was a simple mistake, darling. Miss St Aubyn accepts that. Why can't you?'

'Because I know you better than she does.'

She saw his face tighten with the effort to stay calm. 'It's Christmas, Rachel, and I doubt very much that I'm the only person to have bounced a cheque. We've had a lot of expenses, and I forgot that my bonus wasn't going to be paid until the end of the month.'

'But you don't even know how much your bonus will be.'

He slammed his hand down on the bedside table and she flinched. 'Will you *please* stop making such a bloody fuss! I'll write the woman another cheque as soon as we get home, and that will be that. I don't want to hear another word about it.'

He picked up his book and began to read, but the embarrassment of the last few minutes was still raw in Rachel's memory and she refused to let it drop. 'You promised me this would never happen again,' she said evenly. 'Not after the last time. Why *are* we here, Gerry? Because it sure as hell isn't to celebrate a happy anniversary.'

There was no answer, and she recognised the hostile, brooding silence that invariably warned of trouble. This time, though, something in her wanted to test him: perhaps it was a weary fatalism with life or the familiar desolation of Christmas, perhaps simply the comfort of strangers, in whose presence surely even Gerry would have to control himself, but she longed suddenly for change, and it scarcely mattered whether it was for better or worse. 'I'm going to dress for dinner.' She got up, and felt his eyes on her as she walked over to the wardrobe.

'What are you doing?' he asked. 'I've chosen your clothes for tonight. They're on the chair.'

Rachel looked at the selection he had made on her behalf, a yellow crêpe-de-chine evening dress that he had bought for her several seasons ago. The frills of white silk and a black velvet ribbon bow at the front were ugly and outdated, and she hated the way that the colour always made her look washed out and ill; she had lost weight in the intervening years, and the dress now sat shapelessly on her, ageing her before her time. 'That's kind of you, darling,' she said, unable to resist a sarcastic emphasis on the endearment, 'but I fancy a change tonight. I've brought something special.'

She found the black silk-crêpe dinner dress that the housemaid had hung so carefully in the wardrobe when she unpacked their cases and took it out with a flourish, enjoying the look of astonishment on her husband's face as she held it up and studied herself in the full-length mirror. He was off the bed and across the room in a single movement. She felt his hands on her shoulders, saw his fury reflected in the looking glass, but for once she stood her ground, refusing to let go of the dress. 'Where the hell did that come from?' he demanded.

'I bought it.'

'You've been out shopping?'

'Of course not, darling. I know how angry it makes you if I go out on my own, so I ordered it from a catalogue. What do you think? It wasn't too expensive.'

She met his eye, waiting for the explosion. 'Rachel, you can't possibly wear that thing,' he said, looking at the fitted bodice. 'It's strapless, and . . .'

'You're worried I'll be cold?'

'I'm worried you'll look like a whore.'

A whore with bruises, she thought, watching him panic as he imagined the other guests looking across the dinner table at his wife's arms, already thinking up another careless accident that she might have met with. She twisted away from him and found some nail scissors in her bag to cut the label off the dress, waiting a moment before she put him out of his misery. 'Oh, don't be so pathetic, Gerry. Do you really think I want the shame of that any more than you do? I've been humiliated enough already today.' The elbow-length black gloves that came with the dress were still wrapped in tissue; she tore the paper off and threw it on the fire. 'I'll wear these. Is that modest enough for you?'

'You'll wear what I told you to wear.' He snatched one of the gloves from her and ran the soft black silk through his fingers, then wound one end of it round the palm of his hand. 'Come here.'

She stood her ground, but there was no defying his temper now. He threw her back on the bed and pressed his knee hard into her stomach. 'Not my face, Gerry – please. Think of what people will say.'

There was a knock at the door, and Rachel held her breath,

waiting to see what he would do. Eventually, when the knock was repeated, he released her and threw the glove onto the floor. Rachel straightened her clothes and composed herself, then let the housemaid into the room.

7

Josephine was more than used to theatre and the world of make-believe, but she had never felt as much like an extra on a film set as she did when she, Marta and Archie walked into the library for drinks at six o'clock. The room was intimate and welcoming, far more typical of a traditional country house setting than a castle, and considerably less austere than most of the grander libraries that she had visited: the books set into the cushioned alcoves looked as if they had actually been read, and the pale walls, simple panelling and subtle watercolours gave a soft, understated feel to the space which instinctively married comfort and elegance. If the fireplace was modest by comparison with those in the bedrooms, the size of the low-ceilinged room rewarded its efforts more generously, and the atmosphere was warm and convivial.

But the focal point, for tonight at least, was the baby grand piano in the corner. Josephine had heard the music outside in the corridor, a beautifully played version of 'It Came Upon the Midnight Clear' which she had assumed to be coming from a gramophone record, but as soon as the vocalist joined in, she realised her mistake. Marlene sat on the arm of a chair by the piano, her face veiled in cigarette smoke, and the image was in perfect harmony with the sultry, mysterious quality of her voice – a scene so framed and cinematic that it felt wrong to be viewing it in colour. The actress was wearing a figure-hugging black evening dress which could only have come from a Hollywood wardrobe, and no one in the room seemed able to take their eyes off her. Apart from the footman passing round champagne, the only person to acknowledge their appearance in the doorway was Marlene herself, who singled Archie out with a smile. 'You lucky devil,' Marta whispered in his ear. 'I hope you don't expect us to take the train *back*.'

It seemed they were the last to arrive. Josephine nodded to the Lancasters, who were seated at a rosewood gaming table by another door, then took the opportunity offered by the music to study the guests she hadn't met yet: a dark-haired woman in her twenties, who fitted Archie's description of Barbara Penhaligon; the photographer from *The Times*, who sat in one of the alcoves with his camera in his lap, apparently too captivated even to consider pointing it at Marlene; and an elderly man with a shock of white hair, standing with Hilaria by the piano and looking lovingly past the film star at the woman who was playing for her – they must be the Hartleys, Josephine thought. Hilaria broke away from the group as soon as she saw them, and Josephine was touched by the warmth of her welcome. 'Miss Tey, how lovely to see you again, and you must be Miss Fox. Welcome to St Michael's Mount, both of you, and thank you so much for changing your plans to be here. I hope Archie told you how grateful I am – and not just because you've bolstered the coffers so generously. You really didn't have to do that. It's enough that you've come.'

'Well, Archie did mention that the circumstances were a little unusual,' Josephine said, with a wry glance towards the piano, 'but he certainly didn't have to twist our arms.'

'And the company wasn't the only enticement,' Marta added. 'This is such a special place. Thank you for inviting us.'

'It's my pleasure. Archie and I haven't seen anywhere near enough of each other these last few years. This is almost like the old days.' She smiled fondly at him, and Josephine wondered if their respective families had ever hoped for something more than friendship between Archie and Hilaria. 'Come and meet everyone.'

There was a ripple of applause as Marlene finished singing. She gave a nod of recognition to her accompanist, then got up and headed in their direction. The colour drained from Marta's face until Josephine feared that she might actually faint. The actress held out her hand; the Prussian blue eyes and high cheekbones were so legendary that it was hard to do anything but stare at them. 'I am Marlene,' she said, although it would have been hard to find three more redundant words. 'You must be Archie's friends? He has told me so much about you and your work. Which of you writes the plays, and which the films?' Neither of them spoke, as if the question had been a difficult one, and it was left to Archie to introduce them. 'And you all know Mr Hitchcock?'

'I think it would be fairer to say that Archie and I have crossed paths with him,' Josephine said, still smarting from the liberties that the director had taken when adapting her book, 'but Marta knows him very well. She's worked on several films with him.'

'Were you involved in *The 39 Steps*? I *love* that film.'

'No, that was before my time. I started while he was making *Sabotage*, but my first writing job was on *Young and Innocent*, the film he made from Josephine's book.'

'And your friendship survived that? I have heard he is not kind to his source material.'

Josephine smiled. 'We've got through worse.'

Marlene looked intrigued but didn't pry. 'Everyone talks about the final shot of that film, but the one I really admired was the train under the bridge and the light on the houses – it has such a lovely mood. He is a master of camera work and lighting.'

'He says the same about you. I'm surprised you've never met – you have a lot in common.'

'Tell me – what is he like to work with?'

Marta seemed much more at ease, and Josephine was only too pleased to excuse herself from Hitchcock's fan club as Hilaria continued the introductions. 'Now, Archie – you and Richard must know each other already? Richard was our chaplain here very briefly, just before the war. Surely you met?'

'No, I don't think so,' Archie said. 'I was up at Cambridge then, and I didn't get home very much, although your face looks familiar. Lovely to meet you.'

'And this is Angela, Richard's wife.'

'The music was beautiful, Mrs Hartley,' Josephine said. 'I imagine it must have been quite nerve-racking, playing for someone so famous, but no one would ever have known.'

'I'm afraid I'm not as sharp as I was,' the vicar's wife admitted, although she seemed pleased by the compliment. 'Still, it all seemed to come back to me.'

'Don't be so modest, darling,' Hartley said. 'You've always loved your music, and you've only got better over the years.'

'Actually, Angela, listening to you just now has given me an idea,' Hilaria said. 'Would you do me an enormous favour?'

'Of course, if I can.'

'If the weather doesn't improve, we'll be short of an organist for tomorrow's service – our usual man comes over from Marazion. I don't suppose you'd play for us, would you?'

'Oh, I'd love to!' Angela clapped her hands together with delight, and Josephine noticed how happy her husband seemed for her. 'It'll be just like the old days,' she said, looking at him. 'I so enjoyed playing for Richard at St Clement's when we lived in London.'

The name of the church obviously struck a chord with Archie. 'St Clement's in Notting Dale?' he asked, and the vicar nodded. '*That's* where we've met, not in Cornwall. It was Christmas 1920.' Josephine looked curiously at him, wondering how he could be so specific. 'Mollie Naylor and her children,' Archie continued. 'I was the police sergeant who found the survivors, and you came to collect them.'

Richard Hartley stared at him. 'Of course, I remember now. You were looking after them when I got there.' He shook his head sadly. 'That was one of the worst days of my life. I still have nightmares about it, even now.'

'What happened?' Josephine asked, looking at the stricken expression on Archie's face.

'A woman killed most of her children and then committed suicide,' he said. 'It would have been even worse, but the eldest boy had been sent out on an errand, and he came back just as his mother was turning on his sister. He saved the girl, but Mrs Naylor killed herself in front of them. It happened on Christmas Eve, and I found them hiding in the yard the next morning.'

'Good God, how awful.' Josephine stared at him, horrified. 'What on earth drove her to do it?'

'We'll never know,' Hartley said, 'and I'm not sure we even found out exactly what happened. There was talk amongst the neighbours that it was actually the boy who did it and not Mrs Naylor at all. I think there might have been some truth in that. There were only two people left alive to tell the tale, after all, and his little sister worshipped him.'

'It was idle gossip,' Archie said contemptuously. 'Dangerous gossip at that. Just because there'd been violence in the family when the father was alive, people couldn't wait to tar the boy with the same brush. And the newspapers didn't help – a murder like that on Christmas Eve wrote its own headlines. The bloody scandal mongers couldn't get enough of it.'

'What have we done now?' Fielding asked with a good-natured grin as he tracked the footman down for a refill.

'Sorry, present company excepted,' Archie said, embarrassed to have been overheard.

'No offence taken.'

'What happened to the two children?' Josephine asked.

Archie shrugged. 'I don't know. I tried to follow the case, but my inspector pulled me off it – told me I was being unprofessional. Did *you* keep in touch with them, Richard?'

'Not after the first few weeks,' Hartley said. 'We took them in for a while, didn't we, dear?' His wife nodded, and Josephine was shocked by the intense sadness in her face, so raw that the tragedy might have happened only yesterday. 'But then the authorities got involved, and they were farmed out to different places. I don't know what became of either of them.'

'It must have been painful to be separated on top of so much other grief,' Hilaria said. 'It's hard to see how a child could ever get over something like that.'

She left them briefly to go and speak to the butler, giving Josephine a clear view of the Lancasters; they had been listening intently, she noticed, and she wondered how long it would be before Archie was cornered about every criminal case he had ever worked on. They were saved now by the sound of a gong, and the butler announced dinner. Hilaria led them through to the dining room, obviously enjoying the impact that the room made on her guests. It was a stunning space, a true castle great hall with a high vaulted ceiling and a solid oak table that stretched the length of the room. Josephine could only begin to imagine how such an extraordinary piece of furniture had been carried up the Mount. The sheltered, internal windows held the room's most beautiful feature: a collection of delicate stained glass, some of it clearly very old, which depicted vivid and fantastic flora and fauna, as well as the more traditional biblical scenes. At one end of the room, there was a plaque representing what she assumed to be the St Aubyn family emblem, and the royal coat of arms sat proudly over the fireplace at the other. The hearth was vast, and an entire tree seemed to be burning in the grate.

'What a wonderful room!' Marlene said.

'Thank you. It used to be the monks' refectory. This is the oldest part of the castle.'

'Why did your butler call it Chevy Chase?' Marta asked.

'After the ballad,' Hilaria said, pointing to a plaster frieze which ran round the room, illustrating various hunting scenes. 'It's about a moonlit fight between the English and the Scots in the Cheviot Hills.'

'Which the right side won, of course,' Josephine added.

Hilaria smiled. 'It would be rude to argue with a guest. Please everyone, do sit down.' They all took their places, and Josephine noticed that Barbara Penhaligon and Marlene couldn't have been seated further apart. She, Marta and Archie had been placed near the actress at the head of the table, while Richard Hartley sat at the other end, flanked by his wife, Miss Penhaligon and the Lancasters. Hilaria – both host and referee, Josephine thought – took a seat in the middle, opposite Alex Fielding.

Fortunately, no interventions seemed necessary. The food was excellent – a rich game terrine followed by sole with white wine sauce – and the atmosphere improved as the wine flowed. Hilaria got to her feet as the fish course was cleared away, and the conversation petered out around the table. 'Ladies and gentlemen, I won't interrupt your evening for long, but on behalf of Lord St Levan and myself, I would just like to welcome you all officially to St Michael's Mount. Naturally I'm biased, because I have loved this island all my life and been privileged to live here for many years, but I genuinely believe that it is one of the most special places on this earth, and I very much hope that you will grow to appreciate it in the short time that you're with us. We are here to enjoy ourselves and to have the merriest of Christmases' – she raised her glass and everyone at the table did the same – 'but we must not forget the very serious cause that has brought us together. The world is growing increasingly more dangerous by the day, and it is our duty to offer a refuge to those whose freedom is currently under threat—'

'Hear, hear,' Marlene said, looking pointedly down the table at Barbara Penhaligon.

Hilaria continued before the interruption could get out of hand. 'I'm delighted to announce that, as of today, Lord Baldwin's Fund for Refugees stands at £244,000.' There was a murmur of appreciation around the table, louder in some quarters than in others. 'And thanks to your generosity, St Michael's Mount is able to add another twenty thousand pounds to that remarkable total.' There was a round of applause from everyone except Rachel Lancaster, who looked embarrassed and reached for her glass. Josephine felt sorry for her. An excess of wine had brought a high colour to her cheeks which sat starkly against her pale skin and the yellow, rather outdated evening dress; she had seemed uncomfortable all evening, except when talking to Angela Hartley, the only person in the room who didn't seem to threaten her.

Their hostess resumed her seat and the main course arrived, a spiced side of beef, smelling deliciously of cloves and nutmeg, and decorated with holly. 'Did you like your flowers, Miss Dietrich?' Barbara Penhaligon asked loudly down the table, and Josephine saw Hilaria glance nervously at Archie.

Marlene gave her a frosty smile. 'I appreciate everything that Miss St Aubyn has done to make me so comfortable,' she said innocently. 'The flowers, the Christmas decorations, this wonderful meal – the day is perfect.'

She picked up her cutlery, as if to put an end to the conversation, but the younger girl refused to be so easily diverted. 'And the ones from the Führer? I gather he really is your biggest fan.'

Josephine looked at Marta and desperately tried to think of something to say that might defuse the tension, but things had already gone too far. 'You are just a foolish child,' Marlene said, her voice low and even, 'and you have absolutely no idea what those people you call your friends are like.'

'So you're happy to betray your country?'

'I will always be German to my very soul. *They* are the ones betraying my country.'

'Miss Dietrich is right,' Hartley said, making no attempt to disguise the anger in his voice. 'You're far too young to understand what's coming our way, Barbara. If you had lived through the last war as an adult – if you had had to consecrate *trenches* like I did to keep up with the burials – you wouldn't be talking such nonsense now.'

'Gosh, I'd forgotten how divisive good intentions can be,' Hilaria said, and although the comment was made lightly, there was a note of steel in her voice which was enough to salvage the situation. Marlene apologised and her antagonist seethed in silence.

'Archie was telling us about some of your myths and legends,' Josephine said in an effort to get the conversation back on safer ground. 'He said you found a giant buried in the church?'

Hilaria smiled at her gratefully. 'Something like that. A hermit's cell was discovered about fifty years ago. You can see it now if you look behind the family pews, and inside they found a leather jug and a skeleton which was about seven foot tall. We've no idea who he was or why he was there, but he's buried now in the graveyard.'

'I'll show you the chamber tomorrow during the carol service,' Archie promised, 'and I'm sure Hilaria would be happy for us to look at St Michael's Chair, too.'

'What's St Michael's Chair?'

Archie grinned. 'It's a stone seat on top of the tower, hanging over the edge.'

'It's actually a medieval lantern that was used as a guiding light for fishermen,' Hilaria corrected him, 'but pilgrims used it for prayer, and there *is* a more recent legend attached to it. Newly married couples have been known to race each other to the top of the tower, because it's said that whoever sits on the chair first will be the dominant partner in the marriage.'

'If they live to enjoy it,' Marta said. 'Have you ever seen it done?'

'Twice, and in both cases the winner was the wife.'

'It sounds tempting,' Rachel Lancaster said suddenly. 'We should try it, Gerry.'

She drained her glass and the footman stepped forward to refill it, but her husband reached across the table and covered it with his hand. 'Don't you think you've had enough, darling? You don't want to embarrass yourself.'

There was an uncomfortable silence as the couple glared at each other, but eventually Rachel Lancaster backed down and pushed the glass away from her. The pudding was served quickly, and Josephine began to wonder how many more times the conversation could be rescued and set back on an even keel; this time, Alex Fielding took his turn. 'What is St Michael the patron saint of?' he asked, turning to the vicar as the person in the room most likely to know.

'Grocers and policemen, amongst other things,' Richard Hartley said. Then added more seriously: 'St Michael is the guardian of the Church and the champion of justice. He calls all men to their heavenly judgement and gives each of us the chance to redeem ourselves before passing.'

'Crikey,' Fielding said. 'Then we'd better be on our best behaviour.'

The strengthening wind blew a billow of snow against the window, making them all jump. 'And on that note, I think we should retire to the drawing room and leave the gentlemen to their port next door,' Hilaria said, standing up from the table.

'I didn't think they still did that in the twentieth century,' Marta whispered, as they followed their hostess out of the dining room.

'Neither did I, but the whole evening's been an education in one way or another. I shall be pleased to get to bed.' Josephine stopped by one of the windows and looked out into the night. The snowflakes were thick and restless, as if there were too many for the sky, and they jostled each other in endless fallings to settle on the already blanketed terrace. 'Looks like we're going to be well and truly cut off,' she said, squeezing Marta's hand. 'Happy Christmas.'

8

There was an old-fashioned charm about the Godolphin Hotel, which Violet found all the more welcoming after the last leg of their journey from Plymouth. The weather had worsened steadily as the train moved through Cornwall, delaying their arrival by more than an hour, and by the time they got out at Marazion Station, the wind was howling dismally in from the sea and the whirling flurries of snow had nothing romantic or magical about them. 'Just as well we weren't hoping to get across tonight,' Johnny shouted above the gale, doing his best to shelter her as they hurried down the platform to the station house. 'It'll be a miracle if it's any better in the morning. Once this sets in, it could hang around for days.'

Just her luck that it was the time of year for miracles, Violet thought as she shook the snow off her coat; she could dream up worse things than spending Christmas in the hotel, just the two of them, without the pressure of being nice to Johnny's mother, but she kept her feelings to herself. There was a taxi parked outside the station, but one of the other passengers beat them to it and they could only watch as its tail-lights disappeared down the road towards the village. 'Never mind, we'll wait for the next one,' Violet said, not wanting to make a fuss when he was trying so hard to make things special for her. 'At least we're dry in here.'

Johnny shook his head. 'Don't forget we're in Cornwall,' he said despondently. 'The next one will be along dreckly, and that could be any time between now and New Year's Eve. Wait here a minute. I'll see if there's anyone about.' When he came back, he was in much better spirits. 'We're in luck. One of the lads is knocking off for the night now and he lives in Rosudgeon. He'll drop us at the hotel on his way.'

The guard had made a promise to his young daughter to be home before she went to bed, and he wasted no time in getting them to their destination. 'That was good of him,' Violet said, as Johnny bundled their cases in through the door of the hotel's reception. 'That's what I love about this time of year. It brings out the best in people.'

The entrance hall had been enthusiastically dressed for the season, almost as if each member of staff had been given charge of a corner which bore no relation to the colour scheme of the other three, and Violet had to smile to herself when she saw the overcrowded tree, its red and gold decorations seeming to offer a reflection of the vividly patterned carpet. The hospitable sound of carols, heartily sung, drifted across from the bar, and through another open doorway, she could see a waitress clearing away the last of the dinner tables and re-laying them ready for breakfast. 'Looks like we're too late to eat,' Johnny said. 'I'm sorry, Vi.'

'Will you stop apologising?' she said. 'You can't do anything about the weather. A port and lemon and a packet of pork scratchings will do me just fine.' In the corner, where three rows of paper chains met, pinned to the ceiling, a grandfather clock struck nine. 'This is nice,' she said, squeezing his arm to show how much she meant it. 'Only three hours to go to Christmas Day – our first proper Christmas together. And just think – this time next year we could be sitting by our own fireside on Christmas Eve.'

He smiled, and gave her a peck on the cheek. 'I like the sound of that.'

There was a young woman standing by the reception desk, waiting to check in ahead of them, and Violet looked her up and down, noting the flat-heeled shoes which were the only practical concession to the weather; otherwise, she was attractive and smartly dressed in a royal blue winter coat and matching hat. She seemed anxious, tapping her fingers continuously on the polished wood; when she turned round, sensing their eyes on her, she was obviously pleased to have company. 'It must be the busiest night of the year,' she said with a smile. 'They're rushed off their feet. I was tempted to offer to help.'

A man hurried through from the bar before they could answer, red-faced and welcoming. 'I'm sorry to keep you all waiting,' he said, 'especially on a night like this. Would you like to check in?'

'I suppose I'd better,' the woman said, then blushed. 'I'm sorry – that sounded rude, and I didn't mean to be. It's just that I was supposed to be staying at St Michael's Mount tonight, but my train was delayed by the snow and I gather I've missed the last crossing.'

'Mrs Carmichael?'

She hesitated. 'What? Oh yes, that's right. Carmichael.'

She said the name as if trying it out, and Violet wondered if she was newly married; she certainly couldn't be much more than twenty. 'Excellent,' the hotelier said. 'You're in room three, Mrs Carmichael. I'll get someone to show you up.'

'Oh, please don't bother. You're busy enough as it is and I haven't got much luggage. Just tell me where it is and I'll find my own way.'

He gave her a key and directed her to a room on the first floor. 'Now – would you like something to eat? The kitchen's closed, I'm afraid, but we could rustle up a sandwich or some soup.'

'That would be lovely, if it's not too much trouble.'

'No trouble at all. In your room or in the bar?'

'In my room, please.' She picked up her case. 'The station master told me that Miss St Aubyn has made arrangements for me to go over by boat in the morning?'

'That's right, Mrs Carmichael, if the weather allows it.'

'Is it possible for me to get a message to the castle before that? I was supposed to be surprising someone for Christmas, you see, and it's quite important.'

'The wires are down at the moment, I'm afraid, but I can try again later. What's the message?'

'Just that I've arrived safely and I'll be there as soon as I can.'

'Right-o. I'll do my best.'

'Thank you.'

'Now then,' he said, turning back to Johnny, 'by a process of elimination, you must be our final guest for the night. Mr Soper?'

'That's right.'

'Emily's son, if I'm not mistaken?'

Johnny smiled, and Violet's heart sank; she had been hoping for at least one night of anonymity before the island closed in around them. 'You know my mother?'

'We often have a chat while she's waiting for the boat. Nice woman. I haven't been here long, but she's made me very welcome. And she thinks a lot of you, I know that much. She'll be pleased to have you home.'

'She doesn't know yet. We thought we'd surprise her for Christmas. This is my fiancée, Violet.'

'Lovely to meet you both. Now, if you could just sign the register, we'll get you settled in. It's not a night to be out and about. You're in room number one. I would say nice view, but you might want to draw your curtains tonight.'

He pushed a single key across the desk, and Johnny looked at him in horror. 'But I booked two rooms,' he said, his face flushing scarlet as he glanced apologetically at Violet.

'Did you?'

'Yes, of course. You'll have to find us another one.'

'I'm sorry, Mr Soper. Mrs Carmichael's was the last reservation, and now she's here we're fully booked.'

'But you can't be! What about one of the staff rooms, then? I could sleep there if there's a free bed.' The barman shook his head, and Johnny turned to Violet. 'I haven't done this deliberately, Vi. You've got to believe me.'

'Of course I believe you,' she said, glad now to have told her mother that they were going straight to the island. 'Anyway, it's not the end of the world. You'll just have to sleep on the floor.'

'It's a twin room, Miss.'

'Well then, that's all right. Sign us in, Johnny.'

He hesitated, then carefully wrote 'Mr and Mrs Jonathan Soper' into the register. She watched, feeling suddenly superstitious; it was silly, but she wished desperately that Johnny had filled in their real names rather than tempting fate with a marriage that hadn't actually happened yet. 'You won't tell—' he began.

The barman cut him off. 'Don't worry. It's our mistake and I won't mention a thing.' He repeated the offer of food made to Mrs Carmichael, and they accepted gratefully. 'I'll have it served in the bar for you in ten minutes, when you've had a chance to take your things upstairs. Follow me.'

He led them up the first flight of steps and down a long corridor with creaking floorboards. It was a decent sized room on the seaward side of the hotel, and a welcome fire was already burning in the grate. Their host put some more coal on and left them to unpack, apologising once again for the confusion over the rooms. Johnny hovered awkwardly between the beds, blushing and scarcely able to meet her eye. 'Which one would you like?' he asked, looking at his shoes.

'This one,' she said, choosing the bed nearer the door. 'You can have the view and the draughts.' She smiled and walked over to the window, pulling him with her. 'And will you please stop worrying? I'm glad we'll be together tonight. It's not very friendly out there.'

The curtains had been drawn to prevent the cold night air from penetrating the room, and she threw them back to prove her point. Johnny grinned and put his arm round her, and together they stared out into the blackness. The sea was higher than she had ever seen it, a rolling mass of white horses, and the dark bulk of the Mount – just visible beneath a grudging moon – was the only thing standing in the way of the sweeping blizzards. There were pinpricks of light from the castle, appearing and disappearing amid the pattern of swirling snowflakes, as if someone were switching them on and off, signalling to the mainland. A pair of binoculars stood on the windowsill, and Johnny picked them up and trained them on the island. 'Can you see your mum's house?' Violet asked.

'Just about, but she must have gone to bed early. I can't see any lights on, and she normally has them blazing away. I hope she's not ill.'

'She's probably spent the evening with a friend and been stranded by the weather,' Violet suggested. 'I'm sure she's fine.'

Johnny looked doubtful. 'Perhaps I should have tried harder to get across there tonight,' he said. 'Something doesn't feel right. I'm sure one of the lads with a boat would risk it if the price was right.'

'You are joking?' Violet stared at him in astonishment. 'Try anything like that, and I'll be going across there tomorrow to tell your mother to get her black out again.' She took the binoculars out of his hands and pulled him away from the window, then turned back to draw the curtains. 'There's nothing we can do until tomorrow,' she said firmly, 'and anyway, like I said, I'm sure she's fine.'

9

Rachel Lancaster hung back as the rest of the women made their way to the drawing room for coffee. Even though she would have welcomed something to counteract the effects of all the wine she had drunk, she couldn't bear the thought of yet more conversation, their voices drilling into her as she tried to hide in plain sight at the dinner table. With the exception of Angela Hartley, who seemed as vulnerable as Rachel felt, she had nothing to say to any of them.

Suddenly she craved some air. There was a door to the terrace from the Long Passage, and she was relieved to find it unlocked. Her head started to spin as soon as she was outside, but the shock of a cold night was better than coffee, and she breathed the air in gratefully, feeling instantly better. The snow had finally stopped, except for a few flakes drifting down as an afterthought, and the clouds had moved on, leaving the moon in charge of a clear sky. Swathed in winter, this part of the castle was overwhelmingly beautiful – pure and bright, like a world without a past. She envied its unsullied perfection, even if the peculiar stillness which always followed snow was strangely absent: down below, the churning, restless sea sounded angrier than ever, and she wondered if there was a time when the island felt truly at rest.

She was freezing cold, but it was preferable to being inside, and the area of the terrace where she stood was sheltered from the wind by two long stretches of the castle's walls. The smoking room where the men had lingered after dinner was immediately next to Chevy Chase, and she could see her husband through the leaded windows, drinking his port and trying to fit in. Had she been a stranger, she would still have known that Gerry was uncomfortable in this sort of company. The policeman and the photographer sat together on a wooden bench in the alcove, listening as the vicar talked, apparently at ease with themselves and with each other, although the photographer never quite lost that watchful quality which she supposed was integral to his work, but which made her uneasy nonetheless. Gerry stood at the other end of the room, a child waiting to be invited to the game but unsure of the rules; as she watched, he drained his glass and helped himself to more from a decanter, then went over to study a painting which was out of sight of the rest of the group. Casually, as she had known he would, he took something small from a side table and slipped it quickly into his pocket; she couldn't see what it was, but she knew what it meant, and the shame made her turn away.

She moved further into the shadows, just in case Gerry glanced out of the window and saw her. On the other side of the terrace, the drawing room curtains were closed, but she could hear laughter and music coming from inside and she half wished that she had joined the other women after all. It was too late now to put in an appearance without an explanation; when she went inside, she would have to go straight to bed and apologise in the morning for her rudeness. She found the cigarettes in her bag and began to smoke one, hoping it would kill the last waves of nausea from the drink. High above her, the tower of the church was silhouetted by the moonlight, and in one corner she could just make out the shape of the chair they had been talking about at dinner, a solid lump of stone on the left-hand side, extending further up than the rest of the wall. She stepped back to get a better look, then jumped when she felt the warmth of another body behind her and heard her husband's voice, hushed and tight with anger. 'What the hell are you doing out here?' He followed her gaze up to the tower, and laughed. 'Fancy your chances, do you? Well, let's see how you get on.'

The smile disappeared from his face, and suddenly he was dragging her roughly by the arm across the terrace, kicking snow up as he went. 'Gerry, stop it! What are you doing?' She tried to resist, but his fury made him even stronger than usual, and the only thing left to her was an appeal to his pride. 'They'll hear us, and then what will they think? They're only over there in the drawing room.'

He turned and slapped her hard across the face. 'Then shut the fuck up.'

He pulled her on, past the drawing room windows and round to the door of the church. Rachel hoped desperately that he would find it locked, but it opened easily and he shoved her in ahead of him, then closed the door behind them. The moon was the only light on offer and Gerry paused, allowing his eyes to grow accustomed to the darkness; once he had got his bearings, he quickly located the tower and she protested in horror as he forced her over to the door. The smell of dust and decay hit her, bringing back the nausea with a renewed intensity. She resisted his efforts to pull her inside and up the steps, clinging to the door frame with every ounce of her strength, but he pulled the door roughly shut, catching her fingers, and she screamed in pain. The sound of her fear echoed back off the stone walls, trapped and magnified by the enclosed space, and she began to sob. 'We're supposed to race each other, aren't we?' Gerry said. 'I'll make it easy for you. You go first.'

Rachel stared up into the black nothingness of the tower. 'I'm not going up there.'

'Of course you are. It's what you've always wanted, isn't it? The chance to rule the roost. Well, go on, then. Find out how it feels.' He pushed her again and she fell forward onto her knees, fumbling her way towards the beginnings of a staircase. 'Go on,' he repeated. 'Crawl like the fucking pilgrims.'

It was a kick this time, fuelled by too much alcohol, and she knew that if she didn't do as he asked, he would beat her to a pulp where they stood. She scrambled up the spiral staircase, scraping her arms on the walls as the steps twisted sharply round to the right, hearing his footsteps behind her, driving her on. The space was impossibly narrow, even for her, and she thought for a moment that he wouldn't be able to follow, but his rage was relentless, and she felt his hands on her whenever she faltered. There were window slits in the stone at regular intervals, but the brief respites of slivered moonlight only made her ordeal worse, and she would rather not have seen the cobwebs or the rat droppings which hinted at what lurked in the dark. The ascent seemed endless, but eventually she could go no further and her hands pressed against another wooden door. 'Open it,' Gerry demanded.

'It'll be locked.'

'Open it!'

She did as she was told, and the rush of cold air brought both relief and a fresh hell to face, even worse than the claustrophobic terror of the climb. The doorway was square-shaped, more like a vertical trapdoor than a proper exit, and she struggled to get through it. Outside, a narrow channel ran between a block of stone holding the flagpole and the outer parapet, which was only waist high – an inadequate barrier between her and oblivion. The wind whipped her face, much stronger at this altitude, and the flag strained at its leash, its metal fastenings rapping rhythmically against the pole. *He's going to kill me*, she thought, surprised by how calmly she viewed the idea. *That's what this madness means. After all these years, it's finally over.*

Gerry struggled to haul himself out after her, and just for a second, while his hands were too busy to threaten her, she considered doing the job for him: at least then it would be her choice. One glance over the parapet was enough to change her mind. She recoiled in horror, but he caught her by the hair and forced her to look again, and she thought she was going to faint as the terrace below seemed to rise up to meet her. She twisted her head to the side, and there was the chair, covered in snow and facing out to sea, its stone seat hanging perilously over the precipice. Quietly, she began to whimper like an animal. 'I can't, Gerry. Please don't make me.'

But in one swift movement he turned her round and half pushed, half lifted her onto the wall. She grabbed at his hands, pleading with him not to let her fall, but somehow she was on the chair. The stone felt solid at her back, but it was wet and icy cold. She couldn't bring herself to look down. 'So how does it feel?' he asked, his hands holding her tight around the waist. 'Is power all it's cracked up to be?'

'Just get me off here,' she begged. 'I'll do anything you want me to, anything at all, but please get me down.'

He laughed, momentarily easing his grip, and for a moment she thought he was going to leave her there, but then he put his hands under her arms and began to pull her round, and for the first time in as long as she could remember, Rachel was glad of his strength. She drew her knees up and tried to get a purchase on the parapet with her feet, but the ledge was slippery and she felt herself falling back. In that split-second, before he pulled her to safety, she saw a fear in Gerry's eyes which was every bit as great as her own, and something shifted between them – something that had nothing to do with superstition or St Michael or an ancient piece of stone, but with the sudden realisation that she had the power to hurt him, too.

10

'Your room or mine?' Marta asked, as they walked down the Long Passage to go to bed. 'I know I've got the Christmas decorations, but there's something very tempting about the four-poster bed.'

'Whichever is warmer,' Josephine said, rubbing her hands together. 'It was freezing in that drawing room. The only time I've been warm since we got here was sitting in front of your fire.'

'All right. You come to me.'

'It's probably better that way round. I'm right next to the Lancasters and the Hartleys, and all you've got on your corridor are the missing Mrs Carmichael and two bathrooms.'

'Just how much noise are you planning to make?'

'I meant there'll be less chance of being seen.' She blushed, and returned Marta's smile. 'I hope Mrs Carmichael's all right.'

'Yes, so do I. With a bit of luck, she'll be here tomorrow if the weather calms down.'

'Have you brought an alarm clock? I need to be back in my room by eight to be woken up.'

'I don't even own an alarm clock.'

'Then I'll bring one. I'll go and fetch what I need now, and come back when I'm sure everyone else has stopped moving about.'

'All right. Don't be long.'

Back in her room, Josephine found her nightclothes already laid out on the bed. Feeling guilty for wasting Mrs Pendean's time, she scooped them up into a bag ready to take with her, then waited by the fire until she was sure that the staff had finished their reign of terror for the night. The snow had brought with it a vast, muffled silence, amplifying the noises in the castle's passageways. She heard people saying goodnight in subdued tones, then a voice that sounded like Hilaria's calling something down the corridor about the carol service. Footsteps passed repeatedly outside in a flurry of trips to the bathroom, followed by a sequence of closing doors and a man's loud cough; eventually, the house fell quiet. Josephine left her room, resisting the schoolgirl urge to put a bolster in the bed, and hurried down the dimly lit corridor.

She turned the corner and bumped straight into Angela Hartley, and it was hard to say who was the more surprised as each of their wash bags clattered to the floor. The vicar's wife looked older without her make-up, an impression only emphasised by her pale mauve dressing gown and the anxiety etched deeply on her face. 'I'm sorry to startle you,' Josephine said, when her own heart had slowed a little. 'Is everything all right?'

'Yes, I'm sure it is,' Mrs Hartley said, with an artificial certainty that implied exactly the opposite. 'I was just trying to find my room. It's silly of me, but . . .' She tailed off, looking bewildered, and Josephine knelt down to gather up the soaps and toothbrushes that had been dropped, restoring everything to its rightful bag and noticing that the hem of Mrs Hartley's dressing gown was soaking wet, as if she had been outside in the snow. 'Richard went to speak to someone, you see, and I was waiting to say goodnight to him, but he was longer than he said he'd be, so I went to the bathroom while he was gone. I thought I knew how to get back, but now I've no idea where I am.'

'It's not silly at all,' Josephine said. 'I've been lost myself so many times today. One corridor looks much the same as the next in a strange house, especially when it's as big as this one.'

Mrs Hartley smiled, grateful for the reassurance, and Josephine gestured back the way she had come. 'I think your room is near mine. Shall we try down here?'

She led the way, relieved not to have to explain what she was doing in a completely different part of the castle, and they were soon outside the vicar's door. 'My husband's gone to speak to someone,' Mrs Hartley repeated, 'so at least he won't have been worrying about me. Thank you, my dear. You've been very kind.'

'Not at all. See you in the morning.' She waited until the vicar's wife had gone back into her room, then retraced her footsteps yet again along the corridor. The lull in the wind should have been soothing, but the sudden quiet was somehow more unsettling, and Josephine was glad when it was filled by a peal of now familiar laughter. She paused, then took a short detour to the corridor that Archie shared with Marlene, stopping outside the film star's door. Marlene was talking, although the words were indistinct, and every now and again a man's voice, low and muffled, said something in response. Smiling to herself at the thought that Archie's Christmas had arrived an hour before everybody else's, she made her way to Marta's room.

Never in all her life had Nora been so grateful to finish a shift. The blizzards had blown themselves out by the time she left the castle, but the sea was still high, and she could hear the familiar dull thud of boats knocking against the harbour wall as she made her way down to the village. The Mount's dense canopy of fir trees had protected the higher paths from the worst of the snow, but by the time she reached the old dairy, any shelter had dwindled and the only thing in front of her was a vast lawn of white, exposed and radiant under a three-quarter moon. Something in its cleanness saddened her.

She walked through snow that was two or three inches thick, and felt it begin to soak into her boots as she neared the bottom of the slope. Most of the village houses were gathered together in two terraces that ran parallel with the south wall of the harbour, and all were in darkness except for her own. The lights were confined to the downstairs rooms, and she knew that Tom would be waiting up for her; it must be Christmas Day by now, and he would want to mark it with her, this year more than ever. Nora forced herself on, listening to the whisper of powdery snow beneath her feet. Their cottage was at the end of the row, near the lodge house, and she put her hand on the back gate to let herself into the tiny yard, knowing that Tom would have cleared a path to the door for her. The thought stopped her abruptly in her tracks, a reminder of the love that she had betrayed tugging insistently at her conscience, and suddenly she knew that she simply couldn't bring herself to go home. It was like a physical paralysis, an inability to walk in through the back door and call to her husband as she always did, to pretend that everything was normal. In that instant, Nora realised that she had lost the right to belong in her own life; regardless of how worried she knew Tom would be, she turned and walked away.

The museum was in darkness, covered in its own white shroud, and Nora stood in the shelter of the lych-gate opposite, imagining Emily's body lying still and cold under the sheet, where the woman she thought was her friend had left her. If she had one decent bone in her body, she would go in there now and stay with Emily until someone found them both, but the revulsion of what she had done had only increased as the day wore on, and it had been as much as she could do to lock the door earlier, when the visitors threatened to go inside; now, on the most haunting, emotionally charged night of the year, her friend's death had taken on an almost superstitious horror, and the devil himself couldn't have dragged her over the threshold.

'Nora? What the hell are you doing out here? I've been looking for you everywhere. Where have you been?' The shock of Tom's voice brought her to her senses. He stared at her, and she saw her own despair reflected back in his bewildered expression. 'Christ, Nora, you'll catch your death. What on earth do you think you're playing at? I expected you home ages ago.'

Instinctively, she glanced over his shoulder at the museum, knowing that surely now he would realise as soon as Emily's body was discovered who was to blame for her death. He already sensed that something was terribly wrong, and it was only a matter of time before concern turned to shame and then to hatred. Still, she couldn't bring herself to face it just yet. 'I'm sorry, but they kept me late,' she said. 'Then there was something I forgot to say to Emily when I saw her this morning, so I thought I'd call in and do it now. I was looking for a light upstairs, but she must have gone to bed.'

'Of course she's in bed. It's after midnight. Don't lie to me, Nora.'

'What do you mean? I'm not lying.'

'Yes, you are. This is about Jenna again, isn't it?' Not even in the depths of her depression could Nora have imagined that her daughter's absence would be a convenient excuse for something still worse, but she didn't correct him. 'I know it's hard, love, but we've got to get used to it. This is how it has to be from now on – just the two of us. Is that really so bad?' Suddenly it was all she wanted, but one moment of madness had made it impossible. They had no future now, she knew that, and she couldn't bear the idea of going back with him, taking the lie into the house and getting into bed next to him. 'Come on, love – let's go home. You've got a busy day tomorrow.'

He touched her arm and she flinched, trying not to dwell on the hurt in his eyes. 'I can't, Tom. I need some time to myself after the day I've had. Go home to bed. I won't be long.'

Nora headed up the path before he could argue, turning back once to see him still standing there in the snow, watching her. She had no idea where she was going. Someone was invariably up late in the staff quarters, and no doubt they'd be talking long into the night about the guests, squabbling over who was going to take the German her tea in the morning. She couldn't risk any of the family rooms in this state, just in case she was seen and forced to explain herself, and it really was too cold to stay outside, even if catching her death, as Tom had put it, felt like the easy way out. In her panic and grief, she knew that she was only a breath away from confessing what she had done and taking the consequences; nothing, surely, could be as bad as this constant fear. She saw Tom's face again, knowing how ashamed and disappointed he would be, then thought of Jenna and how untouched she would be by her mother's fate, closeted away with her new beliefs and her new family, hiding behind a different name. In that second, her fear turned to anger again, but the urge to speak was still overwhelming. The only answer lay in the dark silhouette up ahead of her.

She let herself into the castle by the west door, which was further from the bedrooms, and made her way through the downstairs rooms, thankful for her familiarity with the house and the moon for guidance. The church was always left open at Christmas so that the staff could go at any time if their duties prevented them from attending the regular services. Miss St Aubyn was a Christian woman whose faith was important to her, and she encouraged everyone who worked for her to take the Mount's sacred past as seriously as she did. Nora ventured out onto the terrace, noticing instantly that the storm was more reluctant to admit defeat at this altitude. There was a sound of desperation in the moaning wind as it hurled itself across the terrace, and it seemed to chime with her feelings.

Other people had obviously visited the church that evening, because there was a path of trampled snow leading to and from the entrance, but she was relieved to find it empty. She closed the door gently behind her, only to come face to face with the nativity. The sight of Melchior, innocently offering his gold at the crib, sickened her to her stomach and she nearly turned back. Even here, she couldn't escape from what she had done – but that was her punishment, and it was less than she deserved. Her hands were shaking as she lit a candle and walked up to the altar with every intention of praying for forgiveness, but the words wouldn't come. She knelt for a long time on the cold stone floor, finally giving in to the tears that had threatened all day. Never in her life had she felt so alone.

And then she heard a noise behind her. It came from the tower, one loud clatter followed by another and then another, as if something metal had been dropped down the staircase; next came footsteps, shuffling and uncertain, unmistakably the sound of someone coming slowly down in the dark. Nora blew out her candle and listened, trying to decide if she had time to leave before whoever it was came out into the church, but already he or she was fumbling with the handle to the tower door, and in her mind's eye she saw it turn. Perhaps it was her own guilt, perhaps simply the ill-fated presence of strangers in the house, but something told Nora that her unseen companion was dangerous. Quickly, her heart racing, she hurried down the steps to the hermit's cell.

She stood in silence in the musky darkness, willing the intruder to leave and wondering why anyone would want to go up to the tower at this time of night. Any minute now, surely, she would hear the main door open and it would be safe to leave her hiding place, but instead the footsteps came closer, soft but definite across the chapel floor, stopping near the family pews which hid the entrance to the underground chamber. Feeling trapped now, Nora held her breath and moved further back into the shadows, but the sleeve of her coat caught the silver chalice which stood ready for the morning service. It fell to the floor before she could catch it, ringing out against the stone and announcing her presence as surely as if she had spoken. More frightened than ever, she waited to see what the footsteps would do.

CHRISTMAS DAY

I

Josephine made sure she was back in her own bed well before the eight o'clock curfew and braced herself for another strained encounter with Mrs Pendean, but her early morning call came from a young housemaid she hadn't seen before. The girl wished her a happy Christmas and put a tea tray down on the bedside table, then went over to draw the curtains, flooding the room with winter sunlight. Josephine waited until she was alone again, then pulled her dressing gown on and drank her tea by the window. The morning laid out before her was radiantly beautiful, with every ounce of the blizzard's nocturnal ferocity replaced by an unshakeable sense of peace and hope: the ideal expression of Christmas, but so rarely its reality. The castle's turrets and terraces were blanketed in a fairytale white, and down below in the village she could see tiny figures scurrying about their business in the snow, like a scene from a Bruegel painting. There were no boats coming or going from the mainland, she noticed, and it was as if the causeway had never existed: its cobbles were invisible beneath an ever-changing palette of greens, blues and greys – but it was hard to resent being cut off in such a magnificent place, particularly when every conceivable luxury had been catered for. The isolation that had seemed so unsettling under cover of darkness now felt like a magical protection from the outside world, and Josephine was more excited by Christmas morning than she had been since she was a child.

She allowed herself another ten minutes to enjoy it, then dressed quickly in the perfectly pressed woollen suit that somehow looked better than on the day she had bought it. There was no reason to think that the church would be miraculously warmer than the rest of the castle, so she took her coat from the wardrobe and checked her bag for the envelope wrapped in tissue paper that was Marta's Christmas present; as far as she could gather, the day's itinerary was packed with communal activities and they were unlikely to find any private time together until the evening, but she wanted it with her in case the right moment came. It looked a poor thing next to the collection of presents that Marta had brought with her, but Josephine knew how much the gift would mean, and she couldn't wait to hand it over.

The gathering on the terrace outside the church was in high spirits, and the small crowd took her by surprise. There were lots of people she didn't know, as well as one or two familiar faces from the household staff, and she guessed that most of them were islanders who had come up from the village for the service. The terrace had been efficiently cleared of the night's snow, which now rested in large, man-made drifts against the outer walls, proving an irresistible temptation to the Mount's children, who lobbed great handfuls at each other, laughing and shouting when they scored a direct hit, and ignoring their parents' half-hearted instructions to behave. The sheer joy of the game brought the whole scene to life, and Josephine was suddenly conscious that the festivities so far had been strangely muted without the childlike excitement of Christmas; the adults were going through the motions and making the best of it, but there was something missing from the party – some vital element of innocence and sparkle and wonder – that even a Hollywood star couldn't conjure into being.

Two footmen passed among the congregation with trays of hot coffee, rum butter tarts and spicy pepper cakes, and Josephine accepted a cup gratefully, glad of both the warmth and the stimulant. The coffee was laced with brandy, and she took it over to the far side of the terrace to enjoy the views out to Penzance and Newlyn, and then to Land's End. There was no sign of Marta or Archie yet, but Hilaria – a picture of restrained elegance in a tailored burgundy suit that stood out against the snow – was talking to a couple with two young children. She waved when she saw Josephine, and broke away from the group to join her. 'I'm so pleased to see you,' she said, after the flurry of Christmas greetings. 'Everyone must be sleeping late this morning. I was just beginning to wonder if all my guests had defied the tides and fled in the night.'

'I think it's more a case of sleeping off the festive spirit. You looked after us far too well at dinner.' She glanced round the terrace again. 'Am I really the first to arrive?'

'All but Mr Fielding. He's around somewhere, taking more photographs.'

'Of course he is.' They shared a smile, which reaffirmed Josephine's liking for Archie's childhood friend. 'There's plenty to keep him busy here,' she said. 'This is really lovely – a proper traditional Christmas. We could be anywhere over the last two hundred years.' It was true: the scene in front of her, framed by the church, had a timeless simplicity about it. There was a balcony outside the door, accessed by a set of steps on each side, and it had been beautifully decorated with garlands of greenery. Holly berries glinted in the morning sun, picking out shards of colour from the stained glass wherever the church was lit from within, and the peal of bells cut through the air with a gentle civility; although she was no churchgoer herself, Josephine wondered why they all worked so hard each year to smother the heart of Christmas with more elaborate preparations. 'Does everyone on the island come to the service?' she asked.

'Yes, except for one or two of the older residents who find the climb too much these days, and we make sure we have a concert down in the village for them so they don't feel left out. I know we all sigh when Mr Fielding enters the room, but this is the main reason I was happy to let the newspapers in – not for the glamour of Hollywood and not even for the money they're donating to the fund, but for the chance to show off what we do here. I wanted the islanders and the family to have something to be proud of. It feels like the end of something, this Christmas, so it will be nice to have it on record.'

'Were you hit badly by the last war?'

'We lost our fair share of men.'

'And grief resonates in a small community, over and above the personal sense of loss.'

'Yes, I suppose that's true, but we're a resilient lot. Most of the families on the island have lived here for generations, and there are a couple with connections that go back hundreds of years. They're sea-faring people and their ancestors sailed all over the world, so they're no strangers to danger and tragedy. And they're fiercely loyal to the Mount. We're lucky to have them.'

'And they you, I suspect,' Josephine said, admiring the unsentimental respect in Hilaria's words. 'How long have you been here?'

She misunderstood the question and answered on behalf of the family. 'The St Aubyns bought the Mount in 1659, but they were stewards here even before that.'

'And you personally?'

'Oh, I see – sorry. I came in 1908, when I was fourteen. I'll miss it, when the inevitable happens. Two griefs for the price of one.'

And a heavy price, Josephine thought – for Hilaria *and* for the island. It seemed deeply unfair that St Michael's Mount would be deprived of someone who obviously ran it well and cared so deeply about the people who depended on her, but it wasn't the time to discuss the injustices of inheritance and Hilaria didn't seem the type to wallow in self-pity or the sentence of her departure. Even so, the two of them were roughly contemporaries, both at an age when the pleasures of Christmas were also its sadness, and Josephine knew that Hilaria's everyday concerns must have been magnified a hundredfold by the intense melancholy of the season.

They were saved from venturing any further down that route by Marta's arrival, followed shortly by Archie. 'On your own this morning?' she asked mischievously as Archie bent to kiss her, but her hopes for any whiff of scandal were instantly dashed by a disappointing response.

'Yes,' he said, without any hint of coyness. 'Marlene's decided to have a late breakfast in her room, so I can enjoy a brief suspension of duties.'

'What an arduous task you've set yourself,' Marta said teasingly. 'I really don't know how you're putting up with it.'

Archie grinned. 'It's a sacrifice, I know, but all in the course of a day's work.'

'What a shame that Miss Dietrich won't be joining us,'

Hilaria said, a little crestfallen from his news. 'As you can imagine, the carols and prayers aren't the only things that have brought people out this morning – and talking of prayers, I must just go and check where Richard's got to.'

She was saved the trouble by Angela Hartley, who came out of the vestibule to the drawing room with a length of black silk cloth in her hand. 'Richard's forgotten this,' she said, looking at Hilaria with a wry smile. 'It's not often I get to remind him of something these days. Can I take it in to him?'

'He's not here yet. I rather hoped he'd be with you.'

'No, I haven't seen him for a while. He went off to talk to someone.'

They were the same words she had used the night before, Josephine recalled; either the vicar had a lot of people to catch up with or his wife was getting confused, but Hilaria seemed reassured by the explanation. 'Then I dare say he'll be here any minute. Are you still happy to play for us?'

'Of course, if you'd like me to.'

'More than that. We're relying on you. Why don't you come and make yourself comfortable, and we can start getting everyone in out of the cold.' She turned back to Josephine and Marta. 'Come in whenever you're ready, and sit in the family pews on either side of the altar.'

They finished their coffee and made their way over to the entrance, just as the organ music began inside the church, something rousing by Pachelbel or Bach. 'I'm not sure "Von Himmel Hoch" is the most sensitive piece she could have chosen in the current climate,' Archie said dryly, 'but she plays it beautifully. Personally, I'd have avoided the Germans altogether and stuck to Elgar.'

'Perhaps she planned it in Marlene's honour.'

'All the more reason to be careful. Still, at least it's not Wagner.'

The church of St Michael and All Angels was stunning inside, its impact all the greater because of its modest, unshowy exterior. It was filled with light and beauty, a place worthy of the pilgrimage for which the island was so famed, and Josephine paused on the threshold to look round, taking in the glorious rose window and delicate stained-glass panels, the gilt chandelier and its many candles, whose soft, flickering light enhanced the golden stone. She would have found it hard to say what moved her so deeply – the man-made splendour or a rare, less tangible spirituality which she felt as soon as she stepped through the door – but there was no doubt that it was seductive, a gentle nudge of encouragement for optimistic doubters like herself.

'What a beautiful nativity,' Marta said, crouching down to look at the arrangement which stood just inside the door. 'Come and look at these. They're works of art, every one of them.'

The figures were about eighteen inches high, and Josephine touched the nearest – one of the three kings – to see what it was made from. The wood had been skilfully carved, as Marta said, and Josephine marvelled at how naturally the folds in his cloak fell and how convincing the artist had made the texture of the fur. 'They've obviously been in the wars over the years,' she said, noticing the scuffs and imperfections in the wood that only added to the figures' authenticity. The scene was lit from behind, and the gilt paint on the wise man's crown and his gift to the newborn baby shone with a dazzling radiance, but it was the facial expressions that distinguished this from most nativities, the emotion that hovered between joy and reverence and incredulity. 'It's all so natural,' she said, standing up. 'Mary actually looks like a real woman for once.'

They rejoined Archie, who had been talking to an elderly couple near the back of the church. 'Which side is the hermit cell?' Josephine whispered, as the three of them weighed up where to sit.

'It's on the right,' Archie said. 'We used to play in it all the time as kids. I'll show it to you when the service is over.'

'If it ever starts. There's still no sign of the vicar.'

'That's the best sort of church service, if you ask me,' Marta said with feeling. 'A few nice carols, then home for lunch.'

Marta had her own issues with the church, and Josephine didn't argue. They sat in the pews that Archie had indicated, and she turned round to look for the entrance to the underground chamber. All she could see were some steps leading down into shadow from a half-open door, but it was enough to make her shudder at the thought of being enclosed in such a confined space.

'Why on earth would anyone choose to live out their days shut up in a place like that?' Marta asked, echoing Josephine's thoughts. 'How can that possibly be holy? Selfish, I call it.'

'That's if he *did* choose to be there. We've no way of knowing now if he was down there because of fair means or foul. And if it *was* his choice, what was he running away from? I suppose people have all sorts of reasons for retreating from the world.'

'I suppose so.' She looked doubtfully again at the mysterious door. 'I don't mind going down there to have a look with you, but don't ask me to go anywhere near that chair they were talking about last night. If you want a sightseeing trip of that, you're on your own. You can boss me around for the next fifty years and I won't say a word.'

'That'll be the day.'

Marta smiled, and Josephine took advantage of the pause in proceedings to look in detail at the works of art around the altar. The reredos was disappointingly ordinary, but there were three striking alabaster plaques of biblical scenes, and the stained glass here was every bit as distinctive as the panels she had so admired in Chevy Chase the night before. One window in particular caught her attention: a vivid image of the Virgin and child, with St Michael's Mount in the background and a dog at her feet; Josephine had no doubt that the spaniel was a family pet of the time, and the scene seemed to capture perfectly the way in which the sacred and domestic lives of the island had run hand in hand over the centuries. The walls in this part of the church were devoted to the memory of various St Aubyn family members, and Josephine couldn't help but wonder what it must be like for Hilaria to sit regularly amongst such tangible reminders of how quickly time passed.

The buzz of expectant chatter built steadily as the congregation waited for the service to begin, although the family pews were still looking woefully depleted. Hilaria was busy welcoming people at the door, with Fielding hovering just behind her, and Josephine wondered if anyone had bothered to tell him that Marlene wasn't expected. Barbara Penhaligon finally put in an appearance, looking a little hungover, and sat down next to them with a brief nod. There was still no sign of the Lancasters. At precisely a minute to nine, the staff who were on duty that day filed into the church and sat in the row of seats that had been left vacant for them, while Hilaria took her place at the front, glancing nervously at her watch.

A door opened at the back of the church and all eyes turned towards it, but the new arrival would have looked completely out of place in the pulpit. Marlene was dressed in a Marcel Rochas trouser suit, broad at the shoulders and made of the designer's signature grey flannel, a look which somehow managed to be both defiant and uniquely feminine. She walked down the aisle as if she had known the church all her life and took a seat next to Hilaria, much to Barbara Penhaligon's annoyance. The two adversaries glared at each other across the choir, and Josephine hid a smile. 'My God, that woman knows how to make an entrance,' Marta whispered admiringly. 'She's upstaged the Virgin bloody Mary.'

She was right: a collective jaw had dropped amongst the congregation, and although they stopped short of applauding, there would be a few bruised ribs in the morning from the vigorous nudges that passed down the rows. The organ music stopped and there was another expectant hush as everyone looked again to the back of the church, waiting for Richard Hartley to make his entrance, but it began again almost immediately, this time with something a little more strident. Archie caught Hilaria's eye, and Josephine saw her give him a puzzled shrug.

Suddenly she heard a scream outside, coming from the south terrace and growing in hysteria. It was so surreal that for a moment she doubted herself, but one glance at Archie's face was enough to confirm that she hadn't imagined it. 'Keep an eye on Marlene,' he said as he left his seat and headed out of the church, followed quickly by Hilaria, and Josephine wondered if their reaction was connected to the tensions over dinner; it was as if they had been waiting for trouble, and now it had arrived to confirm their worst fears. Not everyone had heard the scream above the music, but the conversation gradually subsided as the urgency of Hilaria's departure sunk in, and when it came again, there was no mistaking it. Marlene looked across at them and stood up, clearly determined to follow the more curious members of the congregation outside, and Josephine and Marta joined her.

They hurried round the former lady chapel to the other side of the church, where Mrs Pendean was standing near the door to the smoking room with a man whom Josephine assumed to be her husband. It was obviously she who had screamed, because she was sobbing uncontrollably, and neither Archie nor Hilaria seemed to be having much success in calming her down or making sense of her distress. It was left to her husband to explain, which he did with a simple gesture towards the tower. Josephine looked up and saw, to her horror, the motionless figure of a man in the left-hand corner, slumped precariously on the stone seat with his legs hanging over the edge. It was unmistakably the Reverend Richard Hartley.

Her stomach lurched as she saw in her mind's eye the sheer drop from such a height, and she felt for Marta's hand. There was a stunned silence as everyone tried to comprehend what they were looking at, and next to her, Josephine heard the quiet despair in Hilaria's voice as she said softly: 'Please God, no.' The obvious futility of her words seemed to act as a catalyst for the horror to take hold, and Mrs Pendean's anguish spread quickly through the assembled onlookers, threatening to spiral out of control. Archie responded immediately, singling out the butler who had been one of the first members of staff to follow Hilaria from the church. 'Stop anyone else from coming round to this side of the terrace,' he said urgently, 'and get everyone back into the church. Tell them to stay in their seats and wait there until I've been up to the tower to see what's happened – and under no circumstances is anyone to follow me.'

'Very good, sir.'

Archie turned to Hilaria, but she pre-empted what he was going to say. 'The telephones aren't working, so we can't call for help. The wires have been down since last night. We're completely cut off.'

He swore under his breath. 'All right. I'll go and see what we're dealing with. Will you take care of Mrs Hartley?'

'Yes, of course.' Hilaria's voice was calm, but Josephine noticed how much she had aged in the time it had taken her to cross from one terrace to the other. 'What shall I tell her?' she asked. 'Is there any chance that he's not . . .' She tailed off, unable to bring herself to say the word.

'Tell her that her husband has been hurt and say that we fear the worst. There's no point in giving her false hope. She's vulnerable enough, and we don't want to confuse her more than she is already by keeping anything from her.' Once again, as she always was whenever she saw Archie at work, Josephine was struck by his sensitivity, even in the most stressful of situations, and she saw that Marlene had noticed it, too; the actress was looking at her escort with something rather more than respect. 'I need someone trustworthy to go down to the Change House and see what the situation is with the tides and the telephone,' he said, oblivious to the appreciation. 'We're going to need help of some sort from the mainland, and the sooner the better. Who do you recommend?'

'Tom Pendean,' Hilaria said without hesitation. 'He's the best boatman we have and he'll know what's possible, but I'm not sure he'll want to leave his wife when she's had such a shock.'

'I will take care of her,' Marlene said. Hilaria looked doubtful, but it was a decision rather than an offer, and the actress was already on her way over to the housekeeper.

Without wasting any more time, Archie followed her and gave his instructions. 'I also need to be sure that no one leaves the island,' he told Pendean. 'Should the causeway and the harbour become accessible again, nobody is to use them without my permission, in or out. Is that clear?'

'Yes, sir.'

'Are there any other access points to the Mount that I don't know about?'

'You can bring a boat in and out via Cromwell's Passage, over on the west side, but it wouldn't be safe in this weather.'

'You're sure?'

Pendean nodded and Archie sent him on his way, then walked briskly back across the terrace, stopping abruptly when he noticed Fielding at the edge of the group. 'Put that bloody camera down,' he shouted, briefly losing his composure. 'If I find out that you've taken so much as a single photograph in the last few minutes, I'll have you out of your job before you even get back to the mainland. Is that understood?'

Fielding nodded and did as he was asked, as Archie headed for the church. 'We keep a flashlight just inside the door to the tower,' Hilaria called after him. 'You'll need it up there. It's not an easy climb.'

'Thank you.'

They followed him back inside, and Josephine watched him make his way over to an arched door halfway down the nave, wondering what cruelty and sadness awaited him at the top of the tower. Hilaria went through to the organ loft, and a few seconds later the music stopped. It was hard to imagine the sorrow behind the scenes, but the sudden silence seemed an appropriate mark of respect for the moment when Angela Hartley was receiving the worst possible news about the person she loved. Josephine hoped that for once her mind's fragility might serve her kindly, protecting her from the enormity of the grief that lay ahead.

2

Penrose found the flashlight where Hilaria had said it would be, and was instantly glad of it when the door closed behind him, plunging him into darkness. As soon as he switched it on, he noticed another torch on the floor and bent down for a closer look. The bulb was broken, as if someone had dropped it down the stairs, and he wondered if it was evidence or merely a coincidence. Already he felt claustrophobic, more so than at any time since the living suffocation of the trenches, but he tried to put the sensation from his mind. The space seemed impossibly small for someone his size, and he realised that the last time he had tried to climb these stairs, he had been a boy of twelve or thirteen. The exhilarating sense of danger he had experienced back then was very different from the deathly apprehension of today, and suddenly all such childish games felt a lifetime away.

He climbed steadily upwards, trying not to breathe in the cloying damp that seemed to cling instantly to his clothes. His mind was racing over what could possibly have led to the dreadful discovery that he was about to make, and – in his panic – he wanted to go faster than was physically possible. He cursed his own clumsiness as he slipped on one of the steps, frustrated by the sharp spiralling of the narrow staircase, and wished heartily that he'd thought to take his overcoat off before starting the ascent; the bulky winter clothes were welcome, but they impeded his progress in the confined space and he paused to remove his scarf and coat before going any further, his fingers fumbling with the buttons in the cold. He shivered as he took his gloves out of his pocket and left the coat on one of the window ledges, but at least he could move more freely now. He pressed on, already dreading the journey back down, and although he tried hard not to pre-empt what could have happened, he was in no doubt of the fear and dread that Richard Hartley must have felt if he had been forced up here against his will. It would be hard to imagine a more inhospitable place to die.

He flashed his torch over the steps and walls as he went, but a cursory glance revealed nothing of any help to him. There would be plenty of time later for a closer inspection; what mattered now was to establish exactly what the situation was at the top of the tower. Already he had seen enough to know that there was very little chance of finding the vicar alive – depending on how long he had been there, the cold alone would have been sufficient to kill him – but it was amazing how forcefully despair and outrage could keep an unrealistic hope alive. At last he was nearing the top, and a change in the light as he made the final turn told him that the door at the head of the staircase had been left open, even before he felt the icy blast of air on his face. He slowed his pace, wary of the snow that had blown into the tower and made the steps even more perilous than they usually were. Bracing himself against the cold and the inevitable sadness, Penrose put the flashlight down on the top step and pulled himself out through the doorway.

He paused before going any further, keen to take in the scene and wary of disturbing anything when the snow made it all so fragile. The corner of the tower which held the chair was directly in front of him, and he could see immediately that Richard Hartley was beyond any help. The vicar's body faced the open sea, his head slumped forward onto his chest – stiff and lifeless, like a deposed king who refused to leave his throne. The body was held in place by a length of rope, tied at the back of the chair, and although Penrose was at the wrong angle to see the actual wound, there was enough blood on the vicar's clothes and the ground beneath the chair to suggest that his throat had been cut. The infinite patterns of crimson on white were shockingly vivid, and Penrose was struck by the peculiar beauty of blood upon snow.

There was a profound stillness about the scene which belied its lonely horror. The covering of snow in the narrow channel leading to the chair was scuffed and kicked, whether from a struggle or in a deliberate attempt to obscure any definite footprints it was impossible to say; either way, the marks would be of no help to him. He moved a little closer, still keeping clear of the area immediately around the body, and looked down at the dead man, noticing the raw, red discolouration on his knuckles where his skin had been exposed to the cold. His eyes were glazed and passive in death, and – perhaps the strangest detail of all – he was barefoot; the cuts and bruises on his feet suggested that he had been made to climb the tower steps without his shoes and socks. Hartley had obviously been killed after the blizzards stopped, but it seemed to Penrose that he had been on the chair for several hours, and he thought about what the vicar's wife had said just now, on the terrace; who was the person he had gone off to see, and just how long ago had that been? It would take an expert to confirm the time of death more accurately; the snow had done its quiet work, affecting the temperature of the body, and there was little point in speculating. In any case, there were questions that interested him far more than when the death had taken place: how had the vicar been persuaded to make that fatal climb out onto the chair, he wondered, and – once he was there – why had the murderer chosen to cut his throat rather than simply pushing him to his death? And then there was the biggest question of all: as far as Penrose could tell, Richard Hartley had been a kind and decent man, so who had hated him enough to contrive this spiteful, dramatic death?

He had been too absorbed in his thoughts to acknowledge how cold he was, but as he stepped back from the body and stood by the parapet, his limbs were stiff and painful, and he tried desperately to rub the life back into his arms. Down below, he saw Hilaria come round from the church and out onto the terrace, staring anxiously up at him; he knew that she was relying on him to know exactly what to do, to take this bewildering act of violence and somehow make sense of it for her, but rarely had he felt more helpless. Cut off from the mainland and with no means of communication open to him, he had no help or support, none of the forensic expertise that was always at his beck and call, and no way of accessing any of the official records that might have made his task a little easier. He realised for the first time how much he took the teamwork of an investigation for granted. Most of all, he missed the professional camaraderie of his colleagues. The isolation – physical and emotional – was new to him, and he was painfully aware that it also carried a far greater significance: Richard Hartley's killer – whoever he or she might be – must still be on the island, and at the moment he couldn't decide whether to treat that as a comfort or a threat.

Reluctantly, he made his way down, nursing a gnawing if irrational guilt at leaving the vicar alone at the scene of his death; the cold and indignity had lost their power to hurt, but it seemed wrong to abandon him, and there was still the question of how long he could decently leave the body in situ while waiting for the island to become accessible again. Hilaria must have seen him leave the roof because she was waiting anxiously for him at the foot of the stairs and showed him into the vestry. 'Well?' she asked.

'I'm afraid he's been killed – sometime late last night or in the early hours of the morning.' He gave her the details as sparingly as he could, knowing that she had a right to the information but reluctant to make things any worse for her if he could help it; she would already be feeling responsible. 'Where is Mrs Hartley?'

'In the drawing room. Josephine and Marta are with her. She's finding it hard to believe, and I can't tell if it's the shock or a more fundamental inability to understand what's happened.' She spoke as always with a quiet authority, but Penrose could see how devastated she was. 'Perhaps it will sink in when we confirm the worst. Can I tell her myself?'

'Yes, of course. I'll need to speak to her, but she's welcome to go back to her room first as long as someone goes with her.'

'I'll take her and stay with her. At least it will feel like I'm doing something useful.'

'No, I'm sorry. There are things I have to check with you before I talk to anyone else.'

'Yes, of course there are. I wasn't thinking. This has all come as such a shock.' She took a deep breath, steadying her emotions. 'Everyone out there is looking to us for direction. What do we have to do first?'

'Will you tell Lee to send the staff back to their duties and take the guests to wait in the dining room until I can come and speak to them? All except Alex Fielding – I've got a job for him, so ask him to wait behind. As I said, Mrs Hartley is welcome to go back to her room or stay where she is, whichever she prefers. I'm sure Josephine and Marta will be happy to stay with her until you and I have finished here.'

'Very well. What about Miss Dietrich?'

'She must stay with the rest of the guests, whether she likes it or not. I don't want her wandering round the castle on her own until we have a better idea of what's going on. I'm sure she'll understand.'

'Do you think Richard's death has anything to do with her being here?'

'I can't see any connections at the moment, but I'm not ruling anything out. Did the Lancasters turn up for the service?'

'No, I haven't seen either of them yet this morning.'

'Then ask Lee to send someone to their room and fetch them. If they're not there, I want to be told immediately. Do you have a doctor on the island?'

'No, I'm afraid not. We have a midwife, who does basic nursing, but if you were thinking of a death certificate, that will have to wait.'

'All right. Is there any news on the boats or the phones?'

'Yes. Pendean called up on the house telephone – that line's still working, thank God – but there's no chance of a crossing, at least until later today. It might be possible for three or four men to walk across at the next low tide if they rope themselves together, but they'd be taking a risk.'

'When is the next low tide?'

'Around two o'clock this afternoon.'

'All right, but I'll take your man's advice on that. We've got enough tragedy here already, without adding to it by recklessness.'

'Haven't we just?' She looked at him, then put her head in her hands. 'Oh Archie, how on earth can this have happened? Poor Richard – he was such a good man. Who on earth could have wanted to do this? It's all down to me, isn't it? If I've invited this evil onto the island, I'll never forgive myself.'

Penrose put his hand on her shoulder and spoke gently. 'Go and give Lee his instructions,' he said, knowing that staying busy was the only thing that would keep her sane. 'Then come back and tell me everything you know about your guests.'

She gave a scornful laugh. 'Well, that won't take long. Inviting a load of strangers into the house! How could I have been so stupid? It was asking for trouble. How on earth am I going to tell my father what's happened? He'll be devastated.'

'Go to Lee,' he repeated, 'and tell Josephine and Marta that I'll come and see them as soon as I can. Tell them to stay together.'

The implications of his warning weren't lost on Hilaria, who looked more horrified than ever. 'What about the villagers? Can they go home?'

'Yes, that's fine. The castle is my priority for now.'

She left him alone, but was back in no time at all. 'Right,' she said, with a new sense of purpose, 'what would you like to know?'

'Let's start with who might have had access to the church last night?'

'Anyone. It's always left open over Christmas.'

Penrose's heart sank. 'You mean anyone can go up there whenever they feel like it? They don't have to get a key?'

His alarm made his tone more judgemental than he had intended, and Hilaria reacted sharply. 'Yes, Archie – that's precisely the point. It's a place of worship, not a high-security prison that you have to be checked in and out of. It's been like that for years – centuries – and I'm not about to stop my staff *or* my guests enjoying a moment of prayer and contemplation on the off chance that one of them is murdered on St Michael's Chair. It's not a hazard that we've ever had to consider before, so don't be so damned ridiculous.'

'No, of course not. I'm sorry.' Penrose forced himself to control his temper, while mentally calculating the number of people – staff and guests – who would now have to be questioned. 'But the *castle* is locked?' he asked tentatively, fearing that he was going to have to add the fifty or so villagers to his inquiries.

'Yes, of course. Lee locks the east and west doors at half past eleven every night.'

'Does anyone in the village have keys?'

'Mrs Pendean, as housekeeper, holds a set, and another is kept in a safe at the estate office on the mainland, just in case of emergencies.'

'When did you last see Richard Hartley?'

'At about eleven o'clock, when the party broke up. He and Angela have adjoining rooms on the same landing as Josephine and the Lancasters. I walked part of the way with them on the way back to my own room, and said goodnight at the head of the staircase. The last thing I said to him was how pleased I was that he was taking the service in the morning, and how much I was looking forward to it. He said he hoped he would do it justice after all this time.'

'What did he mean by that?'

Hilaria shrugged. 'I didn't really give it any thought. I suppose he just meant that it was many years since he'd preached here. I know it meant a lot to him to be asked again.'

'And why *did* you ask him?'

'Quite simply because our usual chaplain was unavailable and Richard was coming for Christmas anyway. He and Angela responded immediately when I first mooted the idea of raising money for the refugee fund. They've been involved in children's charities for as long as I've known them. I've always assumed it was because they didn't have any of their own, but perhaps I'm reading too much into it. They made a very generous donation.'

'And he didn't have connections with anyone else here, staff or guest?'

'*Staff?* Archie, you surely don't think that a member of my staff would do something like this? They love this place, every single one of them, and I can't believe that any of them would defile the church like that.'

'I'm not suggesting that they would, but according to his wife, Richard Hartley went off to meet someone, quite possibly his killer, and I'm trying to establish who it might have been. He lived here in Cornwall . . .'

'And he lived in London for twenty-odd years. Most of the guests are from London – Mr Fielding, the Lancasters, you and your friends. If he had an acquaintance here, it could just as easily be someone he met up country.'

'Yes, I agree with you. It was something you said earlier, though, about inviting a load of strangers into the house . . .'

'What about it?'

'Well, most of them aren't strangers, are they? Not really. The Hartleys, Barbara Penhaligon, me – and I think we can rule out Josephine, Marta and Marlene. So the only people you really don't know are the Lancasters and Alex Fielding.'

'I see what you mean, and even Mr Fielding hasn't *chosen* to be here. He was sent by his editor in exchange for positive coverage and a hefty donation.'

'What about the woman who didn't turn up?'

'Mrs Carmichael?' Hilaria paused. 'She gave an up-country address, but as far as we know she's at the Godolphin Hotel, so I think we can rule her out.'

'So what *do* you know about the Lancasters?'

'Very little, I'm afraid, other than what we all noticed last night – she's very much under his thumb, and he's a rather unpleasant bully. The only thing I can add is that they sent a donation of five hundred pounds, but as I told you yesterday, the cheque wasn't honoured. Mr Lancaster assures me that it was just an oversight which will be rectified as soon as they get home, but I don't hold out much hope of ever seeing the money.'

'So you think they took advantage of the fundraising to cheat their way into a luxury weekend?'

'Something like that, yes. Come to think of it, though, Mrs Lancaster and Angela were getting on extremely well at dinner. They seemed very comfortable in each other's company, but I suspect that was because Angela is so gentle. I rather got the impression that Mrs Lancaster isn't used to kindness, at least not from her husband.' She paused, and gave a heavy sigh. 'I couldn't possibly say this to anyone else, but it would be so much easier if all this did turn out to have something to do with Miss Dietrich's admirers. Another crime to lay at Hitler's door . . .'

He smiled. 'Sadly, I don't think so. That's all about intimidation so that Marlene knows they're keeping track of her. There's no subtlety involved. If there were a Nazi on the island, I think we'd know about it, don't you?'

'Yes, I suppose so. Is there anything else I can do for you? Do you need any of my staff to help with things?'

'Not at the moment. I'm going back up to the tower now with Fielding to get the scene photographed, then I'll speak to the guests, followed by the staff. We just have to hope that the tides will be kind to us, so you could offer up a few prayers in that direction if you like. I desperately need some assistance from the mainland, even if it's only by telephone.'

'I'll see what I can do, and I'll be with Angela if you need me.'

Fielding was waiting outside the vestry, pacing up and down to keep himself warm. He looked pale and anxious, and Penrose regretted not having been more specific about why he was needed. 'Thank you for waiting,' he said.

Fielding smiled. 'I didn't think I had a choice. What's happened?'

'The Reverend Hartley has been killed, and I need a record of the crime scene. Until the weather improves, you're the only expert I've got. Come with me.'

The photographer stared at him. 'I'm not going up there,' he said, his voice full of trepidation.

'Yes, you are. And you *don't* have a choice about that. Come on.'

He headed for the tower, but still Fielding hung back. 'Listen, Mr Penrose, I do society balls, film stars and famous pets. I don't do crime scenes. I'll lend you the camera if you like, but you'll have to take your own pictures.'

Penrose held the door open and stared at his reluctant expert. 'A man has died, and there's precious little that any of us can do except make sure that he has some justice,' he said. 'Please do as I ask.' He led the way, and this time Fielding followed. The ascent wasn't any more comfortable with company, and he wished that he didn't have to put the young man through such an ordeal, but professional photographs would be much more reliable than his own, even if the subject matter was alien to the photographer. Out in the open, Fielding looked everywhere but at the body, and Penrose patiently gave him his instructions, watching as he set his camera, the intense cold and shocking strangeness of the situation conspiring to make him clumsy. Eventually, he was confident that the outline of the scene had been captured on film, and he moved in to take a closer look at the body.

The wound was every bit as vicious as he had anticipated, a cut so deep that it had partially severed the windpipe. Penrose would have taken comfort from the fact that Richard Hartley had died instantly were it not for the torment and fear that must have preceded the injury. Standing where he was now, he could see that a garland of holly lay in the vicar's lap, its prickles snagged in the wool of his clothes, and a series of barely perceptible cuts on his scalp showed that it had fallen from his head. A crown of thorns, Penrose thought, wondering what it signified; sacrifice, perhaps, or simply a mockery of the vicar's faith. Hartley's hands were clasped together in front of him, and Penrose could just make out something clenched in them. 'Take some close-ups,' he said to Fielding, pointing each time to the area he wanted photographed. When he was satisfied that every angle had been covered, he leaned forward to get a better look, gently prising the vicar's hands apart and removing the item.

'What is it?' Fielding asked, his earlier hesitation now replaced by curiosity, but Penrose didn't answer. He stared down at the old-fashioned decoration, a cotton-wool snowman exactly like the one that had hung on Marlene's Christmas tree, except that this one was stained with blood. Now he realised what it had reminded him of, that niggling moment of recognition that he hadn't quite been able to place. The sight of Richard Hartley with his throat slit – just like the children they had been discussing only the night before – took him back to that house in the slums as if it were yesterday, to that scruffy tree, so pathetic in the truest sense of the word, and to the deep, inconsolable sadness that always resurfaced at this time of year in his work, even if it belonged to a different crime and a different family, to a different human tragedy but one which was nonetheless connected on some fundamental level with those that came before it.

'What is it?' Fielding asked again, and Penrose realised how strange his silence must seem.

He held the decoration out in his hand. 'Make sure you get every detail,' he said, and waited quietly while Fielding did as he was told, appreciating a moment to think. It was the second time in two days and the first time in years that he had thought of those children, and he wondered what had happened to the brother and sister who survived the massacre. He had tried to keep in touch with the case, driven by an unprofessional but inevitable attachment to the orphans he had found in such distress, but once they were surrendered to the authorities they were lost to him – and of course they would have been given new names, as if that could wipe out their past. Would he recognise them now, he wondered? If one of them passed him in the street, would he even know?

'Give me the camera,' he said, when Fielding had finished his work.

'Why?'

'Because although I'm fairly sure you're not stupid enough to give these photographs to your editor or sell them to the highest bidder, I'd rather remove the temptation completely.' He smiled, taking the edge off his words. 'Hand it over. I'll make sure any photographs that are yours are sent back to *The Times* as soon as they're developed.'

'Yes, sir.'

Penrose took the camera and rewound the film, then removed it and put it in his pocket. 'Thank you, but you don't have to call me sir – not unless you're applying for a job.'

Fielding shrugged. 'A change of scene might do me good. We'll have to see how the pictures turn out.' He removed a hip flask from his pocket, and waved it at Penrose. 'You don't mind if I have a drink? I could do with one after this.'

'Go ahead. You can join the others in the dining room now if you like, but I need you to give me your word that you won't discuss this scene with anyone else here. Is that understood?'

'Yes, of course. Do you want a drop of this before I go?' He held the flask out and Penrose accepted, grateful for the warmth of the whisky. 'Why do you think he died?' Fielding asked, lingering at the door.

If he could answer that, Christmas really would be a time for miracles, Penrose thought. 'I honestly don't know yet,' he said, 'but there's someone here who does, and it's only a matter of time before I find out who that is.'

It was said as much in hope as in faith, but Fielding seemed reassured. He left Penrose on his own to take one last look at the scene before facing the practicalities of removing the body and starting his investigations, but the grim theatricality of the murder became more surreal and impenetrable under his scrutiny; there were no answers here, only endless questions. Once again, he felt that odd sense of betrayal at leaving the body behind, and before he headed down to the castle to begin his work, he reached up to the flagpole and tugged at the rope to pull the flag to half-mast. With luck, someone on the mainland would notice and at least be alerted to the fact that something was wrong – and if nothing else, it offered a small affirmation of compassion to contradict the degrading injustice of Hartley's death.

3

Personally, Josephine thought it might have been better to take Angela Hartley somewhere further from the scene of her husband's death than the drawing room, but the vicar's widow scarcely seemed to notice her surroundings. She had had to be led gently but forcibly from the church; the initial shock, followed swiftly by the confirmation of her worst fears, had sapped all her energy, and now she sat next to Marta on a powder blue sofa – the sofa once used by Queen Victoria, Josephine recalled from the night before; how long ago that evening suddenly seemed. She looked with concern at Mrs Hartley, who was deathly pale. Her hands shook in her lap as she repeatedly wound and unwound the tippet, and its black silk now struck a horribly prophetic note. She had yet to cry; a numbing fog seemed to have smothered her emotions, along with a sense of disbelief that Josephine shared. All the theatre of Christmas gave a heightened, surreal quality to the tragedy, and she felt as if she were observing things from a distance, unable to take part. The tea and brandy that one of the footmen had brought sat untouched on the table in front of them.

Outside, she saw some of the islanders beginning to leave the church by the north door. They walked in twos and threes across the terrace, heads bowed in respect or against the cold, and Josephine knew that they had no choice but to use the walkway which ran immediately round the drawing room. She got up to pull the curtains across the windows, partly to give Angela Hartley some privacy, but mostly to prevent her from seeing the fuss that would no doubt ensue when the departing congregation reached the south terrace; the last thing she needed in her grief was to witness people pointing up at the spectacle on the tower. Josephine shivered as she crossed to the windows, although the fire was doing its best to placate the chill of the day. The drawing room was actually made up of two individual spaces, divided by the chimney breast, and the blue walls and ornate white plasterwork were utterly out of character with the rest of the castle. The contrast had been less stark the night before, when the room was filled with lamplight and shadows, but now it had a completely different feel – cool and elegant, certainly, but a little austere, like a Wedgwood vase amongst everyday earthenware. The beautiful Christmas tree, which had sparkled along with the warmth and laughter of Christmas Eve, now looked redundant and out of sorts in the corner.

Angela Hartley misunderstood Josephine's wistful glance in its direction. 'I'm so sorry,' she said, her voice deceptively strong against the silence, 'we shouldn't be spoiling everyone's Christmas like this when Hilaria has gone to such trouble. You ought to be enjoying yourselves, not shut up in here with me.'

Josephine looked at Marta, baffled that the pressure to make every Christmas a happy one was so deeply rooted in the English psyche that not even murder could get in the way. 'Please don't think about it,' she said, horrified that Mrs Hartley should be blaming herself on top of everything else she must be feeling. 'I'm just so sorry there isn't more that we can do. It's precious little consolation, I know, but your husband couldn't be in better hands. Archie won't rest until he finds out who did this.'

'But it's all my fault.'

Marta took her hand, so affronted by the idea that she spoke almost angrily. 'Of course it isn't. Why on earth would you say that?'

'Because it's true. Richard only came here to make me happy. We don't usually go away for Christmas, and I know how special he was trying to make it for me – and why. There's an irony in that, don't you think? In wanting to make it memorable. Only for this to happen.' She wound the silk round each hand and pulled it tightly, as if she could take her frustrations out on the material. 'We've tried not to let it spoil our marriage, but we never thought . . .'

The emotion in her eyes was too much, and Josephine had to look away. The shock of finding herself so suddenly alone would be devastating enough for Angela Hartley, but her obvious reliance on her husband made her even more vulnerable now that he was gone. 'How long had you been married?' Marta asked.

'The fifth of September 1910, before we moved to London. I wish we'd never come back, really, but Richard was only trying to help.'

'Did something happen last night, Mrs Hartley?' Josephine asked, and then, when there was no response: 'When did you last see your husband?'

'I've been trying to remember. I know it's important, but the harder I try, the more confusing it becomes.'

'Take your time.'

'It's all so muddled, you see.'

Marta gave Josephine a warning look, discouraging what was beginning to sound like a police investigation, but she ignored it, spurred on by a troubling suspicion that she should have done more to help last night; if she had waited with Mrs Hartley, or even gone to look for the vicar herself, things might have turned out very differently. 'We bumped into each other in the corridor,' she prompted gently, 'and you said he'd gone to talk to someone. Do you know who it was?'

'Oh yes, I remember now. You were very kind, and you showed me the way back to my room.'

'That's right. Then what happened?'

'I was cold, so I got into bed and waited for Richard to come and say goodnight, but I must have fallen asleep because I don't remember him coming back.'

'So you didn't see him again, last night or this morning?'

'I didn't *see* him . . .'

'But?'

'But I heard him. That's right – it's coming back to me now. He must have woken me when he got back to his room. We'd left the adjoining door open, you see, and I could hear him moving about. I remember thinking that he'd be anxious about the service. He often had trouble sleeping, especially before an important day.'

'But you didn't see anyone, so you can't be sure it was him?'

'Who else could it have been?'

'No one,' Marta said firmly, before Josephine could answer. 'Of course it was your husband.'

'Unless I dreamt it,' Mrs Hartley said, suddenly doubting herself again. 'I might have done. I really can't be sure.' She looked to Josephine for reassurance. 'Did I go to look for Richard?'

'You said you were lost on your way back from the bathroom, but your dressing gown was wet, as if you'd been out in the snow. Do you remember going out on the terrace?'

'Why would I do that?'

'I don't know.'

'Perhaps I went to the church.'

'Is that where your husband was planning to meet someone?' Josephine might have imagined it, but the expression that passed briefly across Angela Hartley's face looked less like confusion than fear. 'Is that why you went outside?'

'I needed to give Richard his tippet before the service started. I found it in the case while I was getting dressed, and I knew he'd need it.' She began to cry, and it would have been futile to ask anything further, even if Josephine had had the heart to. 'This is all such a muddle,' the vicar's wife protested through her tears. 'Where *is* Richard? Why isn't he here to make sense of things for me?'

It was impossible to tell if the question was a symptom of the anger that so often accompanied sudden bereavement, or of Angela Hartley's general state of mind; either way, Josephine could think of no response to the injustice of it, and was relieved to see Hilaria making her way across the terrace to take over from them. They stood helplessly by as she tried to comfort the vicar's wife, who eventually asked to go back to her room, then headed for the dining room to join the remaining guests.

'If there *is* a war, they'll be after you for the interrogation unit,' Marta said as they walked down the Long Passage.

'What was that third degree all about? Surely you don't suspect her of killing her own husband on top of a tower in the middle of the night?'

'Of course I don't. That wasn't what it seemed like, was it?'

'A little. Carry on in that vein and you'll make Archie look like a rookie copper on his first big case.'

Josephine smiled, in spite of the circumstances. 'Well, I doubt that all the experience in the world will get him any further with Mrs Hartley.'

'What exactly do you think she can tell him?'

'I think she knows – or at least suspects – who her husband was going to talk to.'

'But why would she hold something back that might help catch his killer?'

Josephine shrugged. 'Oh, I don't know. Perhaps I'm wrong, and she really can't remember. Or perhaps she's frightened of being targeted herself.' She stopped before they reached Chevy Chase and took Marta's hand. 'It hadn't even occurred to me until now, but what if this isn't the end of it? What if someone else is in danger?'

'I'm sure it's occurred to Archie,' Marta said. 'Why else would he want us all gathered together in one place?'

It had obviously occurred to their fellow guests, too, because every member of the group seated in the dining room seemed on edge as Josephine and Marta walked in. The atmosphere was oppressive, like the heavy silence that invariably follows a row, and when Rachel Lancaster looked up nervously to see who the newcomers were, Josephine was shocked by the livid purple marks on her temple and cheekbone. Breakfast had been laid out along one side of the room, but no one had touched it, and the long refectory table now seemed absurdly large for the dwindling number of guests. The Lancasters, Marlene and Barbara Penhaligon were clustered together at one end, an improbable attempt at solidarity that only served to emphasise the desperate situation in which they found themselves. Each place setting was finished off with a small Christmas stocking, personalised to a particular guest, and Josephine counted it a blessing that Fielding and his camera were absent from the room: it would have been hard to imagine a picture which contrasted more sharply with Hilaria's hopes for the weekend than the scene in front of her, and she wondered where the photographer had got to.

Marlene followed her gaze to the stockings and picked up the one in front of her. 'It was kind, wasn't it? Miss St Aubyn doesn't deserve to have such sadness brought into her home. It will never be the same again for her.' She got up and walked purposefully across to the bank of silver dishes, as if doing something practical could somehow salvage Hilaria's good intentions. 'We should have coffee and something to eat. It will help us to think more clearly.' She began to put eggs, bacon and toast onto six plates, and Josephine remembered what Archie had said about her kindness on the journey down; a motherly instinct was not something she would have associated with the film star, but she liked her all the more for it. No one argued as she passed the food round, but there was very little appetite amongst the group, and Marlene herself ate less than anyone.

'How is Mrs Hartley?' Rachel asked, pushing her plate away and looking directly at Josephine and Marta, as if daring them to mention the bruises that hovered unacknowledged on the edges of the conversation. 'I can't imagine how she'll cope. They were so happy together.'

It was a very definite statement for such a brief acquaintance, and Josephine wondered if the two women had confided in each other the night before, or if happiness was simply the accepted thing to assume after a death; somehow, she couldn't imagine the same formality being extended to the Lancasters if one of them had been murdered in the night. 'She's in shock,' Marta said, 'and it's hard to know how much of what's happened has really registered yet. Hilaria has taken her to her room to lie down.'

'I'll call in on her later, if that's allowed.' Josephine noticed Gerald Lancaster glance sharply at his wife, but he said nothing. He, too, was pale and heavy-eyed from the excesses of the night before, and she could only speculate as to what had gone on after the couple retired to their room.

Marlene got up again and poured the last of the coffee into her cup, then rang the bell for more. 'I think I must have been the last person to see the Reverend Hartley alive,' she said, drawing the focus of the gathering as deftly and surely as she did a camera's. 'He came to my room last night. We had a drink, and we talked.'

'Why?' Barbara Penhaligon asked, and there was a childish note of petulance in her voice, as if she resented the fact that Marlene seemed on the verge of taking the starring role in another, far more important, drama.

'Because I invited him.' Barbara repeated her question, this time even more vehemently, and in the pause that followed, Josephine realised that she had been completely wrong about the voice she had heard in Marlene's room; no wonder Archie had ignored her innuendo. 'I met him in the corridor last night on my way to bed,' the actress said. 'He was upset – crying, actually – and I thought it was because of the talk of war at dinner.' She looked pointedly at Barbara. 'He was chaplain at a clearing station near the Somme during the war, and it cannot be easy to live with those memories.'

'And was that the reason?' Josephine asked, conscious of how intently they were all awaiting the answer.

'No, it wasn't. It was because of his wife. He had been talking to her about their wedding, but she couldn't remember it. She pretended to, but he could see in her eyes that it was lost to her. It was the first time that had happened, and he knew it was going to get worse, because he had seen it all before. He couldn't bear the thought of losing the only person who shared his most intimate memories. Happiness was like guilt, he said; it only existed if someone could bear witness to it.'

There was a long silence in the room as everyone considered the vicar's words and what their significance might be. 'Mrs Hartley told us that her husband had gone to talk to someone,' Marta said eventually. 'Do you think he meant you?'

'Me? No, I don't think so. We made no arrangements to meet – it happened by chance, and he came straight to my room. If he told her he was going to talk to someone, he must have meant someone else.' She thought about it for a moment, then added: 'Lots of things seemed to be troubling him. He said how ironic it was that his wife should be losing her grip on the past, while his was coming back to him when he least expected it.'

'Did you ask him what he meant by that?'

'No. Again, I thought he was talking about the war. It's only because of what has happened that I'm wondering about it.'

'You'll have to tell Archie all this as soon as he gets here,' Josephine said.

'Yes, of course.' Marlene sat down and lit a cigarette, staring at Barbara Penhaligon through the smoke. 'You seemed very anxious to know about Reverend Hartley just now,' she said, as the pause became uncomfortable. 'Is there something bothering you?'

'He's dead. Of course I'm bothered.'

Barbara lit her own cigarette, gesturing with it like a weapon, but the effect wasn't quite the same without the film star's cool self-assurance. 'No other reason?' Marlene persisted.

'Like what?'

The actress shrugged. 'Perhaps you're wondering if your friend really did go back to the mainland?'

'Just what are you suggesting?'

She was prevented from answering by Alex Fielding, who was shown in by the butler. 'Where the hell have you been?' Lancaster demanded, and the tension that had been building between the two women shifted seamlessly to a different part of the room. 'We were told that everyone had to gather here immediately, so what's so special about you?'

Fielding ignored him and went straight over to the fire. His shoes and the turn-ups of his trousers were soaked through, and he was obviously chilled to the bone. As he rubbed the life back into his arms, Josephine noticed the moss stains and cobwebs that had dirtied his mackintosh. 'I've been up that bloody tower,' he said, when he was finally beginning to get warm. He gestured to the camera that he had dumped on the table as he came in. 'Penrose wanted me to take some photographs. Believe me, Lancaster, I'd much rather have been sipping coffee here with the rest of you. Get off your high horse.'

'So you've seen his body?' Barbara said. 'What exactly happened to him? No one will tell us anything.'

Fielding glanced at Josephine, and she wondered if he would have been less discreet if Archie's friends hadn't been in the room. 'I can't tell you anything either,' he said. 'Sorry. Strict orders from on high to keep schtum.'

More coffee arrived, and once again Marlene did the honours. Fielding took a hip flask from the pocket of his coat and poured the last of its contents into his cup. Josephine noticed how badly his hand shook as he drained the coffee in one go and accepted another. Although he had kept his promise to Archie, the ordeal of what he had witnessed – presumably in intimate detail, if the photographs were to be used as evidence – was written all over his ashen, haunted face, and Josephine's sadness for the Hartleys only deepened.

Fielding seemed lost in his thoughts, isolated from the rest of the group, and she tried to think of something to say to distract him, but Marlene beat her to it. She got up and disappeared briefly into the library next door, returning with a pile of the week's newspapers that Hilaria was keeping there as a record of the Mount's recent publicity. 'I have been meaning to congratulate you,' she said to Fielding. 'There was a picture of yours that I so admired in here, and I wanted to talk to you about it.'

The photographer seemed pleased but a little apprehensive, as he always did when the film star singled him out for attention. 'Which one is it?'

'The river at dusk,' Marlene said, flicking through the pages. 'That was you, wasn't it? With the trams and the skyline and the reflection of the lights on the water?'

'Probably. We have to take so many, especially at this time of year. And with an assignment like this on the horizon, some of the more run-of-the-mill stuff gets forgotten.'

She smiled. 'Mr Fielding, do not be so modest. You should be proud of such a picture.' She found what she was looking for and beckoned him over. 'See? You have composed it very well, but lots of people can do that. It's the light that brings it to life, those things that we were talking about last night.' They looked at the photograph together, and Josephine was struck again by Marlene's kindness as she tried to replace the recent, traumatic images in Fielding's mind with a different, more innocent picture. 'Such a lovely interplay of soft lights and shadows and half-tones that you could almost believe it was colour. The sky was a deep blue, yes?' He nodded. 'I thought so. The best time to photograph a city. In film, we call it the magic hour, just before everything fades to black. And you?'

'The same,' Fielding said, becoming more animated. 'That's exactly what it feels like when you get it right – magic.'

'Well, you most certainly have got it right here. Look at the light trails on the bridge. A fast shutter speed, I suppose?'

'Of course. As you said, it's the magic hour, and an hour isn't long to get what you need.'

'Indeed.' Marlene nodded thoughtfully, still looking at the picture. 'I hope your photographs of me turn out as successfully, Mr Fielding.'

The room fell into silence again, and Josephine was beginning to wonder where the next minor skirmish would erupt when Archie appeared in the doorway. He gave a cursory glance round the room to make sure that everyone he expected to see was there, then sat down at the end of the table nearest the fire, refusing Marta's offer of coffee. 'As you will all know by now, Richard Hartley was murdered . . .'

'What we all *want* to know, Penrose, is how quickly you can get us off this fucking island.'

Archie glared at Lancaster. 'I'm afraid no one is leaving this island until the circumstances of Reverend Hartley's death are more firmly established.'

'But that's outrageous!' Barbara argued. 'What will my father say? You can't keep us here against our will.'

'Actually I can, Miss Penhaligon, but even if I couldn't, I think you'll find there's little point in arguing when the tides are running in my favour. Now, it would save us all a lot of time if you co-operated with these inquiries rather than obstructed them. I'm sure your father would give you exactly the same advice, and I'm more than happy to check with him as soon as the telephones are working again. In the meantime, perhaps you'd be kind enough to give me the benefit of the doubt and tell me where you were late last night and in the early hours of this morning?'

'In bed, of course, like everyone else.'

'Except two people, at least. So you went straight to bed after leaving the drawing room?'

'That's right.'

'And you didn't leave your room again until this morning?'

'Only once, to go to the bathroom.'

'Thank you.'

Marlene spoke next, repeating everything that she had told them earlier. 'Did he say some*thing* or some*one* from his past?' Archie asked when she had finished.

'I don't know that he was specific. If he was, I don't remember.'

'Did you bring any Christmas decorations here with you?'

The change of subject came from nowhere, and Marlene looked at him curiously. 'No, of course not.'

'Not even something small and sentimental? A toy you've had for a long time, or something to remind you of your daughter?'

Most of the people round the table were looking at Archie as if he had lost his wits. 'No, nothing like that,' Marlene insisted. 'I have a lucky doll called Zola, and she travels with me everywhere, but she is not a Christmas decoration.'

Archie nodded, apparently satisfied with her answer. 'I need to talk to all of you now about last night, and please be as detailed as you can in the information you give me, even if it seems irrelevant to Reverend Hartley's death.' Josephine half expected him to lead them off into separate rooms, just like the dull middle section of a country house murder mystery, but either he was pressed for time or he wanted to see how the guests would react to each other's evidence. She answered his questions like everyone else, telling him about her late-night encounter with Mrs Hartley but omitting to mention that she had been on her way to Marta's room at the time; she could come clean privately later, she thought, justifying the deception by telling herself that it could hardly be of importance and that he probably knew already. Marta was next on Archie's list, declaring truthfully that she had not strayed from her bed all night.

After the content of their very first conversation, Josephine expected Gerald Lancaster to be in his element while taking part in a real life criminal investigation, and she wondered if he would offer Archie the same sort of guidance and criticism that he had bestowed on her own

Inspector Grant, but Lancaster seemed increasingly nervous as the questioning went on, and looked at Archie with barely disguised hostility when his own turn came. 'You left the party early last night, Mr Lancaster,' Archie said. 'You didn't come with us to the drawing room when we went to join the ladies, and I didn't see you again. Where did you go?'

'To find my wife,' Lancaster said, and Josephine couldn't decide if his tone was suspicious or simply cautious. 'She'd had a fair amount to drink, as I'm sure you noticed, and I wanted to make sure she was all right.'

'So you went back to your room to look for her?'

He hesitated. 'I found Rachel in that long corridor with all the paintings. We went back to our room together.'

'That's a lie, Gerry.'

Everyone turned to stare at Rachel Lancaster, including her husband. For a moment, Josephine thought he was going to get up and reach across the table to her, but Lancaster clenched his fists in his lap and struggled to keep his tone even. 'You don't remember, darling, because you were a bit worse for wear. I had to practically carry you back to our room because you were feeling so ill.'

She stared defiantly at him, and Josephine could only admire her courage. 'I remember last night very clearly, *darling*,' she said, 'and the only place you carried me – well, carried, pushed, kicked if we're going to be strictly accurate – is up that tower.'

'What?' Archie looked first at one of them, and then the other. 'You were both in the church last night?'

'Yes.'

'She's lying, Penrose. Don't trust a word she says.'

'Be quiet please, Mr Lancaster. I'd like to hear what your wife's got to say.' He turned to her and spoke more gently. 'Is that how you got the bruise on your face, Mrs Lancaster? By being forced up to the tower against your will?'

Lancaster banged the table with his fist. 'That's none of your damned business.'

'Go on, Mrs Lancaster. Take your time.'

Josephine hoped fervently that Archie had a plan to keep husband and wife apart after he had finished his questions; Lancaster's rage was enough to bring on a second murder, regardless of whether he had had anything to do with the first. 'I went out onto the terrace after dinner,' Rachel said. 'Gerry's right about that – I did have too much to drink, and I was feeling unwell so I went outside for some air. He found me there, and he was angry.' She laughed to herself, but there was no humour in it. 'He gets angry very easily, always has, and he wanted to pay me back.'

'For what?'

'For what I said at dinner about that chair. Gerry doesn't like to think of a woman getting one over on him, or anyone else, come to that, so he thought he'd show me who's boss – didn't you, darling?'

'What time was this?' Archie asked.

'I couldn't say exactly, but not long after we left the dinner table. You were still in the smoking room with the vicar and Mr Fielding – I could see you through the window from the terrace and I thought Gerry was with you, but he took me by surprise.'

'And he forced you into the church?'

'That's right.' She looked directly at her husband, and Josephine saw sadness in her eyes rather than fear. 'I honestly thought he'd gone mad, but it was just hatred, pure and simple. Our marriage has been heading that way for a long time.'

'Did you go right to the top of the tower?'

'Yes. He made me climb out onto the chair.' There was a collective intake of breath around the room and Josephine exchanged a look of horror with Marta; even Archie seemed temporarily thrown from his questioning. 'It doesn't seem to have changed much between us, though,' Rachel continued. 'I'm still the one with the bruises.'

'What happened next?'

'Gerry helped me back down. To be fair, I think he'd frightened himself as much as he frightened me. I nearly slipped at one point, and that was going further than he had intended, so he left me alone after that. I came back down when I was feeling strong enough, and went straight to my room, hoping not to bump into anyone, but I think you'd all turned in by then. There were no lights on in our corridor.'

'And your husband?'

It was the question she seemed to have been waiting for, and she didn't hesitate in giving her answer. 'I left him on his knees in the snow, and I didn't see him again until much later.'

'That's a fucking lie!' Lancaster launched himself across the table, but Fielding – seated next to him – forced him back to his chair. 'She's trying to set me up, Penrose. Isn't that obvious?'

'So you deny being in the church last night?'

He hesitated. 'No, that bit's true, but—'

'And yet you lied about it, so why should I believe you now?'

'Because we went back to our room together. I swear it. For Christ's sake, Rachel – tell them. Do you even know what you're saying? They'll have me down for murder.'

'Do you stand by what you said, Mrs Lancaster?' Archie asked. 'Did you leave the church alone?' She nodded. 'And did you see anybody else on your way back?'

'No. As I said, everyone seemed to have gone to bed by then. It was just before midnight – I know that, because I heard a clock striking the hour shortly after I got back to my room. I remember thinking that it was a strange way to start Christmas.'

'How much later did your husband come back?'

'I can't say exactly. I know I heard the clock strike one, but after that I must have fallen asleep. When I woke again, he was there beside me.'

'I was there beside you all the time, damn it, and you know I was.'

Archie ignored the interruption. 'Did you notice the snow outside the church? Had anybody crossed the terrace before you and your husband?'

She thought for a moment before answering. 'I'm sorry. I don't remember.'

'What about on top of the tower?'

'Definitely not. The snow was untouched up there. It would have been beautiful if I hadn't been so frightened.'

'Mrs Lancaster, why did you come here this weekend?' For the first time, she didn't hold his eye, and Josephine wondered if Archie already knew the answer to his question. 'Does either of you have a connection to anyone else here, guest or resident?'

'Oh no, nothing like that – at least . . .' She left the sentence unfinished, and Archie looked questioningly at her. 'It was something Gerry said yesterday, as we were crossing the causeway. He told us that he came here as a child with his grandmother – you remember that, don't you?' She turned to Marta and Josephine, and Marta nodded. 'That was the first I'd heard of it. Gerry doesn't usually mention his family.'

'So I came here as a boy – what of it? Lots of people do.'

'Did you have any connection to Reverend Hartley before you met him yesterday?' Archie asked. 'He would have been living here in Cornwall when you were a child, so your paths might well have crossed. And I would advise you to think very carefully before you answer. There's a lot at stake.'

Lancaster began to look genuinely frightened now, as the pattern of the questioning became clear to him. 'I've never set eyes on the man,' he said, a note of panic creeping into his voice. 'Honest to God, I haven't.'

'Or anyone else here?'

'No.'

'So why did you come? I know it had nothing to do with giving to a worthy cause.'

'Oh, I don't know. Maybe I wanted to be one of *them* for a change,' Lancaster said, jabbing with his finger at the coat of arms above the fireplace. 'Maybe I'm sick of bowing and scraping to people all year round. I saw the advertisement in the paper, and I remembered how deferential my grandparents used to be.'

'Deferential to whom?'

Lancaster hesitated. 'To the St Aubyn family. My grandfather was a fisherman here years ago, and my grandmother worked as a housemaid at the castle. They lived in one of those houses behind the harbour – until he retired, that is, and they had to give the house up and move back to the mainland.'

'And they resented that?'

He scoffed. 'No, not at all. They wouldn't have a bad word said about the family – that was just the way things were, according to my grandmother. There was no sentiment about it, and they were loyal to the day they died – but I resented it. I loved it here as a kid. Those holidays were the only happy times I knew, and suddenly we couldn't come anymore. We didn't belong. So when I saw the paper, I jumped at the chance to come back here and be what my grandparents could never have dreamed of being, even for a couple of days.'

'It's a funny sort of tribute – to con your way into a home that your grandparents had such respect for, and cheat the family they served so devotedly. I can't see them being proud of that, can you? Did you really know nothing about this, Mrs Lancaster?'

'No, I didn't,' Rachel said, and Josephine believed her. 'As far as I was concerned, the reason we're here is in our wardrobe, all packed up in Gerry's suitcase and ready for a swift departure.'

'Rachel! For God's sake!'

'Tell me what you mean.'

'My husband's a thief, Mr Penrose, no matter who his grandparents were – a conman and a petty thief, and *I'm* the one who should be ashamed. If she looks carefully around the castle, I'm afraid that Miss St Aubyn will find some of her most precious belongings missing.'

Josephine saw the relief pass across Archie's face. Gerald Lancaster seemed to have no alibi for Richard Hartley's murder, but the only evidence to that was his wife's word against his; if the accusations of theft proved to be true, at least there would be something to charge him with and an excuse to keep him away from Rachel for the time being. Archie rang the service bell, and the butler appeared so quickly from the staircase down to the kitchens that Josephine could have believed he was waiting there to be called. 'Lee, I'd like you to come with me and Mr Lancaster while I search his room. Get one of your staff to join us, will you?'

'Certainly, sir.'

He did as Archie asked and the four men left the room together. 'Bloody hell,' Fielding said, as their footsteps drifted away. 'I wouldn't want to be in his shoes.'

Marta got up and went to sit by Rachel Lancaster. 'That was very brave,' she said quietly. 'Are you all right?'

'I have absolutely no idea. I'm just glad that he's gone – for now, at least.'

She started to cry, and although Josephine felt every sympathy for her, she couldn't help but recall how well Rachel seemed to know Angela Hartley; it was overly suspicious, perhaps, but the thought crossed her mind that if Lancaster genuinely didn't have an alibi for the early hours of Christmas morning, then neither did his wife.

4

Violet slept later than she had planned, soothed sub-consciously by the rhythm of the sea outside the window. When she finally came to, it took her a moment to make sense of the unfamiliar ceiling and oddly matched furniture, then she remembered the storm and the hotel, and the expression on Johnny's face when he had learned that they would have to share a room. She turned over, enjoying the simple luxury of being warm on a cold winter's day, and looked at her fiancé in the next bed. Johnny was every bit as dead to the world as she had been, and it was nice to have him at her mercy for once, unselfconscious and without the distraction of trying to please her. He looked so young in his sleep, with a lock of fair hair fallen forward over his eyes and his arm outstretched on the pillow, but it was a strong face as well as a handsome one, she thought – definitely a view she could get used to, and not a bad start to Christmas Day.

A smell of bacon and toast from downstairs tempted her out of bed, and she pulled on her dressing gown and tiptoed across the floor, hoping that they hadn't missed breakfast. Her handbag was by the dressing table, and she sat down in front of the mirror to redo her hair and put some lipstick on before Johnny woke up. The fire that had been so welcome the night before had long died down, but she had remembered to hang the wet clothes they had arrived in by the grate when it was at its fiercest and now she was pleased to find them nearly dry. After supper, they had undressed shyly in the dark, and Johnny's shirt and trousers were thrown untidily over a chair: he could knock that on the head, she thought, going over to pick them up; his mother might have been happy to run round after him, but she wasn't. To her surprise, the clothes were wet through, soaking the arm of the chair and dripping water onto the carpet. Bewildered, she went over to his bed and shook him roughly awake. 'Have you been out in that storm again?' she demanded, giving him no time to register what was happening. 'I told you not to do anything of the sort. You're a bloody idiot, Johnny Soper. You could have been killed.'

'I wasn't, though, was I?' He grinned at her, but she wasn't in the mood to be charmed. 'I'm sorry, Vi. I was worried and I couldn't sleep, so I walked down to the jetty to see for myself if there was any chance of getting a boat across there safely. I wouldn't have done anything stupid, I promise. Why would I? I've got you to think of now.' He smiled again, and this time she thawed a little. 'Do I get a Christmas kiss?'

'Yes, but you can dry your own trousers. Now look the other way – I'm getting dressed.'

'Spoil-sport.'

He did as she asked, burrowing back under the sheets while she hurriedly chose clothes that might make a good impression on his mother. 'All right, I'm decent now. Your turn.' While he was dressing, she walked over to the window and drew the curtains back, pleased to see that the weather was greatly improved from the night before, even if the sea still looked threatening. She picked up the binoculars and trained them on the Mount, hoping to see a cheerful plume of smoke rising from Mrs Soper's chimney, but there was nothing, and suddenly she began to share some of Johnny's anxiety. 'It's much brighter now,' she said cheerfully, hoping that he wouldn't notice the artificial tone in her voice. 'Surely those waves will die down soon.'

'Let's hope so.' He came to join her, and reluctantly she passed him the binoculars. 'Oh no,' he said after a second or two, and the dread in the words was even worse than she had expected. 'Oh God, Vi, I knew it. Something's wrong – look at the church tower.'

She snatched the glasses back and looked again, and saw instantly that the flag which marked the highest point of the island was flying at half-mast. 'But Johnny, that doesn't mean . . .'

'Come on!' he said. 'We need to get packed up and downstairs. Perhaps someone here knows what's going on.'

In a panic, he started piling wet clothes into his suitcase, and she went over and took his hands, forcing him to stop and look at her. 'Calm down, love, and let's think this through. I'm not being funny, but why would they lower the flag for your mum? She's not one of the toffs, is she? That doesn't make sense.'

'No, I suppose it doesn't.' Johnny smiled at her, as the logic of what she said sank in. 'That's probably why she wasn't at home last night. If there's been a death at the castle, it'll be all hands to the pump, especially if it's the old man. They all love him over there.' He held her tight, and she could feel the relief pass through his whole body. 'I wouldn't wish ill on anyone, Vi, but thank God it's not Mum.'

5

The clutch of stolen items was in Lancaster's suitcase, just as his wife had described. It was mostly silverware – a sugar vase and an Elizabethan chalice, several elaborately decorated ladles, all easily pocketed – but Penrose also recognised a circular snuff box that had been on the side table in the smoking room, and several miniatures, including one of Charles I which he knew to be valuable. Lancaster seemed visibly to shrink under the disapproving stare of the other three men in the room. 'I can only begin to imagine how ashamed your grandparents would be if they could see you now, Mr Lancaster,' Penrose said. 'What was their name?'

'Pascoe. Frederick and Joan Pascoe.'

'And is Gerald Lancaster your real name?'

'Of course it is.'

'And what do you do for a living?'

'I'm a railway porter.'

'For which company?'

'London, Midland and Scottish.' Penrose made a note of the details, and the simple act of committing evidence to paper seemed to focus Lancaster's fear. 'I didn't kill him,' he said repeatedly. 'You've got to believe me. I didn't know the man. Why on earth would I want to kill him?'

'I don't know, but I can't imagine why you would force your wife to climb onto St Michael's Chair either, so forgive me if I don't automatically take your word for it. But you stand by your statement? You left the church with your wife and were in your room with her all night?'

'Yes, absolutely.'

He seemed sincere, and Penrose couldn't rule out the possibility that Rachel Lancaster had seen a solution to her unhappiness in refusing to give her husband an alibi, salvaging her freedom from his guilt; he wouldn't have blamed her for it, but he couldn't make assumptions either way. 'Mr Lancaster, when we get back to the mainland, you will be taken to a police station for further questioning about Richard Hartley's death, and charged with theft and fraud. I will also be asking your wife if she would like to press charges for assault. In the meantime, you'll be kept under supervision at all times, and you're not at liberty to move about the castle or speak to your wife or any of the other guests. Is that clear?' Lancaster nodded. 'Good. Please go with Mr Lee.'

Penrose watched them go, relieved at least that the suspect wasn't putting up a fight. He fastened the suitcase to take with him, and ran into Hilaria in the corridor outside. 'What on earth is going on?' she asked. 'I was just leaving Angela's room when I saw Mr Lancaster being escorted downstairs. Did he kill Richard?'

Penrose brought her quickly up to date. 'You'll be glad to have this back. It was quite some stash that he was planning to get away with. Does the name Joan Pascoe mean anything to you?'

'Vaguely. Why?' Hilaria listened as he explained Lancaster's connection to the Mount. 'I still don't see why that would give him cause to murder poor Richard.'

'No, neither do I, other than raising the possibility that they met before Richard moved to London. I suppose there's a chance that Richard might have cottoned on to what Lancaster was doing.'

'Even so, it seems a very extreme reaction. Better just to put the stuff back and deny all knowledge of it.'

Penrose agreed. 'How is Mrs Hartley?' he asked. 'Josephine told me just now how distressed and confused she is, but I *will* need to speak to her.'

'She's staying in her room for the time being, and I've asked someone to sit with her. You're welcome to go in now, but I doubt you'll get anything coherent at the moment. She's very anxious about Richard's body and how long he'll have to stay up there, and she doesn't seem capable of focusing on anything else. I told her I'd ask if you intended to bring him down soon.'

It was the question that Penrose had been wrestling with, both morally and practically. He would dearly have loved a forensic opinion on the murdered man in situ, but that might not be possible for hours yet, and there was decency to consider, as well as the body's vulnerability to birds and other predators. 'I don't suppose you have an undertaker on the island?'

'No, I'm afraid not. We use Brooks, but his workshop is at the other end of the causeway. There are some good men in the village who would do it respectfully, though, and it seems right to let Richard rest in the church while he's with us. I'm happy to oversee it now if I have your authority. To tell you the truth, I'd be pleased to have something useful to do.'

'All right, thank you. I'd appreciate that, but please make

sure that the church is locked at all times now. I'm sorry if that compromises its importance for you.'

'I understand. These are hardly normal circumstances.' Not for the first time, Penrose was grateful – in the absence of his professional colleagues – to have support from someone so calm and dependable in a crisis. 'Why do you think he was killed up there?' she asked tentatively, as if she were half afraid of the answer. 'Was it just an obscene gesture, or is there a meaning in it that ties his death to the Mount?'

'I'm trying to keep an open mind at the moment,' Penrose said. 'I'd have said the latter if we hadn't been talking about St Michael and the chair at dinner – after that, everybody knew that it's freely accessible and what it symbolises, so it doesn't have to have been an insider.'

'What it symbolises?'

'Yes – dominance, prayer, judgement. St Michael was the weigher of souls at the Last Judgement, wasn't he? Separating the blessed from the damned. Perhaps someone thought the Reverend Hartley set himself too high in the world. Or perhaps it was simply the most frightening death imaginable. Either way, I've rarely seen a murder that looked more staged.' His words had hardly reassured Hilaria, so he tried to offer something more positive to offset them. 'I'd really like an up-to-date assessment of the tides. Short of a confession, there's only so much I can do without some outside help. If I can call the Yard, I can at least ask some questions about the people here who are strangers to us. Something useful might come up. And I'd like to talk to Richard's sister-in-law. She's local, isn't she?'

'St Ives way, I believe. I expect Angela will go to her, for the time being at least.'

'And she might be able to give me a better picture of Richard's life and associates. I feel as though I'm fumbling in the dark at the moment.'

'Would you like me to send for Pendean so you can talk to him about getting across to the mainland?'

'Yes please, and I'll make a start on questioning the staff.'

'Do you want to speak to them individually?'

'No, it will save time if I see them all together, perhaps in the servants' hall? If I'm honest, I don't hold out much hope of their being able to tell me anything specific enough to be of use.' He rubbed his hand wearily across his face. 'In fact, hope of any sort is in pretty short supply at the moment.'

'You'll get there, if anyone can – and don't forget that some of the staff bedrooms overlook the north terrace, so somebody might have seen something. I'll go downstairs and tell them all to gather in ten minutes.'

'Make it fifteen. I want to look at Richard's room first, and I'll try not to keep them from their duties for too long.'

She smiled sadly. 'Suddenly their duties don't seem very relevant, do they? It hardly matters if lunch is late, when no one has an appetite. Have you had anything to eat?'

'No, I've been too busy.'

'I'll make sure there's something downstairs for you.'

She left with a renewed sense of purpose, and Penrose tried to do the same, although his hopes of finding something out from the dead man's room yielded nothing more useful than evidence of an orderly disposition and a liking for Agatha Christie; a brand-new copy of *Hercule Poirot's Christmas* sat waiting to be read on the pillow, but the bed had obviously not been slept in. He headed back to Chevy Chase, conscious that his abrupt departure with Lancaster had left everyone else without any definite instructions. The guests seemed to have paired off, he noticed. Marta and Josephine were sitting together by the fire, and the Lord Lieutenant's daughter was talking earnestly to Rachel at the other end of the table. Marlene was in full flow, holding a coffee cup and pacing up and down as she talked to Fielding about Hollywood. She broke off as soon as she saw him. 'Is there any news?'

'Nothing at the moment, I'm afraid.'

'Where's Gerry?' Rachel asked anxiously. 'Has he gone back to our room?'

'No, he'll be kept apart from everyone else until I've had a chance to speak to him again, this time under caution.'

She looked relieved. 'But you found the stuff?'

'Yes.'

'Rachel's worried sick that she'll be incriminated, too,' Barbara said. 'I've told her she's got nothing to be frightened of. That's right, isn't it?'

Penrose ignored the question and spoke to the group as a whole. 'You're welcome to stay here now or go back to your rooms, whichever you prefer. I would ask you to be vigilant at all times, though, and if anything out of the ordinary happens, please report it straight to me or to Miss St Aubyn. She'll talk to you about the plans for the rest of the day.'

'It's hardly going to be charades round the fire now, is it?' Fielding said. 'Can I call the office? We'll need to re-plan the feature.'

No prizes for guessing the direction that the coverage would now take, Penrose thought, but he didn't blame Fielding for prioritising his work; this assignment was a gift to his career already, but now even more so. 'There are no telephones working at present,' he said, glad not to have to worry about headlines for the foreseeable future, 'but you can speak to your editor when there are, as long as you don't give away any information which might jeopardise the investigation.'

'Is there anything we can do to help?' Josephine asked.

He appreciated the concern in her voice. 'Nothing at the moment. I'll come and talk to you all again later.'

The stairs down from the dining room were a short cut to the servants' quarters. The smell of Christmas hit him, a rich, nostalgic blend of sage, roast turkey, bacon and spices, and just for a moment he allowed himself the luxury of its normality, finding something comforting in the illusion of the day played out as it should have been: the familiar, dissonant sounds of ordinary tasks, hollowed and amplified by the cold, stone floors; a distant babble of female voices, whose easy gossip was such a welcome contrast to the grief and fear upstairs. The castle's vast kitchen rattled to the sound of pans boiling steadily on the range, but the room itself was strangely deserted and he realised that he was late for his rendezvous with the staff.

Mrs Pendean was looking out for him and she showed him through to the servants' hall, where around a dozen members of staff were seated at benches on either side of a long wooden table. The room struck him as particularly cheerless, painted a drab shade of green with no carpet and very little furniture, but its chilliness was probably a welcome relief to those whose faces were flushed from the heat of working in the kitchens. The buzz of conversation ceased as soon as the housekeeper set foot in the room, and Penrose wondered if their respect was for the role or for Mrs Pendean personally.

She introduced him and he thanked them all for coming, then outlined the basic circumstances of the vicar's death. 'Which of you was responsible for looking after the Reverend Hartley while he was here?' he asked, and a footman put up his hand. 'Didn't you think it was strange that he wasn't in his room this morning?' Penrose persisted, when the evening routine had revealed nothing of interest.

'I didn't know, sir. I asked him what time he'd like to be called this morning and he told me not to bother because he was an early riser and wanted to go to the church first thing. He didn't even want morning tea, and I got the impression he preferred to be left alone. Some guests are like that. They don't want the fuss.'

'And Mrs Hartley?' The housemaid who responded was similarly unforthcoming, except to say that Mrs Hartley was a nice lady, whose only difficulty had been in making up her mind about her clothes. 'What about the other guests? Did anyone see Mr or Mrs Lancaster after dinner? Or someone in a part of the castle that seemed strange to you?' There was silence around the table and Penrose knew that he was wasting his time. 'Which of you have bedrooms overlooking the north terrace?' he asked, and three housemaids raised their hands, glancing nervously at each other. 'Did you see anyone coming and going to and from the church last night?' Two of them shook their heads immediately, but the third girl – the one who had been waiting on Mrs Hartley – hesitated, and Penrose looked at her. 'Did you see something out of place?' he asked again.

'Not really out of place . . .' She broke off, torn between honesty and discretion, and Penrose waited impatiently as she looked to Mrs Pendean for guidance.

'Is it me you're thinking of, Rosie?' the housekeeper asked, and the girl nodded vigorously, obviously relieved to have the decision made for her.

'You were at the church last night, Mrs Pendean?' Penrose asked, trying to keep a note of judgement out of his voice as he wondered why she hadn't said anything before.

'Yes. I always go last thing on Christmas Eve, just to make sure that everything's ready for the following morning. The church is my responsibility, you see – always has been.'

'And what time was this?'

'Oh, quite late. Just after midnight, I'd say. Would that be about right, Rosie?'

'Something like that, Mrs Pendean. I saw you as I was drawing my curtains, so it must have been around then.'

'Thank you, Rosie,' Penrose said. 'Does anybody else have anything to say? In that case, I've kept you from your work long enough, but if I could have a private word with you, Mrs Pendean?'

'Yes, of course.' He waited while she dismissed her staff and instructed one of the kitchen maids to bring him some breakfast, which arrived almost immediately. 'How are you?' he asked, when she had settled again. 'It must have been such a shock for you.' She stared at him, thrown by the change of tone. 'To see the vicar's body this morning?'

'Oh, yes. Yes, of course. It's a terrible thing to have happened here. This is a quiet place these days, in spite of its history. We're not used to violence.'

How inconsiderate of Richard Hartley to have brought it here, Penrose thought cynically, but he wasn't surprised that the islanders' first thought was for the impact on the Mount's tight-knit community; things would no doubt be different if one of their own had been killed. 'Were you in the church for long last night?' he continued.

'No, not long at all. Ten minutes at the most, I'd say.'

'And did you go there on your own?'

'Yes. Other people had been coming and going, obviously, because there was a path trodden through the snow, but that's not unusual. It's a beautiful church and most of us use it, especially Miss St Aubyn. It was empty when I went in, though.'

'But it's possible that somebody could have been in the tower?'

She looked suddenly frightened. 'I didn't go to the tower. Why would I?'

'No reason at all, and that wasn't what I meant. I just wondered if you saw or heard anything out of the ordinary while you were in the church? Anything at all, even if it didn't seem significant at the time.'

She considered the question, then answered it reluctantly. 'I did hear someone in the tower last night.'

'Go on,' Penrose said, resisting the temptation to curse her for not saying so earlier.

She shrugged. 'That's it, really. I heard someone coming down the steps, so I hid in the hermit cell.'

'Why, if you were doing nothing wrong?'

The 'if' obviously grated on her, but she didn't argue. 'It was late, and I didn't want to see anyone, so I waited there until I heard the main door close. Then I left and went straight home.'

'So you have no idea who it was?'

She shook her head. Penrose studied her face, noticing how tired she looked. He remembered what Josephine had said the night before about her being upset, and wished he had taken more notice. 'How long have you worked here, Mrs Pendean?' he asked.

She seemed more guarded as the questions took a personal turn, but answered them readily enough. 'All my adult life,' she said. 'I grew up here, and my first job was as a stillroom maid. That was the best part of forty years ago now.'

'And you've worshipped at the church all that time?'

'Yes.'

'So you'll have known the Reverend Hartley before he moved to London.'

'I knew *of* him, that's all. You don't know someone personally just because you've heard him preach or waited on his wife.'

'Of course not, but I wondered if you could think of any reason at all why someone might want to do this to him?'

'No, absolutely not. It's a wicked thing to do.'

There was a knock at the door, and Tom Pendean put his head round. 'Miss St Aubyn said you wanted me, sir?' He looked with concern at his wife. 'Everything all right, love?'

She stood up, obviously embarrassed by the term of endearment while she was at work, and Penrose thanked her for her help. 'Mr Penrose was just asking about the Reverend Hartley,' she explained. 'He wondered if I could remember anything that might help, back from when the vicar used to be chaplain here.'

'You should talk to Emily Soper, sir, if you want to know anything about the island.'

'Who is that?'

'She's got the museum at the head of the causeway, and what she doesn't know herself she can always look up. There are photographs and newspapers going back years down there, as well as all the general displays.'

'Mr Penrose isn't here for a history lesson, Tom,' the housekeeper said impatiently. 'He's got more important things to do than look for a needle in a haystack, and you know how Emily likes to talk. It's you he wanted to see.'

'Actually, that might be very useful,' Penrose said, looking at his watch, 'but first I need to know if there's any chance at all of getting to the mainland? I know low tide isn't for an hour or two yet, but is there anyone who would be prepared to take a boat across with me?' Pendean looked doubtful. 'I don't want you to take any risks, but I really can't stress how urgent this is.'

'All right. I'll take you, but I'll need some help.'

'Tom! It's not safe!'

'Let me talk to some men down in the village,' Pendean said, ignoring his wife's protestations. 'If you can wait, the best thing might be to go for the causeway at the lowest point of the tide. We've done it before, with a few of us roped together, so if I can get a couple of volunteers, I'm happy to give it a go.'

'Thank you,' Penrose said gratefully. 'Will you see what you can do now? And I'll come down to the village with you and have a look at the museum.'

As they left the servants' hall together, Penrose couldn't help but feel guilty at how distressed the housekeeper seemed by her husband's offer to risk a sea crossing. God forbid that anything should happen to them, he thought; the last thing the Mount needed today was another tragedy, especially one brought about by his own recklessness. He accepted the long oilskin jacket and boots that one of the footmen found for him, and was glad of their protection as he followed Pendean down the winding cobbled paths to the village. The wind caught at their heels and the early brightness of the day had long since disappeared, replaced by a light but insidious rain. He turned to look back at the castle, and offered a silent prayer of thanks that at least Richard Hartley's body was no longer exposed to the elements.

The snow was entirely gone from the lower parts of the village. Even though the tide was on the wane, the water levels in the harbour were still high, and Penrose could tell from the seaweed and other debris along the front that the sea, at its worst, must have pounded against the most exposed line of houses, all of which now had boards and sandbags across their doors and windows. He parted company with Pendean by the graveyard, and crossed the narrow road to the museum on the corner. The ground floor was in darkness, so he knocked hard on the door and waited. When there was no answer, he went round to the side of the building to look for another, more private entrance, but there were only two sets of windows, which showed him nothing but a counter and a variety of packed display cases. Disappointed, he returned to the front door and tried again.

'No luck?' Pendean called, coming out of the Change House.

'No, she's obviously not at home. How about you?'

'Trannack's up for it, as long as you're happy to wait for low tide, and he says he'll get John Mathews to come as well – he's our postman, and he's seen a fair few rough crossings in his time, so you'll be in safe hands.' He looked with concern at the museum, and knocked on the door himself. 'The chaps in the Change House say they haven't seen Emily all day. I hope she's all right.'

'Does she live alone?'

'Yes, since her husband died.'

'And she couldn't have gone away for Christmas?'

'Not unless it was a last-minute thing. Her son's up country in Plymouth now, and she's supposed to be coming to us later. It was her first Christmas on her own, so Nora asked her over for supper. I think she'd have let us know if her plans had changed.' He rattled the door, but it was firmly locked.

'Do you want to force it?' Penrose asked.

'No need. Nora keeps a spare on her castle keys. I'll ask her to nip down if she's free.'

He went back to the Change House to use the house telephone and Penrose walked over to the causeway, trying to assess how difficult the task ahead would be. The sea swelled and churned against the harbour wall, its surge still strong even at a fraction of its power, and he hoped that he hadn't made the wrong decision.

6

So this was how easily it happened, Nora thought, as her husband rang off and the line went dead. One slip, followed by another and then another, until someone noticed the inconsistencies and your life unravelled in front of you. She had lied to the guests on Christmas Eve about Emily's absence from the museum, and then to the policeman about her time in the church, and now he would be waiting for her in the harbour because Tom was so hell-bent on doing the right thing. Ironic, she thought, that her husband's simple wish to help should have sealed her fate.

Her fear dogged her progress down the Mount like a physical disability, making her footsteps heavy and slow, clutching at her heart until she found it hard to breathe. There was something malignant in the wind today, something in the fury of it that frightened and tormented her, perhaps because it reminded her of those last, terrible breaths that had taken Emily from the world; she heard them still in the wind's persistent moaning, until it felt as if her friend would never let her rest. Above her, the branches of the ancient pine trees creaked and strained under the pressure, threatening to snap at any moment, and she knew exactly how that felt.

And there they were, below her in the harbour, waiting by Emily's door. Her stomach tightened and she stopped in her tracks, wondering which of the two men she feared more. For a moment she was tempted to turn back, to make an excuse about her work and try to delay the inevitable, but that was all she would gain by prevarication – a few more hours of this desolate, insidious fear, and she honestly didn't know how much longer she could stand it. It would almost be a relief to stop the charade now, no matter what the consequences.

She pressed on, arriving flustered and out of breath. 'Don't look so worried, love,' Tom said when he saw her. 'I was wondering if Emily went over yesterday and got caught on the mainland. That would make sense, I suppose, but it's best to be on the safe side.' He squeezed her shoulder and she had to turn away, caught on the other side by the policeman's sympathetic smile; he was obviously touched by her apparent concern for her friend, and she wanted to scream at him not to be so kind, when kindness was the last thing she deserved. He moved away from the door to let her unlock it, but Nora hesitated and handed the keys to her husband. The wind rushed in ahead of them, as if determined to get to the truth, and the rustle of dried seaweed across Emily's carefully swept floor was the only sound that broke the silence.

'Emily?' Tom called as he walked over to the counter. 'Emily, are you here? It's Tom, we've just come to see if you're all right.' She waited for him to stop in horror, to turn and look back at her with shame or disgust, but his behaviour was so natural that she caught herself waiting for Emily to reply. He rummaged in a drawer for some matches and passed them to her. 'Light the lamps, love, or Mr Penrose won't be able to read anything.' She did as he asked, and a warm glow filled the room. 'Those albums are here, next to the postcards,' he added, pointing them out to Penrose. 'Take whatever you think might help.'

'Thank you.'

Nora braced herself to join the two men at the counter, standing where she had stood during that fateful conversation. She looked round, then closed her eyes, convinced that her mind was playing tricks on her, showing her what she dearly wished to see rather than the reality of her terrible deed; so seductive was the illusion that she had to will herself to look again, but still there was nothing there. Emily's body, the dust sheet and the boxes, the blood that had spread in pools and rivulets across the floor – it was all gone.

'Emily?' Tom called again.

'She *must* be here somewhere,' Nora insisted, a note of panic in her voice. She stared round, utterly bewildered. 'Where *is* she, Tom? Why isn't she here?' The only response to her question was a loud, indignant mewing as a tiny black-and-white cat appeared from a back room and began to rub round each of their legs in turn. 'Oh God, I forgot about Charlie,' she said. 'He hasn't been fed.'

'I must have been right, then,' Tom said. 'She'll have gone to Marazion and been stranded by the tides.'

'But she *can't* have done.'

Her voice began to rise hysterically. Penrose found her a stool, but she waved it away. 'No, I'll be all right in a second. It's just the day, and everything that's happened. I've got to feed Charlie, though. Emily would never forgive me for letting him go hungry.'

She made to go upstairs, but her husband put his hand on her arm. 'Let me go, love,' he said. 'You stay here with Mr Penrose. Show him Emily's albums.'

She watched him walk through the workroom and draw back the curtain that covered the staircase. He hesitated, glancing back at her and quickly pulling the curtain across again, but she had already seen her friend's body lying at the foot of the stairs.

'Don't go any further, Mr Pendean,' Penrose ordered. 'Come back and look after your wife.'

He tried to hold her back, but Nora forced her way past him. 'I need to look at her,' she cried. 'Please let me look at her.' If she hadn't known better, she would have said that Emily had fallen down the stairs. She stood over her body, looking at the awkward, crumpled way she was positioned, and it seemed so obvious that she wondered if Emily had still been alive when she left her after all? Then she remembered the blood, so much blood, and that terrible, stertorous breathing.

'She must have fallen,' Tom said, and Nora wanted to tell him to stop, to give her time to think, but he ploughed relentlessly on. 'Look, her shoelace is undone. What a bloody awful thing to happen. I'm so sorry, love. I know how close you were. Come here.'

He put his arm round her and led her gently away.

'Do you live nearby?' Penrose asked.

'Yes, just behind the harbour.'

'Then take Mrs Pendean home and stay with her. I'll ask Miss St Aubyn to send someone to check on her.'

Tom nodded. 'What about the causeway?'

'Don't worry about that now. I'm sure the three of us can manage if necessary.'

'All right, but be sharp about the timing or you'll never make it across.'

He turned back to Nora and held her close, and she clung to him as the only thing that made sense. 'Come on, love – let's go home. You've had a terrible shock.'

She wondered if he would ever know how true his words were. 'What about Charlie?' she said, suddenly remembering the cat. 'We can't just leave him, Tom.'

'All right, all right.' He scooped the cat up and gave him to her to hold. 'You were a good friend, Nora,' he said. 'Emily was lucky to have you.'

7

As Tom Pendean led his wife from the building, Penrose watched them go, trying to make sense of what was happening on the island and what his priorities should be. He locked the museum and went straight to the Change House to call the castle and speak to Hilaria. She took the news calmly, but he could hear the strain in her voice, and he knew that these tragedies would take their toll once the anaesthetising practicalities were dealt with.

Deep in thought, he returned to Emily Soper's body, conscious of having a limited amount of time before low tide offered the only opportunity to access the mainland. The bizarre surroundings of the scene struck him anew as he entered the room, even though this time he was prepared for them. Mrs Soper had obviously been a talented taxidermist in her own right, as well as a collector: a workbench was covered in the tools of the trade, and the gimlet eye of a jay in full flight stared across at him – a work in progress, now garishly lifelike by comparison with its creator.

He went back to the foot of the stairs and crouched down by the dead woman. Her dull eyes looked past him as if hoping for someone more important to enter the room, and her hair was matted with viscous, sticky blood – although there was very little on the floor beneath her head. Curious, he fetched one of the lamps from the museum and placed it on the step beside her body, then gently lifted Mrs Soper's head and examined the wound on her temple. The laceration was ragged and deep, and as he peered more closely in the fitful light, he could see tiny fragments of something – most probably wood or paint – embedded in the skin. He considered the significance of what his eyes were telling him, keeping an open mind to other possible explanations until an expert opinion was available, but one thing now seemed certain: however Emily Soper had died, it wasn't from an accidental fall down these bare stone steps; a fatal blow to the head was far more likely. He lifted her arms, one after the other, pulling her sleeves back to examine the skin; there was no sign of bruising from an attempt to defend herself, suggesting that the attack had taken her completely by surprise, but that was the only blessing he could find. Her skin was grey and cold to the touch, with rigor well developed, and had he been forced to hazard a guess at the time of death, he would have put it at several hours before Richard Hartley.

Penrose stood up and looked round for a possible murder weapon, but there was nothing immediately obvious in this bizarre collection of dead animals and Victorian mourning dolls, all waiting to be repaired, and neither could he find anything remotely out of place in either of the upstairs rooms. The museum might hold more possibilities, but he was wasting time with uneducated guesses when everything he needed to know for the time being had already been established: there were two suspicious deaths on the island, not one. It was reasonable to suppose that they might be connected, but for the life of him he couldn't see how.

He knelt quietly again by Mrs Soper's body, as if respect could help him to find an answer to his questions, but it only served to deepen his sadness. It never ceased to amaze him, this indefinable but crippling sense of rage that he was capable of feeling for a stranger – shamefully more powerful than the emotions which underpinned many of his longstanding friendships – but he clung to it as the essence of who he was, and he knew that if it ever let him down, it would be time to concede defeat.

When he was ready to leave, he blew out the lamp and went back to the museum to collect the photograph albums from the counter where he had left them. The smell that he had noticed there before and thought nothing of now seemed more significant – a faint but unmistakable odour of disinfectant. The floor had obviously been recently washed, and he knelt down to look for any evidence that might have been missed; the cleaning was a reasonably thorough job, but he knew how difficult it was to eradicate everything and his patience was soon rewarded by a spatter of blood on the wall, and other marks on the floor leading through to the back room. No doubt a proper forensic examination would reveal more, but Penrose was satisfied for now that regardless of where Mrs Soper had been found, the attack had taken place here, at the counter.

Looking round the museum again, he noticed that one of the cases was open. It was devoted to a collection of sweetheart jewellery, sent home from South Africa by migrant Cornish miners, but some of the contents were missing from the neatly labelled shelves and the detail struck him as odd. His first thought was of Gerald Lancaster, but he doubted very much that petty theft was at the root of either death. Still brooding on what might link the two victims, Penrose pulled the blinds and locked the door, then hurried back up to the castle.

He was shown to the study, where Hilaria sat staring out of the window. 'Emily Soper lived on this island her whole life,' she said sadly, without any other greeting. 'She was a nice woman – a *decent* woman. She shouldn't have died alone.'

'I'm afraid there's more to it than that,' Penrose said. He could see by the shock on his friend's face that she had understood his meaning immediately, but he outlined everything carefully to avoid any misunderstandings.

'Please tell me that the deaths are connected, at least,' Hilaria said. 'I don't think I could bear the idea of harbouring two murderers under this roof.'

'You mustn't—'

'Don't tell me not to blame myself, Archie. You know me better than that. Have you got *any* idea what is going on here?'

'Not yet, but I'm going over to the mainland now with the men that Tom Pendean recommended. I hope to have some answers for you when I get back.'

'Will you do something for me while you're there?'

'Yes, of course.'

She picked up a piece of paper from her desk and handed it to him. 'This is the address we have for Emily's son, Jonathan. Can you arrange for someone to go and break the news? He should know what's happened as soon as possible. I'd hate him to read about it in the newspapers, and we shouldn't forget that we have a journalist in our midst.'

'I'll make sure it's done.'

'When will you be back?' The question was business-like enough, but there was a deep anxiety in Hilaria's voice and he knew that she was at a loss to know how to keep everyone safe. 'And what can we do to make sure that nothing else happens while you're gone? Should I warn the islanders?'

'No, not yet. At the moment, everyone thinks that Mrs Soper's death is a tragic coincidence, and I'd rather it stayed that way for now. If people start to panic, it might trigger an extreme reaction from the killer, and that's the last thing we're in a position to deal with. I'd much rather wait until we can get reinforcements onto the island.' She nodded reluctantly, and Penrose prayed that he wasn't being reckless by keeping people in the dark about the extent of the violence. 'I won't be gone long,' he promised. 'I'll make sure to be back before the tide turns again, and by then we'll have people doing all they can up country to get to the bottom of this.'

He must have sounded convincing because Hilaria seemed reassured, and that in itself felt like a betrayal, when in reality he couldn't remember ever feeling so helpless. 'Are those albums from the museum?' she asked, nodding to the pile he had put down on the desk.

'Yes. I thought I'd ask Josephine and Marta to look through them to see if there's anything interesting about Richard Hartley. Unless you'd rather do it?'

She shook her head. 'No, by all means hand them over. Everybody's getting more restless by the minute, so I'm sure they'd appreciate a mission.'

'Is everyone still in Chevy Chase?'

'Yes. I've cancelled lunch by mutual agreement, but we'll have a cold table later. Until then, what would you like me to do with everyone?'

'The important thing is for no one to be on their own, guest or staff member. None of you must take any risks. Lancaster is to stay under lock and key, and be vigilant about Mrs Hartley, too, just in case she's in danger because of something she knows about her husband. I was hoping to speak to her before going over to the mainland, but that was before we found Mrs Soper and there isn't time now. Will you make sure that there are plenty of staff around Marlene while I'm gone?'

'Yes, of course.'

'Thank you. I'll go and speak to Josephine and Marta now.'

'Archie?' He turned back to her from the door. 'Please be careful.'

In the dining room, the restlessness that Hilaria had mentioned was palpable, and he had to fend off several demands to know what was happening and what he intended to do about it before he could shepherd Josephine and Marta into the library for a private conversation. 'You can't seriously be considering that!' Josephine said angrily, when he had brought them up to date and told them about the causeway crossing. 'What the hell is the point of getting yourself killed?'

Penrose looked to Marta for solidarity, but she managed to make it perfectly clear that she agreed with Josephine without uttering a word. 'Those men wouldn't have agreed to accompany me if it was dangerous,' he said tersely, knowing there was no time to argue reasonably. 'Anyway, it's your safety I'm here to talk about, not mine. Make sure you stay together while I'm gone, and look through these for me. If there's something relating to Richard Hartley – or anything else of interest, for that matter – tell me when I get back.'

'*If* you get back.'

'*When*, and promise me you'll do as I ask.'

Knowing she was beaten, Josephine agreed. 'Can we take these to one of the bedrooms?' Marta asked. 'I know it's a tasteless thing to admit, but I'm sick to death of all the nervous energy in that room.'

'Yes, but lock the door. I'll see you later.'

He went back to Chevy Chase to issue one final round of instructions, but was delayed by Marlene at the door. 'Can I speak to you before you go?' she asked. Penrose doubted that the star had ever been asked if what she was about to say was important, but she took it with good grace. 'Yes, I think so.' She glanced meaningfully at Barbara Penhaligon. 'Could we go somewhere private?'

Intrigued, he led her through to the smoking room and closed the adjoining door. 'What is it?' he asked, wondering if she had remembered something else about her conversation with Hartley.

'The photographer from *The Times* isn't who he says he is.'

'What?' Penrose stared at her, utterly unprepared for what she had just said. 'What do you mean?'

'Mr Fielding – he is a fraud. Didn't you notice yesterday, when we arrived? He had no idea what photographs he wanted to take, and he was so clumsy with the camera . . .'

'But that was nerves, surely? You're a little out of his league, and I'm not surprised he was intimidated. I was, too, the first time I met you.'

'Were you? You did not show it.' She smiled, but it soon faded. 'Please take what I am saying seriously. How did he behave when you asked him to take your photographs?'

'He was competent, I suppose, but . . .'

'Competent? But he is supposed to be one of their best men. Believe me, Archie, I have met thousands of photographers in my lifetime, and he is not the man that *The Times* would send on an assignment as important as this one.' He thought about what she had said, remembering how awkwardly Fielding had behaved on the tower, and how reluctant he had been to go in the first place; again, Penrose had put that down to nerves and the horrific circumstances of the task, but perhaps there was more to it. 'I gave him a test just now,' Marlene admitted, 'because I thought you would ask me for something more than instinct.'

'What sort of test?'

'There is a photograph in Wednesday's newspaper that has his name on it, but he knows nothing about it. It was taken at dusk, and I talked to him about the magic hour and the technicalities of the light, but I could tell he was out of his depth. He did not correct me when I talked about the shutter speed, and he had obviously never heard of the magic hour. You know about it?' Penrose shook his head. 'It's that moment at twilight, before the sky goes completely black, but the phrase is misleading because it's never an hour, just a few minutes. The man who took that photograph understands that with every fibre of his being. The man in there' – she gestured towards the dining room – 'does not.'

'Does he know you tricked him?'

'No.'

'Good. Let's keep it that way for now, and don't mention this to anyone else. I'd rather not alert him to our suspicions until I've had a chance to check him out with the newspaper. But you're sure?'

Marlene nodded. 'It doesn't make him your murderer, I know, and there might be a perfectly innocent explanation. Perhaps *The Times* had to send someone else at the last minute and didn't want to admit that he was a junior, or perhaps the wrong name is on the photograph. But if Alex

Fielding took that picture, then this man is most certainly not Alex Fielding.'

'And what about the Lord Lieutenant's daughter?' Penrose asked.

'What about her?'

'You gave her a very pointed look before we left the room. I thought you were going to tell me something about her.'

'Ah, that was just to put Mr Fielding off the scent – and anyway, I do not like the woman. If she worries, that is a bonus.'

Penrose shook his head in admiration. 'You've missed your vocation, you know. Hollywood's loss would be the country's gain.'

It was meant as a light-hearted compliment, but she took him at his word. 'When the war comes, there will be plenty for me to do, no doubt. Now, can I ask you a question? Why did you ask me about Christmas decorations?'

'A snowman exactly like the one on your tree was found with Richard's body.'

'And you thought it *was* mine?'

'It crossed my mind that it might be. I haven't forgotten those letters you showed me, and now it seems we have an impostor amongst the guests. He could be here for any number of reasons, but it's not inconceivable that he's conned his way here to get to you.'

'But how would he do that? How would he even know I was here? It wasn't made public until yesterday.'

'Nothing is ever completely confidential. People here had been told you were coming, and I dare say there were a few quiet rumours circulating at *The Times*. Your luggage was sent on ahead, so people at Claridge's knew where you were

233

spending Christmas, and they have access to your hotel room. Any number of railway porters could have seen the luggage between Paddington and Marazion,' he added, thinking of Gerald Lancaster. 'And of course we have our German friends, who seem to be everywhere at once and always a step ahead of us.'

She nodded thoughtfully. 'You really believe that Richard's death had something to do with me?'

'No, in my heart I don't. But I'm not ruling anything out, and even if it doesn't, there's still the possibility of someone here with an entirely different agenda. Just be careful, and whatever you do, never be on your own with this man who's calling himself Fielding. Stay with Hilaria, or some of her more senior staff.' He thought for a moment, then added: 'Actually, even that's not safe enough. I need to get him off the Mount.' They went back into the dining room, and Penrose addressed Barbara Penhaligon. 'I'd like a word with you as soon as I get back,' he said, unable to think of a better sleight of hand than the one that Marlene had created already. 'I need some information on the man you came over here with.' He turned to Alex Fielding, who was staring into the fire. 'You wanted to speak to your editor?' Fielding nodded. 'Then come with me now to the mainland and telephone from there. We're a man short on the rope, so you'll be doing me a favour.'

Fielding's eagerness to oblige was convincing, and Penrose wondered if that suggested he was genuine or had simply seen an opportunity to get off the island; either way, he was pleased to be removing a potential threat from the castle. He requested more waterproof clothing, then took Fielding down to the Change House, where Trannack and Mathews were waiting. The level of water across the causeway was noticeably lower now, and Penrose waited impatiently while someone called Jim tethered the four men tightly together, then diligently checked each knot. Eventually, he was happy with his work, and the line – Penrose and Fielding in the middle, flanked by the two islanders – moved steadily down the shingled slope to the sea.

The receding tide swept over his feet, slashing and nipping at his legs like an angry dog, and he caught his breath as a burst of spray hit his face. There were no words to describe how cold it was, and above the howl of the wind he heard Fielding cry out as the shock of the icy water hit him. Trannack paused when they were nearly up to their waists, allowing the less experienced men to get a sense of the rhythm and power of the waves. At first, Penrose was relieved that the surge wasn't stronger, but he underestimated how tiring it would be to push on relentlessly against such steady pressure, and long before they were halfway across, the water began to feel almost unbearably heavy against his body. Strands of seaweed wrapped themselves around his legs, throwing him off balance, and he was grateful for the sturdy bulk of the man next to him; without it, he might have been tempted to turn back. The islanders seemed prepared for the weak links in the chain and took turns to offer shouts of warning or encouragement, and in spite of his reservations about Fielding, Penrose could not help but be impressed by his courage. He set his sights firmly on the snowy hills that framed Marazion, and gradually their dogged solidarity paid off as the markers were reached one by one: the cross that stood at the midpoint of the causeway; the dark bulk of Chapel Rock; and finally the mainland itself, gloriously solid beneath his feet.

He was shivering and soaked to the skin, his throat raw from the effort of shouting above the elements, but just for a moment the sheer relief of the achievement made Penrose forget the circumstances that had driven them to attempt it in the first place. A curious welcoming party waiting outside the Godolphin Hotel served as a sober reminder. 'Looks like we've caused a bit of a stir, arriving like this,' Trannack said, as his frozen hands wrestled with the knots in the rope. 'You see that lad coming towards us?' Penrose nodded, watching the young man break off from the group and make his way across the beach. 'That's Jonathan Soper, Emily's boy.'

'But I thought he was in Plymouth?'

Trannack shrugged. 'Obviously not. Looks worried, doesn't he?'

Penrose shook off the ropes and headed up the shingle, rehearsing news that he had not anticipated having to deliver. The boy's unexpected arrival left him with a dilemma; he didn't want to make the reality of Mrs Soper's death public yet, but neither did it seem right to lie to her son. He was still deciding what to do when the young man took the initiative. 'Is it Lord St Levan?'

'Lord St Levan?'

'Yes. We noticed the flag was at half-mast this morning, then we saw you coming over and knew it must be serious, so we thought . . .'

'No, it's not Lord St Levan. He isn't even at home for Christmas. We lowered the flag for one of the guests.'

'Oh, thank God!' Soper looked mortified. 'I'm sorry. I didn't mean that disrespectfully, but my mum . . .'

'Emily Soper?' Penrose clarified, too bothered by the

unfounded relief on the young man's face to let him go any further.

'How did you know that?'

He looked frightened again, and Penrose could hardly bear to confirm his worst fears. 'I'm Detective Chief Inspector Archie Penrose, Mr Soper. I'm so very sorry to tell you that there have been *two* recent deaths on the Mount. Your mother's body was found earlier this morning, although I believe that she died some time yesterday.'

'No!' Soper bellowed the word, a raw, despairing act of denial, and he looked so angry that Penrose thought for a moment that he was going to lash out.

A young woman hurried over to join them and took Soper's hand. 'Johnny, what is it? What on earth's wrong?'

He shook her off, but still she took the brunt of his grief. 'I *knew* something was wrong. I should never have listened to you. We might have been able to save her if I'd gone over last night like I wanted to.'

'But you couldn't get across.'

'How do *you* know? You're not from round here. We could have tried harder.'

'The young lady's right, Mr Soper,' Penrose added gently. 'You arrived late last night?' He nodded. 'Then there was nothing you could have done. We've had to wait until now to come across and get some help.'

'We were going to surprise her, weren't we, Vi?' He took her hand, all hostility now forgotten. 'She wasn't expecting us, but we wanted her to be the first to know.'

'We've just got engaged, you see,' Violet explained. 'Johnny wanted to tell his mum.'

'I wish I'd written now,' Jonathan said. 'At least then she'd have known we were on our way. She could have looked forward to it. It was her first Christmas on her own. She probably thought we didn't care.'

'Don't be daft, Johnny. Of course she knew you cared about her. Why else would you have half drowned yourself last night?'

'What do you mean?' Penrose asked.

'Johnny couldn't sleep last night, so he went out to try and find a way across. I've spent most of today drying his clothes.' She squeezed his hand lovingly. 'So don't beat yourself up about not trying hard enough, love. Your mum couldn't have had a better son – she always said so herself.'

Mathews put his hand on Johnny Soper's shoulder and Penrose was relieved to have someone there who knew the family. 'Come inside, lad, and let's get a drink down you.' He looked at Penrose. 'That's all right, isn't it?'

'Of course it is.'

They headed towards the hotel, but Soper turned back. 'How did she die?' he asked.

Penrose's dilemma returned and he chose a middle path. 'We found your mother at the bottom of the stairs. She died from a head injury.' It was the truth, but not the whole truth, and he felt a pang of conscience as Emily Soper's son accepted it and turned away.

'What a tragic fucking coincidence that is,' Fielding said. 'Poor bloke. Christmas will never be anything but misery for him now.'

There was no trace of anything but sincerity in the words, but Penrose decided to test him. '*If* it's a coincidence,' he said, waiting for the reaction.

His meaning took a second or two to sink in, but when

it came, the surprise seemed genuine. 'You mean she was murdered as well?' Fielding asked. 'It isn't just Hartley you're after someone for?'

The barely suppressed enthusiasm for the idea was exactly what Penrose would have expected from a journalist; if Fielding *was* an impostor, he was a good one. 'Keep that to yourself for now. Let's go and find the landlord and get those calls made.'

The warmth of the hotel was almost as welcome as the prospect of contact with the outside world. A convivial Christmas lunch was obviously drawing to a close in the dining room, and as they waited in reception, a room full of revellers wearing coloured paper hats stared in bemusement at the new arrivals and their wet, dishevelled clothes. Penrose introduced himself and asked to use the telephone, and the hotelier pushed it across the desk, mercifully too busy to engage in much conversation. 'Isn't there somewhere more private?'

'There is, but not with a telephone,' the man said in a beggars-can't-be-choosers sort of way, and Penrose considered himself told.

'Go and wait in the bar,' he said to Fielding. 'I might be some time, so get yourself a drink on me. It's the least I can do after this morning. Make it a large one.'

Fielding took his whisky to an empty table – near the islanders but not with them – and Penrose positioned himself carefully to keep an eye on the bar while making his calls. As luck would have it, there was far too much rowdiness for him to be overheard as he asked to be put through to Scotland Yard, and then to his detective sergeant, Bill Fallowfield, who had drawn the short straw of Christmas Day duties.

'Happy Christmas, sir,' Bill said, when he finally came to the telephone. 'We didn't expect to hear from you today. Fed up of hobnobbing with film stars, are you?'

'No, Bill, I'm fed up of trying to guess how two people have died.' Fallowfield was one of Penrose's closest friends, as well as his most reliable colleague, and usually he found the sergeant's relentless good nature a welcome contrast to his own, more cynical, personality; today, he had no patience for anything but the task at hand. There was a silence at the other end of the telephone, and he took advantage of it to bring Fallowfield succinctly up to date.

'Are Miss Tey and her friend all right?' Bill asked as soon as Penrose had finished.

'Yes, they're fine, but I can't be sure that the violence will stop here because I've absolutely no idea if there's a connection between the two victims, or why anybody would want to kill either of them. There's so much I need, Bill, and I haven't been able to access any of it from the Mount. We've even had to wade across the sea to use the bloody telephone.'

'Fire away, sir. I'll get straight onto it.'

'First of all, get hold of someone from *The Times*, preferably the editor, and ask him to confirm that he sent a photographer called Alex Fielding on this assignment. Get a full description of Fielding – there's a chance that the man here isn't who he says he is.' He watched Fielding down his drink and get up to order another, wondering if he had unwittingly asked a suspect to photograph his own crime scene. 'Find out anything you can on Gerald Lancaster and his wife Rachel. If he's telling the truth, Lancaster works for London, Midland and Scottish Railways, so check him out there and see if he's got any previous convictions for theft or violence. Hartley was the vicar at St Clement's in Notting Dale . . .'

'Nice part of town,' Bill muttered sarcastically.

'He was there for a few years after the war. Get the file out on the Naylor murders. It's probably a needle in a haystack, but if there's anything that might help us track down the surviving children, I want to know about it.'

He gave his sergeant the details and waited while he noted them down.

'What about the dead woman?' Fallowfield asked.

'Emily Soper, an islander all her life. I think the answer to her death *must* lie closer to home, but obviously let me know if her name comes up in connection with anything else.'

'Right-o, sir. Anything else?'

'Yes. Telephone Claridge's and ask someone to go and look at Marlene Dietrich's Christmas tree.'

'Her *Christmas* tree?'

'That's right. I haven't got time to explain, but I need to know if it's still got a snowman on top.'

'Of course you do, sir.'

Penrose smiled. It was a relief to talk to someone who could not only help, but who also understood the pressure that he was under, and he felt better simply for giving the instructions. 'I'm going to call the local force down here now and get reinforcements over to the Mount as soon as possible, together with some forensic help. I'll also try to track down Hartley's sister-in-law and break the news – she might be able to tell me something useful – but I want any information as soon as you have it. If the line is engaged, just keep trying – there's only one bloody telephone here.'

Fallowfield rang off, and Penrose noticed Jonathan's fiancée waiting to speak to him. 'Can I help you, Miss . . .'

'Carter. Violet Carter. I can see you're busy, so I won't keep you, but I just had to ask if what you said to Johnny about last night being too late to help was right, or if you were just being kind?'

'No, I wasn't being kind. We'll have to wait for an expert to confirm a more precise time of death, but I'm as sure as I can be that Mrs Soper died much earlier in the day.'

'Thank God,' she said, looking relieved. 'It was me that held us up, you see. Johnny would have been hell-bent on getting there last night, but I talked him into booking us in here. We didn't always get on, me and his mother, so I wasn't in a hurry to get over there. Now I feel awful about it, but you know what it's like. Families at Christmas . . .'

He smiled. 'How well did you know Mrs Soper?'

'Not very well at all. We'd only met a couple of times, but that was enough to remind me that no girl will ever be good enough for a boy's mother.' She shrugged. 'It wasn't personal, but Johnny meant the world to her. He wasn't as close to his father – always said his dad never really wanted to take him in.'

'Take him in?'

'Yes. Johnny was farmed out when he was a baby.'

'And his real family?'

'He doesn't know, and he's never wanted to. I'd be curious, but perhaps that's a woman's thing. He's not bothered.'

'Do you know Mrs Soper's maiden name?' Penrose asked, wondering if it had been an informal adoption within the family or something more official.

'No, sorry.' She glanced back to the bar, where her fiancé was sitting silently with Trannack and Mathews. 'He wants to go back to the Mount with you. Will that be all right?'

'Yes, of course.'

'They look after each other over there, don't they?' she said, and he couldn't tell from her tone if she meant it as a blessing or a curse. 'What an awful thing to happen. I bet that other woman's pleased she missed it now.' She noticed his bemused expression, and added: 'One of the guests who was booked in at the Mount. She was here last night when we arrived.'

'Mrs Carmichael?' Penrose asked, remembering Hilaria's missing guest.

'I don't remember her name, but she signed in just before we did. She said she was here as a surprise for someone.'

That was strange, Penrose thought; Hilaria hadn't said anything about a surprise. He wondered which guest the late arrival was connected with, and looked round for the hotelier to see if there was any information he could add, but he was far too busy in the dining room with a Christmas pudding and a bottle of brandy. Violet thanked him again and returned to the bar, and Penrose went back to the telephone but it rang before he got there. 'What have you got for me, Bill?' he demanded, much to the surprise of the woman on the other end who was calling about a last-minute room for the night. 'I'm sorry, you'll have to call back later,' he said, replacing the receiver. It rang again immediately. 'We're fully booked,' he barked down the telephone.

'Moonlighting again, sir?'

'Bill, thank goodness. Anything useful?'

'I tracked Dick Robertson down over his Christmas dinner,' Bill said, and Penrose recognised the animated tone of voice that the sergeant always used when he had something important to report. 'I thought you'd want to hear this straight away.'

'Go on. Have you got a description?'

'I have, but I don't think you'll need it.'

'Why not?'

'Because whatever your bloke looks like, I'm sure he doesn't answer to the name of Alexandra.'

'Alexandra?'

'That's right, sir. Alex Fielding – the one who works for *The Times*, at any rate – is a woman.'

Penrose was quiet for a moment, trying to take in the news. 'So where is she?' he said, as much to himself as to Bill. He looked at the man who called himself Fielding, now sitting with the rest of the islanders and engrossed in conversation. 'And who the hell is he?'

'I can't help you on the second one, but I've got Miss Fielding's address. It's in Southwark. Do you want me to send someone round to have a look while I carry on here?'

'No. Give the phone calls to someone else and go yourself. I need every scrap of help from that house, and you're the best pair of eyes I know. What do we know about her?'

'Young, ambitious and very talented, apparently. She's put a few people's backs up to get where she is, and she doesn't always play by the rules.'

'What do you mean by that?'

'The first thing Robertson said when he knew who I was calling about was "What's she done now?"'

'But as far as he was concerned, she was at St Michael's Mount? There wasn't a last-minute change of plan?'

'No. Miss Fielding had a train ticket for Thursday, but he hasn't heard from her since she left the office late on Tuesday night. She was supposed to telephone him on Christmas Eve with an update, but he wasn't surprised that she didn't. He told me that she pretty much pleases herself once she's on a job, and he puts up with it because she's good enough to get away with it. As tough as any of the boys, apparently.'

'What about her personal life?'

'That was interesting. Robertson said he knows nothing about her at all, even though he's been her editor for five years. He's asked to be kept informed – in confidence, obviously.'

'All right, thanks. And you say he's at home?'

'That's right, sir, and he'll be there all day. I've told him you might want to speak to him.'

Penrose took down the number. 'Good. You'd better get going, Bill, while I decide what to do. If I leave it too long, we won't be able to get back across to the Mount, but I'd rather not take Fielding back there until I've heard from you. Telephone me here as soon as there's some news.'

8

Their house felt safe after the confusion of the day, but Nora knew it couldn't last. For now, though, she let Tom fuss around her without criticism, using the wrong tea and forgetting to warm the pot – all the things that usually drove her to distraction, but which suddenly felt like the small acts of love that might just save her. She watched him in silence, afraid to open her mouth in case she said something that destroyed the closeness between them. Now that she had had the peace and time to think about it, she knew what he had done for her in Emily's house: nothing else made sense.

He put the pot down on the table and took her hand. 'Tell me what happened, Nora. It'll be all right, I'll make sure of that, but you've got to trust me. I need to know everything, or I can't help you.'

She touched his face, wondering why it had taken something so dreadful to bring them together again after the strain of recent months, why one grief could only be repaired by another. 'You can't help me, Tom – no one can. Not after what I've done, but I love you for trying.'

There were tears in his eyes now, and she was ashamed of what she had done to him and their life together. 'Don't give up, Nora,' he begged. 'Promise me you'll do as I say. I'm *not* losing you. I can't. We just have to make sure they can't prove anything.' He didn't understand, because his faith had never been as strong as hers, but she would be punished, whether or not the police discovered the truth. '*Promise* me,' he urged again, and she nodded.

'All right. I'll do whatever you want me to.'

'Start by telling me what happened.'

She forced herself to relive the previous morning, stopping only to answer his queries, grateful that he offered no judgement on anything she said. 'How did you know?' she asked when he was satisfied. 'How could you possibly know what needed doing?'

'I saw you go in while I was working down in the harbour,' he said, 'and I watched for you to come out, because I'd been so worried about you, what with not hearing anything from Jenna and how upset you'd been. When you left, you went home, not up to the castle like I thought you would, and I wondered if something was wrong.'

'So you checked on Emily?'

'Not exactly. I went to ask her advice. Anything I did, anything I said just seemed to make things worse between us recently, and she was always so wise. I thought if anybody could help us come to terms with Jenna, she could.'

And he was right, Nora thought; in the most tragic of ways, Emily had helped. 'I didn't mean to hurt her, Tom. Really I didn't. I'd do anything to change what I've done – anything.'

'Of course you didn't mean to do it, and it's my fault as much as yours. I should have talked to you instead of bottling everything up. That way, you might not have felt so alone. But it's done now, love, and there's no undoing it. We just have to stay calm and decide what to do. Which of the nativity figures was it? I'll go up and get it tonight, when everyone's gone to bed, just in case you didn't clean it properly. We'll need to get your keys back from Penrose.'

Nora could have wept with shame to think of it there, in the church – a thing of evil now, hiding so innocently in the crib. 'You can't, Tom. Even if you had my keys, the policeman's said no one's to go in there. They're probably watching it for all I know.'

'All right, it doesn't matter. He won't think to look there, and anyway – who's to say he'll be looking for anything? As far as he's concerned, it was an accident.'

There was a knock at the door, and Nora froze. 'Don't answer it,' she pleaded, clutching at his hand, but he stood up and pulled away. 'Just ignore it, Tom.'

'I can't. We've got to behave normally, and hiding ourselves away is the worst thing we could do.' He must have seen the fear in her face, because he turned back and kissed the top of her head. 'Stay here. You're grieving for a friend, and no one can blame you for that. I'll deal with it.'

She did as she was told, waiting urgently for the voice to see how much she should fear it. Tom showed their visitor through to the kitchen, and Nora was relieved to see that it was only one of her neighbours.

'Mary's just come to see how you are, love,' he said. 'Miss St Aubyn asked her to call in, just to be on the safe side.'

Mary put her nurse's bag down on the table. 'That's right. She thought you might need something for the shock. It's quite an ordeal, what you've been through today. Poor Emily, God rest her soul.' She shook her head, and Nora wondered how many times she would have to go through this conversation. 'She fell down the stairs, I hear?'

'That's right,' Tom said, and answered the subsequent questions so patiently that Nora scarcely knew where he got his strength from.

'Do you want something to help you sleep?' Mary asked, when she had finished her examination.

Nora shook her head; she craved nothing more than a merciful oblivion, but she didn't trust it. 'No, thank you. I'll be going back to work in a bit. Keeping busy will help me more than anything else.'

'All right, but let me know if you change your mind. And you take it easy, Nora. Miss St Aubyn was concerned about you, and Emily wouldn't want you making yourself ill over her.' Nora choked back a sob, willing Mary to leave and give her the freedom to cry, but she turned back at the kitchen door. 'Oh, I nearly forgot. I've been meaning to give you this for days. I accidentally picked it up with my post at the Change House, and it's been knocking round in my bag ever since.' She laid an envelope on the kitchen table, and Nora stared in horror at Jenna's handwriting. The Christmas card had been posted on the fifteenth of December.

'How long have you had this?' she asked, not caring if it sounded like an accusation.

'Best part of a week, probably.' Mary laughed, and shrugged her shoulders. 'You know how it is at Christmas – you get busy and things are forgotten. Makes you wonder why we worry, though, doesn't it, the news we've had today? Emily's death puts things in perspective.' She sighed, oblivious to the effect her words were having. 'I hope the card wasn't important.'

'Important? Do you have any idea—'

'All right, love, don't get yourself worked up.' Tom glanced apologetically at Mary, and showed her to the door. 'You've got to be more careful,' he insisted, when they were on their own again. 'Think about what you're saying.'

'I can't do this, Tom,' she said quietly, knowing as soon as she had spoken the words that there was no going back on them. 'It's all been for nothing, and I can't keep lying, not even for you. This is so wrong.'

He took her face in his hands and she began to resent the despair in his eyes, the only thing now that was stopping her from ridding herself once and for all of this crippling guilt. 'Please Nora, just trust me,' he begged. 'If we hold our nerve, we can get through this. It was an accident, for God's sake. You didn't mean to hurt her. I've only made it look like what it was.'

'But what if they find out what you've done? Penrose isn't stupid. They might be able to prove that Emily didn't fall down the stairs.'

'Even if they can, they won't suspect you. Sooner or later, they'll find out who killed the vicar, and the chances are they'll lay Emily's death at the same door.'

He had thought it all through, she realised, and the knowledge that he was prepared to sacrifice someone else to save her filled her with a bewildering mixture of horror and gratitude. Then another thought struck her. 'But Penrose knows I was in the church,' she said, with panic in her voice. 'What if he thinks that *I* killed them both?'

9

The address in Southwark wasn't a house but a basement flat, part of a tired-looking building in a terrace of similar properties, all skulking in a maze of narrow streets off the Blackfriars Road. Kids were playing up and down the street as Fallowfield arrived, full of energy in the joy of their release from family duties, and he smiled as a volley of snowballs hit the car on its way past. It seemed that the children were the only ones left standing in this cold, mid-afternoon lull, the footnote to Christmas morning and still far too early for the evening revelries to begin. As he parked outside the address he had been given, it seemed to Fallowfield that most of the city had retreated behind drawn curtains to its fireside.

He got out and stood at the top of the basement steps, noticing that the chaste white snow – undisturbed as far as the door – seemed out of place in this run-down part of London. There were no lights on that he could see, here or in any other room of the house, and he guessed that the flats above were empty or deserted for the Christmas holidays; either way, Alex Fielding's most immediate neighbours would be of no use to his inquiries. The one window at basement level had its curtains tightly drawn, so he went straight past and knocked firmly on the front door. As he had expected it to, the house frustrated him with its silence.

There was no question that he had to get inside, through fair means or foul. He could waste time looking for a back entrance to try, or he could go with an instinct that the woman he was looking for was in no position to complain about forced entry. A second knock, and then a third, brought no response, so he went back to the car to fetch a jemmy. The wood gave easily, and he found himself in a dark hallway with three doors leading off it and a rear exit to a yard. 'Miss Fielding?' he called, his voice unnaturally loud in the silence. 'Miss Fielding, are you all right?' His breath fogged the air and he shivered; there was barely a noticeable difference between the temperatures inside and out, and the flat reeked with the earthy smell of damp. A man's overcoat, scruffy and frayed at the sleeves, hung on a hook inside the door, and he wondered if it belonged to the photographer.

The room on his right – the one with the window to the street – was a bedsit, sparsely furnished with a couple of shabby armchairs pulled up to a gas fire and a metal army bed in the corner, unmade and covered in a couple of thin grey blankets, woefully inadequate for the time of year. Old copies of *The Times* were piled high at the head of the bed and used as a makeshift side table; a half-drunk cup of tea and an empty cigarette packet had been left on top of them, and there was a gas ring and kettle on the floor, but no evidence of other home comforts, and he guessed that Fielding lived for her work. Even so, after the festive atmosphere of the last few days it was strange to walk into a home so devoid of Christmas; the hardest of hearts and the busiest of lives usually succumbed to some grudging acknowledgement of the season, but here there was nothing – no decoration or card, no treat or luxury, no sentimentality of any sort. Perhaps she had simply been too busy, he thought, or had decided that any preparations were a waste of time when she was going away.

The smell in the flat changed unmistakeably as he walked further down the hallway, and he knew then what he was going to find when he opened the second door. Alex Fielding's body was on the floor beside her bed. Her blood had drenched the threadbare rug where she lay, and the spray marks on the sheets and walls testified to how viciously her throat had been cut. The assailant seemed to have taken her by surprise because there were no signs of a struggle in the room; on the contrary, a half-packed suitcase sat neatly on the bed, filled with clothes that seemed at a glance much smarter than the pullover and trousers she was dressed in, and a new, emerald green evening dress – still with its price tag – hung on the wardrobe; something in its hopefulness saddened him. Reluctantly, Fallowfield covered his nose and mouth with a handkerchief and bent over the dead woman. Decomposition had been slowed down considerably by the freezing cold temperatures in the flat, but the body was beginning to look bloated and discoloured. Outside, the sound of children playing in the street seemed suddenly absurd and out of kilter.

He gave the rest of the room a cursory search to make sure that he hadn't missed anything that might tell him more about Alex Fielding or her killer, but there was nothing. As far as he could see, there were no cameras or photographic equipment of any kind in either of the rooms he had checked so far, and the third door led only to a bathroom, stark and impersonal like the rest of the flat. He went back to the room he had started in, wondering who slept in the army bed. It was reasonable to assume that Fielding's killer had taken her camera and was, in all probability, now using it as part of his deception on St Michael's Mount – but was it someone she knew, perhaps even someone she had lived with? Hopeful of offering Penrose answers as well as more questions, Fallowfield scoured the flat for anything that might provide a clue to the impostor's identity or Fielding's death, but every new idea – from the yard to the bathroom cabinet – drew a blank.

He was on his way back to the car to radio for help when he remembered the suitcase on the bed. On the off chance that Fielding was taking something more interesting than smart clothes to Cornwall, he stepped carefully around her body to examine the packing, but the only other items in the main compartment were two pairs of shoes and a wash bag. He had more luck in the side flap, where he found a notepad and a sheaf of photographs. The pad contained ideas for the assignment at the Mount, together with scribbled notes about the island and even more information on Marlene Dietrich – background research which proved little more than Fielding's diligence. The photographs, too, seemed to be of the film star – nothing remarkable, just shots of her leaving a hotel or arriving at a social engagement, usually with a handsome escort on her arm, and Fallowfield flicked quickly through them, assuming that they were the photos which Fielding herself had taken for *The Times*. He stopped abruptly when he arrived at the last few images, astonished to see himself in one of them; he was leaving an inquest with Penrose, and he remembered the photograph appearing in *The Times* a few weeks ago, part of the newspaper's coverage of a recent murder, where a man had killed his wife and three children in Kensington. Quickly, he laid the other pictures out on the bed, wondering why Fielding had been so interested in this particular case, but it soon became obvious that the connection between the photos wasn't the case at all, but the man investigating it. Every one of the dozen photographs featured Detective Chief Inspector Archie Penrose as its main subject – at a murder scene or a trial or a police station – and some of them went back years.

There was no time to speculate on what any of this might mean. Aware that Penrose was waiting for news, with time stacked against him, Fallowfield hurried to the police box at the end of the street to telephone for help.

10

'Who do *you* think did it?' Marta asked, pouring them each an early sherry in the welcome peace of her room. 'My money was on one of the other guests at first, when we thought it was just the vicar, but after what Archie told us about the woman from the museum, I'm inclined to suspect someone closer to home.'

It sounded like they were discussing the plot of a crime novel, Josephine thought, struck by the peculiar situation in which they found themselves: the momentous sequence of events that had taken place since they got to Cornwall was as shocking as anything she had ever experienced, and yet – because the people who had died were strangers, and they were struck by sadness and injustice rather than grief – it was impossible not to speculate. 'I can't make my mind up, but I do know we should have told Archie about yesterday. I was so worried about him that I didn't think to say anything, but *we* could have discovered Emily Soper's body if the housekeeper hadn't come between you and your enthusiasm for tin mining.' She frowned, staring at the fire. 'I know it's ridiculous, but Mrs Pendean was *very* keen for us to stay out of that museum. She said it was closed because of family commitments, and that's obviously not the case. Archie said Mrs Soper was spending Christmas alone.'

'Didn't you say she was nearly in tears in your room? Perhaps that's connected.'

'I thought it was to do with her daughter, because she'd just mentioned her, but that could have been a coincidence.'

'What about the vicar, though? Could he have seen something incriminating?'

'So she forced him up the tower and slit his throat?' Josephine shook her head. 'It's ridiculous that we're even *having* this conversation.'

Marta drained her sherry. 'I'm not sure I can face a cold table. Perhaps we should just go to bed and hope it's all been a terrible dream.'

Josephine knew exactly how she felt. As a child, she had always dreaded the end of Christmas Day, clinging like Cinderella to every last bit of magic, as if that could somehow delay the stroke of midnight; now, she couldn't wait for the day to be over.

There was a knock at the door, and Marta got up to see who it was. 'Do you mind if I join you for a moment?' Hilaria asked.

'Of course not. Come in.'

'Is there any news from Archie?' Josephine asked.

'Not yet, I'm afraid.' Hilaria looked at the photograph albums that he had brought from the museum. 'Have you been through those?'

'With a fine-tooth comb, but we haven't found anything.' The albums had been meticulous in their recording of every significant moment in the Mount's recent history – royal visits, family weddings, losses during the war – but they had given up no secrets relating to Richard Hartley or his death. 'We know a lot more about the island,' Marta added, 'but that's all.'

'How is Mrs Pendean?' Josephine asked. 'It must have been a terrible shock for her.'

'Yes, it was, but she's remarkably resilient. I've just been down to see her, and she's insisting on coming back to work to keep busy, even though there's very little for her to do. This isn't quite the house party we were planning.' Hilaria smiled sadly, then added: 'She's a strong woman, and she knows her own mind. That hasn't always made for the easiest of working relationships, I have to admit, but I can't fault her loyalty.'

'And she has a daughter?' Josephine said.

'Jenna, yes. She left us earlier this year, so it's the Pendeans' first Christmas without her. That can't be easy.'

'Do you mean she died?'

'What? Oh no, that wasn't a euphemism. Jenna took holy orders.'

'She's a nun?' Josephine had to hide a smile at the unabashed horror in Marta's question.

'A novice, yes. She takes her final vows in a couple of months.'

'Then she might as well be dead as far as her mother's concerned,' Marta said. 'I'm not surprised Mrs Pendean's upset.'

'Upset?'

Josephine repeated their conversation from the night before, and Hilaria sighed. 'Yes, she's still grieving, I suppose – that *is* the only word for it. It's put a great strain on them both, but on her in particular. She and Jenna were always so close.'

'It's not the sort of loss you expect to have to deal with, is it?'

'No. It's a great source of pride for the island, of course, a link back to our past, but at what personal cost?' She paused for a moment, and Josephine wondered what she was going to say. 'The convent asked me for a letter of testimony,' she admitted. 'It's standard procedure, apparently, to ask people about the candidate's life, but it put me in an impossible position.'

'Because she wasn't suitable?'

'No, precisely the opposite. It felt like a betrayal either way – the girl's wishes, weighed against the mother's love. I was having that very conversation with poor Richard only last night.'

Josephine was quiet for a moment, struck by the intense, everyday sadnesses that were simultaneously hidden and aggravated by Christmas, borne stoically behind closed doors. 'Did Mrs Pendean know Emily Soper well?' she asked.

'Oh yes, they've been friends for most of their lives. She was telling me just now how guilty she felt about her death, when—'

'Guilty?'

'Yes. She was punishing herself for not checking on Emily as soon as she realised that she wasn't at the morning service. She wouldn't have missed that for the world. I told her it would have made no difference by then, but she wouldn't have it.'

'Did *you* tell her that Mrs Soper was missing from church?'

Hilaria looked surprised by the question. 'No, I didn't mention it. She brought it up, so she must have noticed herself.'

'But she couldn't have done,' Josephine insisted. 'The Pendeans arrived late, if you remember, and they never got to the church. Mrs Pendean was so upset by what she saw on the tower that she went straight back to the castle. She wouldn't have had a chance to look at the congregation, so how could she possibly know that Emily Soper wasn't there?'

I I

Penrose put the telephone down, shocked by the brutality of the news from London, even though he had feared the worst. Had Alex Fielding been murdered simply to pave the way for someone with a very different agenda to take her place, he wondered, or was there more to it? The details of the photographs that Fallowfield had found in her suitcase bewildered and troubled him. Thinking back, he vaguely remembered a woman among the crowd of regular journalists who covered the city's high-profile crimes, but he hadn't known her name or even which newspaper she represented, and she had certainly never spoken to him. If that *had* been Alex Fielding, he was at a loss to know why she had found him so interesting.

He glanced at his watch, assessing how long he might have to wait for the back-up from Penzance; he would rather not make an arrest until they arrived, but neither did he want to waste time. Looking through to the bar, he studied the suspect now firmly in the frame for at least one murder, and was annoyed by his own reluctance to believe it – annoyed because the feeling had nothing to do with evidence or logic, but with the simple fact that he had come to like the man who called himself Fielding. There was no doubting the deception, though, and something as audacious as this could surely only have been achieved by someone familiar with the photographer, or at least with her

260

lifestyle; the impostor had been convincing enough to fool most of them, and if Marlene had been less knowledgeable about photography, he would probably still be getting away with it.

Dick Robertson's line was engaged, but he got through to the editor at the second attempt. 'Mr Robertson? It's DCI Archie Penrose. One of my colleagues should have been in touch with you . . .'

'Yes, just now. I'm still trying to take it in. Have you got the bastard who did it?'

'That's why I'm phoning. I was hoping you might be able to help me identify the man who's been passing himself off as one of your photographers.'

There was a silence at the other end, as Robertson considered the implications of what Penrose had said, and the instinct for self-preservation kicked in. 'You think he's connected to this paper?' he asked guardedly. 'Unless you're sure, Penrose, I'd be very careful—'

'I'm not saying that the newspaper is in any way culpable for Miss Fielding's death, but it's reasonable to assume that the man who has taken her place knew her routines and her schedule for this weekend. He obviously knew where she lived, and he was convincing enough for his deception to go undetected, at least at first.'

'Go on, then. What does he look like?'

'He's about thirty, with sandy brown hair, worn quite long, and a beard. Six foot, or thereabouts, and a London accent. Are there any reporters or photographers who fit that description?'

He heard the relief in Robertson's voice. 'No, sorry. There's no one like that on my staff.'

'What about past employees? Anyone who might hold a grudge against Miss Fielding?' A police car drew up outside and the landlord glared at Penrose as two men in uniform joined him by the reception desk, adding very little to the festive atmosphere, or to the hotel's reputation for a warm welcome.

'Not that I can think of,' Robertson was saying. 'The only person who looks anything like . . .' He tailed off, and when he spoke again, his tone was anything but dismissive. 'Christ, he was in the office with us – of course he was. But why would he . . .'

'Who was in the office?' Penrose demanded impatiently.

'Jack Naylor. But he's just the cleaner, for God's sake, he couldn't possibly have anything to do with—'

Penrose put the phone down without waiting to hear what Jack Naylor could or couldn't do. 'I'll need your dining room,' he said to the landlord, and signalled to the two policemen to follow him. 'Jack Naylor?' he called across the bar. Naylor realised his mistake as soon as he turned round, but the response had been instinctive and it was too late now to go back on it. He looked up, and it was the expression rather than the face itself that Penrose found so familiar. The muddle of fear, grief and curiosity was the same now in the man as it had been in the eyes of the boy staring back at him from the coal bunker, eighteen years ago to the day – and he looked so vulnerable that, for the briefest of seconds, Penrose was there again in that snow-covered yard, chilled to the core and feeling the raw, helpless despair that he had back then. In spite of the circumstances, his overwhelming emotion was sadness. 'You *are* Jack Naylor?' he said quietly, and the man nodded. 'Then, Mr Naylor, I'm arresting you on suspicion of the murder of Alexandra Fielding, Richard Hartley and Emily Soper.'

Naylor stood up, and Penrose was relieved that he made no attempt to argue. 'Where do you want to do this?' he asked.

'Please come with me.'

Everything had happened so suddenly that it took the other people round the table a moment to catch up, and Penrose and Naylor were on their way out of the bar by the time Johnny Soper launched himself across the room. 'You bastard! What did you do to my mother? I'll fucking kill you.'

The policemen pulled him away while Naylor just stood there taking the blows, then watched as Trannack tried to calm Soper down. Penrose waited to see if his prisoner would deny responsibility for the third charge against him, which seemed so different from the others, but he didn't. 'It's terrible to feel that kind of rage,' he said instead. 'It eats you up inside, and then you're lost.'

Penrose heard the emotion in his voice, and realised that this was the first time in his career that he had wanted to be wrong. They went through to the restaurant, leaving one of the policemen in the bar to keep an eye on things there. The room had been emptied but not cleared, and still smelt strongly of roast turkey and alcohol, and Penrose tried in vain to remember a more inappropriate setting for an interview. He chose a table that couldn't be seen from reception, and swept the spent crackers and discarded novelties onto the floor. 'Sit down, Mr Naylor.'

'What happened to "Jack"? You were friendlier last time we met.'

'Last time we met, you hadn't killed anyone.' Naylor gave him a sad, faintly pitying look, as if he had failed to understand some fundamental truth, and Penrose remembered the conversation in the library the night before, when Richard Hartley – in Naylor's hearing – had raised the possibility that there was more to the horror in the slums than had ever been revealed; suddenly he wondered if he had been wrong to dismiss the rumours so readily.

He took the snowman decoration out of his pocket and slid it across the table. 'You kept this all those years.'

Naylor nodded, satisfied. 'I wondered if you'd recognise it.'

'That was taking a risk, wasn't it? Leaving something I'd recognise with the body.'

'Only if you assume I wanted to get away with it.' He shook his head to emphasise the words. 'No, this all started at Christmas, and it's right that it should end there.'

'But it doesn't end, does it?' Penrose said, angered by Naylor's arrogance in deciding the course of the story. 'Not for the people left behind. You should understand that better than anyone. It doesn't end for Angela Hartley or for Johnny Soper, just because you say it does. It doesn't end for Alex Fielding's family or her colleagues at *The Times*. She was a young woman with a bright future ahead of her. Who knows what she might have achieved? What gives you the right to decide who lives and who dies?'

Naylor smiled, but there was no malice in it. 'So you *don't* know everything,' he said, 'but you're still taking her side, just like everyone else did. They all favoured her, even then – the vicar and his wife, the newspapers, the authorities. She was the little girl, the clever one, the angel.'

'You mean Alex Fielding . . .'

'Was my sister, yes. Alice, as you knew her, although she

never acknowledged that when she grew up.' He accepted a cigarette from the packet that Penrose passed across the table. 'Alex was my sister, and she looked out for me – putting me up in her living room, getting me a run-of-the-mill job in the place where she shone, sweeping me the crumbs off her table. But that was all right.' He obviously sensed Penrose's scepticism, because he added: 'Really, it *was*. It was all right because I loved her and she loved me. Even what happened eighteen years ago was bearable because we faced it together. She never forgot your kindness, you know. Neither of us did, but *she* worshipped you.'

It came again, that familiar feeling of desolation that Penrose would have found hard to explain. 'And what *did* happen eighteen years ago? Do we know the truth, or was there more to it?'

Naylor ignored the question, lost in his thoughts, and Penrose knew that he would have to wait for the story to unravel in its own time. 'My sister said you saved her life that day. I always thought *I'd* done that, but apparently not.'

'What did she mean?'

He shrugged. 'That you'd given her a sense of purpose, I think. Do you remember? After you found us, we had to go back inside the house to wait for Hartley to come and collect us, and that policeman's case was at the bottom of the stairs. You caught us playing with one of the cameras, and we thought you were going to tell us off, but you sat us both down and showed us how it worked. You'll have noticed from my efforts this morning that Alex listened better than I did.' His fingers moved restlessly, absentmindedly fastening and unfastening one of the buttons on his jacket. 'You showed her how to take her first photograph, and you promised to bring it to her when it was developed. I didn't believe you, but you kept your word – that time, at least.' Naylor reached into his jacket pocket and pulled out a tattered image of himself as a little boy, and the forced smile in the picture seemed out of place against the pale face and haunted eyes. 'Alex treasured this. It killed her when you stopped coming to see us.'

'It wasn't my choice,' Penrose said, compelled to explain himself by the guilt he had always felt for making promises that he could never keep.

'No, I'm sure it wasn't, but Alex hoped for a while that you'd take us in.'

'I could never have done that.'

'It doesn't stop kids wishing, though, does it? We were split up not long after that. Alex was luckier than I was. The Fieldings were a nice family. Ordinary, but kind. They treated her well, and worked hard to give her what she wanted.' It was what he didn't say about his own fate that brought tears to Penrose's eyes, that and the idea of two young, grieving children nursing secret hopes that a stranger would save them just because he had been kind. The regret was so sudden and so powerful that he had to look away, but not before Naylor had noticed. 'Do you remember what I asked you when you found us?'

'Yes,' Penrose said immediately, the sadness of the question seared permanently into his memories of that day. 'You asked me why you weren't special enough to die with the others.' The boy had been sent on an errand that fateful Christmas Eve, and Penrose could easily understand why the question would always haunt him: why, on the day that his mother chose to remove herself and everything she loved from the world, had he been sent away? 'I couldn't give you an answer then,' he admitted, 'and I can't now.'

'It's all right. I have my answer.'

'Go on.'

'It was going to be a special Christmas for us,' Naylor said. 'The vicar had found my mother a position – did he ever tell you that?' Penrose nodded. 'It was something to do with his wife and one of her charities. We were moving away, leaving that terrible place behind and starting again, outside London.'

'Hence the note and the settled bills.'

He nodded eagerly, still the child at Christmas that every adult yearned to be. 'I was so excited. She sent me to pay the bread bill, and it seemed significant, like she'd trusted me with something that was symbolic of a new start. I remember running home that evening and thinking to myself that I wouldn't want to be anyone else in the world. That was a change for me. Normally, I'd have been ready to swap places with anybody, and just for an hour or two I understood what it was to be happy.' His face darkened and Penrose waited impatiently for him to continue, sensing that the narrative wasn't going to be the one he had most feared. 'I heard my ma screaming and shouting halfway down the street, and as I got closer, I heard Alex, too. She was crying, and I couldn't get upstairs fast enough. All I could think about was how Maisie and Emily could possibly be sleeping so soundly with such a racket coming from the next room. Then I saw that they weren't asleep.' Perhaps it was because Penrose had seen the aftermath of the tragedy for himself, but the pictures were so clear that he felt as if he were there at the boy's shoulder, watching the scene unfold. 'When I went next door, Tommy and Alfie were already dead and Ma and Alex were fighting over the knife. She had it at Alex's throat and Alex was trying to push it away. If I'd have been a couple of minutes later, that would have been it.'

'So you *did* rescue your sister,' he said, resisting the temptation to ask why you would save a life, only to take it years later.

'Somehow I pulled her away. She was hysterical, they both were, and I was so frightened but I managed to get in between them. Ma just kept coming, though. She tried to get at Alex again, and I knew she was going to kill her.'

He looked at Penrose, pleading with him to finish the story and say the words he couldn't bring himself to speak. 'Did you kill your mother, Jack?'

Naylor nodded. 'I didn't mean to. I just wanted her to stop, so I grabbed her hand and pushed her against the wall. The next thing I knew, the knife was in her neck and everything was quiet. I couldn't believe what I'd done. It all happened so quickly.'

'But it was self-defence,' Penrose insisted, trying to reconcile the remorse that was so evident in Naylor's face with the ruthlessness it must have taken to kill Richard Hartley. 'People would have understood. *I* would have understood.'

'Really?' He shook his head, unconvinced. 'As it was, some people thought I'd killed all of them. You were thinking that just now, when you brought me in here. I could see it in your face – you didn't want to believe it, but you did.'

It was pointless trying to deny it. 'I still don't understand, though,' Penrose said. 'If your mother had a new life to look forward to, why would she do something so terrible?' Naylor

268

said nothing, challenging him to find the answer to his own question. 'Tell me, Jack. Please.'

'If I'd had the choice, I'd have died on the spot rather than be left behind. I remember thinking that on the day of the funeral.' Penrose closed his eyes, remembering that bleak January day – hundreds of people crowded round a double grave as four tiny coffins were laid next to their mother, each with a bunch of snowdrops placed on top. 'I've spent my whole life feeling guilty for what I did, wondering if that's the reason Ma treated me differently that day. Perhaps there was always something bad in me, and she could see it. Alex did her best to heal that over the years . . .'

'So why punish her?'

'Because she didn't tell me the truth, not until this week. She could have taken all that pain away, but she didn't. She made me live with it, and rely on her to make it bearable.' Again he waited for Penrose to catch up, then continued half impatiently. 'You don't have to be a photographer to know that your eyes can play tricks on you. When I went into that bedroom, I saw my mother trying to kill my sister, but perhaps that's what I *wanted* to see. Perhaps it was better than the alternative.'

'Which was?' There was a long silence as the answer finally dawned on Penrose. 'You mean that *Alex* killed the other children?' he asked. Naylor nodded. 'Are you sure?'

'Yes, she admitted it.'

'Why now, after all this time?'

'Because I drove her to it. She didn't mean to say anything, but we were having a row and she said something in the heat of the moment that she couldn't take back.'

'What was the row about?'

'Christmas, of course. What else, at this time of year? It's a terrible time for us, for obvious reasons, but we've always got through it together.'

'And this year she was going away.'

'Yes, but it wasn't that. Alex was looking forward to the weekend, and I was pleased for her – she'd let me into the secret about Marlene Dietrich, and I knew how important it was for her career. And if I'm honest, I was quite looking forward to being on my own for once – just an ordinary bloke on Christmas Day. I think I'd even kidded myself that the memories might go away if Alex wasn't there to remind me.'

'So what changed?'

'I found out the truth. I heard your name by accident when I was in the editor's office, and I knew straight away that it wasn't Marlene she was excited about seeing. It was you. There was an old list of guests in the bin, so I read it to make sure that I hadn't got it wrong, and there you were – you *and* the Hartleys. Alex kept all that from me, and I didn't know why, so I confronted her with it when I got home. I asked her to take me with her, but she refused, and all those old insecurities came back. I was still the one left out in the cold, the one who wasn't wanted. I'd always be the kid who was sent away, and suddenly that made me angry rather than sad. I told Alex that she owed it to me after what I'd done for her – one weekend didn't seem too much to ask for saving her life. I wouldn't let it go, and in the end she just turned round and screamed at me that she didn't owe me anything because all I'd done was finish what she started.' He closed his eyes and screwed his hands into fists, digging his nails into the palms of his hands to stave off the tears. 'I couldn't believe what she was saying at first, but then it all made sense. That's why Ma turned on her – because of what she'd done to the others.'

That part did make sense, and although Penrose still recoiled from the idea that a twelve-year-old girl – a girl he had cared for – could be a murderer, he was experienced enough to know that history suggested otherwise. 'Do you know why she did it?' he asked, wanting at least an explanation if he had to accept the fact.

'Because she found out that the family was going to be split up. Ma could only afford to take the little ones with her, and we were old enough to stay behind and work. She hadn't told us everything because she didn't want to spoil Christmas.'

Such a natural thing for a mother to do, Penrose thought: keeping a painful secret to protect the last Christmas they would share as a family. He tried to imagine the grief and horror that Mollie Naylor must have felt when she saw what her daughter had done, and realised why she had done it; had she been there to testify, he wondered if she would have thanked her young son for unwittingly putting her out of her misery. 'People always said that violence was in our family,' Naylor added. 'My dad used to knock us around, so they thought it ran in the genes. Perhaps they were right, but they blamed the wrong kid – and Alex let them go on thinking it.'

'And she destroyed your love for your mother,' Penrose said. 'You've spent your life hating her for things she hadn't done, things she would *never* have done.'

Jack nodded, grateful for his understanding. 'I clung to Alex because she was the only person who could possibly know how it felt to have your family snatched away from you, the only person left alive who knew what I'd done and understood why, but even she wasn't who I thought she was. It was all a lie.'

'So you killed her in the heat of the moment?' Penrose said, wishing it to be true.

'No, not then, but I told her I was going to come here and tell you the truth – you *and* Hartley. She just laughed.'

'She didn't believe you?'

'She said that Hartley knew already. Apparently she told him all those years ago while we were staying at the vicarage, and he promised to protect her. It would be impossible for me to tell you how much I hated her in that moment – how much I hated them both. I've spent my whole life resenting something I didn't understand, but I've never felt a rage like that.'

Could it really be true that Richard Hartley had conspired to keep the truth of that day a secret? Penrose wondered. It was hard to contemplate, and the vicar's comments the night before had seemed genuine enough, yet he also knew how difficult it would have been for *him* to betray the girl's trust if he had been put in that impossible position; he would have done it, but it would have destroyed him, and the Hartleys had known both children much better than he had. In fact, he had always wondered why they didn't adopt the orphans themselves; perhaps now he knew the answer. 'When did you confront Richard Hartley?' he asked. 'You were obviously the past that he hadn't expected to see. Did he recognise you?'

'No, not at all. I think she did, though.'

'Mrs Hartley?'

Naylor nodded. 'She kept looking at me over dinner, like she knew me and couldn't place me, but nobody took any notice. She obviously didn't say anything to him, because it came as a shock when I told him. I did it as we were leaving the smoking room together, when you'd gone off to find Marlene. He'd just been telling us that he was going to preach a sermon about love, if you remember, so I thought I'd show him what love was really capable of.'

'You asked to meet him in the church?'

'Yes. After all that talk about the chair and St Michael, it seemed right that someone should judge *him* at the end. He spent his life deciding who to damn and who to save . . .'

'Not consciously,' Penrose argued. 'He was trying to do his best. He didn't deserve to die, especially not like that.'

He could see that his words had disappointed Jack. 'Neither did my mother,' he retaliated angrily, 'and she certainly didn't deserve to be blamed for it – so who gets to decide what's right and what's wrong? Whose secrets are kept and whose reputations are destroyed? Whose lives are worth protecting, and whose can be thrown away? Everybody passed a judgement that day, including you, and some of us are still living with it.'

And some are not, Penrose thought. 'Did Richard Hartley admit that he knew what Alex had done?'

'No. He swore she'd never said a word to him, but he'd have said anything last night. He was begging for his life.'

A note of doubt had crept into his voice. 'You could hardly bear to look at him this morning, when I asked you to photograph his body,' Penrose said.

'Of course I couldn't. I thought it was a trap.'

'There was more to it than that. You were worried that he'd been telling the truth, weren't you? The more you thought about it, the more you began to suspect that Alex had fooled you into killing for her all over again.'

'No! Why would she tell me that Hartley knew if he didn't?'

'To stop you coming here. To protect herself. She'd been lying for years to do that, so why baulk at it now? Richard's was a horrific death, Jack. You didn't just kill him. You tormented and humiliated him – a good man, who had always tried to do his best. How could you let yourself be manipulated like that?' Penrose heard the fury in his own voice and knew that he had overstepped the mark; Naylor's devastation was obvious, and nothing *he* said could make the man's remorse any more profound than it was already. In truth, it was himself that he was angry with, not Jack Naylor: they should all have asked more questions about what happened that Christmas, and he should have got to the truth eighteen years ago – not now, when it was far too late.

Naylor picked up the snowman from the table and looked at the bloodstained cotton. 'I thought of myself differently after Alex told me the truth,' he said. 'Does that make sense? Until then, I'd killed but I wasn't a killer. There was a reason for it, and I could always tell myself that it was for the best, no matter how terrible it seemed at the time. All that changed last week. I killed my mother, the person I loved most in all the world, who loved me. Nothing else mattered after that, or at least I thought it didn't. By the time I got here, it was just the end.'

'You didn't kill Mrs Soper, though, did you?' Penrose asked, and Naylor shook his head.

He got up and walked over to the Christmas tree that stood in the corner, and Penrose watched as he rubbed the pine needles between his finger and thumb and smelt their scent. 'My mother loved Christmas, did I ever tell you that?'

'I don't think so, but I remember the tree you had and how much love had gone into it. I remember the presents.'

'We never opened them because of what we thought she'd done. She worked so hard to get them for us, and they were just thrown away. It's funny, isn't it, the things that haunt you. After Alex told me what had happened, all I could think about was how ungrateful that was, and how hurt Ma would have been if she'd known.' He brushed a hand across his cheek and turned to Penrose. 'Every year it comes back, you know. Every year, when the music starts and the lights go up, I can't wait for Christmas to be over. It's actually quite a comfort to know I'll never see another one.'

12

As the afternoon wore on, Josephine and Marta decamped to the other bedroom, where there was a better view of the route across to the mainland. 'Any sign of Archie?' Marta asked as Josephine peered out into the semi-darkness.

'No, not a thing. Even if there was a boat on its way back to us, I'm not sure we could see it from here. We'll just have to wait and hope that he's all right.'

'I never want to hear the words "Christmas" and "house party" in the same sentence again as long as I live,' Marta said with feeling, as she put the parcel she had brought with her down on the bed. 'Still, at least I can finally stop lugging this around. It'll be your responsibility once you've opened it.' She tried to patch the wrapping paper where it had been torn in transit, but quickly gave up. 'Go on, you might as well open it now and finish the job.'

Intrigued, Josephine unwrapped the box and took out a black leather case which held an exquisite gold-plated Corona typewriter. 'This is beautiful,' she said, lifting it out and trying the keys. 'What a wonderful present.'

'I'm glad you like it, because it's a selfish gift really. I thought if we have to spend some time apart while I'm in America, the least we can do is write to each other. I want a letter from you every day, and I can't possibly read that much of your handwriting. It's ruined my eyesight already.'

'But glasses suit you.'

Marta laughed, then added more seriously: 'This goes with it as part of the present.' She handed over an envelope with Josephine's name typed neatly on the front. 'I thought I'd better try the machine out before I gave it to you. The bell has a particularly nice ring, I noticed.' Josephine removed the sheet of notepaper and read the words 'Come with me'. 'Consider it an IOU for the air tickets,' Marta added. 'The typewriter's portable, so if we don't need the letters, you can always bring it with you and write your next book on it instead.' She sat down next to Josephine and took her hand. 'You don't have to decide anything now, and this probably isn't the best time to discuss it. I know it might not even be possible, but it makes me feel better to think that we have a choice.'

'Of course we have a choice. I'm not any happier than you are about being on different continents.'

'So you'll think about it?'

'Yes, I'll think about it. Now, wait there.'

She fetched her bag and handed over the tissue-wrapped envelope. Marta opened it, looking first confused, then astonished. 'But these are the deeds to your cottage. You can't just sign half of it over to me.'

'Why not? It's always been *our* cottage, and it would mean nothing to me without you.' Marta began to object, but Josephine silenced her with a kiss. 'If it makes you feel any better, the cottage is a selfish present, too. I thought it might give you a reason to come home.'

'You're the only reason I need to come home – and it's not for ever. I promised you that.' She looked at the two gifts and smiled. 'They don't seem very compatible, do they?'

'Oh, I don't know. I think they sum us up quite nicely.'

The sound of the dinner gong drifted up from the hallway, and Marta looked at her watch. 'I thought supper was going to be later?'

'It's supposed to be at six.' The noise persisted, clearly a summons to go downstairs, and Josephine sighed. 'God knows what's happened now. We'd better go and see.'

13

The tide was in Penrose's favour when he was finally ready to go back to the Mount – by boat this time, and with the welcome support of the local police. It had taken him a while to explain to Johnny Soper why the man detained in custody was not being charged with his mother's murder, and Penrose was all too conscious that he had no alternative scenarios to offer. He was exhausted, the physical effort of crossing the causeway matched only by the mental strain of his interview with Jack Naylor, and he didn't relish the task ahead: Naylor's confession had stirred up too many memories, and Emily Soper's death – at the heart of this proud, tight-knit community – had all the hallmarks of another domestic tragedy, of other lives destroyed in the saddest of circumstances.

It was early evening as the boat sailed into the little harbour, and the lights from the front row of cottages were deceptively welcoming; as they docked at the east pier, he could almost believe that the sun had set on a normal day. Only the museum was in darkness, with one of the islanders standing guard outside, and he watched Johnny's face as he and Violet climbed the steps. 'She shouldn't be in there on her own,' Violet said, anticipating his next dilemma. 'Can we go to her? Pay our respects?'

'Not tonight, I'm afraid,' Penrose said. 'The pathologist is coming first thing in the morning, and I can't allow anyone else into the building until he's been, not even you. I know how wrong that sounds, but I do promise you that there's a reason for it. It will give us the best possible chance of finding out who did this.'

They accepted his explanation, but walked over to the building anyway and stood quietly outside. Penrose left them to their thoughts until they were ready to come up to the castle with him, and sent some of his Penzance colleagues on ahead to deal with Gerald Lancaster, glad to hand that particular inquiry over. He was just beginning to consider what to do first about the village murder when he saw Josephine and Marta coming towards him along the harbour. 'We've been looking out for you,' Josephine said. 'You've been gone so long. We were worried sick.'

More pleased to see them than he could possibly have said, Penrose brought them quickly up to date. 'I've got to tell Hilaria what's going on, so as soon as Mr Soper and his fiancée are ready, I'll take them up to the castle. She'll want to talk to them.'

'She's not there,' Marta said. 'She wanted to do something for the village after everything that's happened, so she's organising a memorial for Mrs Soper and we were summoned by gong to help. It's in that building down at the end.' She pointed along the harbour to a granite sail loft and workshop. 'Obviously we couldn't have it in the church.'

'It was a spur-of-the-moment thing, but all the islanders and staff are going,' Josephine added. 'Hilaria thought it would bring everyone together. Marlene's there with her.' She looked closely at him, obviously concerned. 'This has been a terrible day, hasn't it? That poor boy.' It was typical of Josephine to refuse to see things in black and white, and Penrose was grateful to her for articulating what he felt but could not allow himself to say. 'It's going to get worse, too,' she added. 'We've got news of our own.' He listened in surprise as she repeated a conversation they had had with Hilaria about Nora Pendean. 'Hilaria wanted to tackle her about it straight away, but we persuaded her to wait for you.'

'I'm glad you did. God knows how she might have reacted, innocent or guilty, when emotions are running high like this.' He was quiet for a moment, thinking about the housekeeper's behaviour at the museum; she had been so certain that her friend couldn't have gone to Marazion, and so upset – guilty, almost – about the cat, and yet her surprise at seeing the body had seemed genuine enough. 'I'll have to go and talk to her, but I need to see Hilaria first. She might want to be there when I question her. Where are the other guests?'

'All together, up at the castle,' Josephine said. 'Barbara Penhaligon is packed and ready to go on the first boat out, and Rachel Lancaster is looking after Mrs Hartley. She's going to stay with her for a bit, I gather.'

'Mrs Hartley isn't going to her sister?'

'Not immediately, no. She wants to be at home, where she was happy with Richard. That's understandable, I suppose. And Rachel is vowing to divorce her husband, so I suppose that's the weekend's silver lining.'

'God knows we could do with one. I'd better go and find Hilaria. Are you coming to the memorial?'

'No, we thought we'd leave them to it. They were very welcoming, but they don't need outsiders at a time like this. And anyway, we promised Hilaria we'd keep an eye out for Mrs Carmichael. She's expected, now that a crossing is possible.'

'Surely she won't come at the eleventh hour? Especially if she knows what's been happening here?'

'Oh, I think she will,' Marta said. 'It meant a lot to her to be here.'

Josephine smiled and Penrose looked at her curiously, but there wasn't time for any more conversation. Over by the museum, Violet was gently encouraging Johnny to come away. 'Miss St Aubyn is hosting an event in the village tonight to remember your mother,' Penrose said, when they rejoined him. 'She'll be glad to know you're here.'

'That's kind, isn't it, Johnny?' Violet said, but he just nodded, looking utterly lost and dazed now that the news had sunk in. The small group walked along the harbour to the building on the other side of the tram shed, a large carpenter's workshop which was traditionally used for village gatherings. The chairs were still laid out from the Christmas concert of a few days before, but all the decorations had been respectfully removed and the only trace of the festive season was a practical one: a series of trestle tables running along one end of the room, gradually filling with food from the castle. It was typical of Hilaria to have come up with such a simple, unifying gesture, and the only thing that was out of place was the apron that Marlene was wearing as she helped the staff to butter bread. Under different circumstances, the expression on Violet Carter's face would have been priceless.

'Archie, thank God you're back,' Hilaria said when she saw him. 'We were all so worried about you. Is there any news?' Before he had a chance to answer, she noticed Johnny standing behind him. 'It's Mr Soper, isn't it? I thought you were in Plymouth, but how fitting that you're here. I'm so very, very sorry for your loss. Your mother was a fine woman.'

She took his hand and spoke with such sincerity and warmth that Johnny seemed comforted for the first time since hearing the news, and Penrose waited impatiently for Hilaria to be free; he was keen to get on with his unfinished business, but he couldn't possibly discuss Nora Pendean in front of Johnny.

'Mr Penrose?'

Penrose turned round, so deep in thought about the housekeeper that it startled him to see her husband. 'Mr Pendean, what can I do for you? How is your wife?'

'Nora's all right, but I need to speak to you. It's urgent.'

'Tom!'

A series of fleeting emotions passed across Pendean's face when Johnny Soper called his name – surprise, followed by affection and then awkwardness. 'What are you doing here?' he asked, half in anger. 'You're supposed to be up country.'

'We came down to tell Mum the good news. Vi and I have just got engaged.'

His eyes filled with tears again, and Penrose expected the older man to comfort him somehow, or at least offer his condolences, but he didn't. 'What did you want to talk to me about, Mr Pendean?' he asked.

The question was ignored, and Tom spoke first to Johnny. 'I'm so sorry, lad,' he said. 'I killed your mum. I didn't mean to, and I wish to God that things had been different, but I can't let you go on wondering.' He turned back to Penrose. 'I killed Emily Soper,' he repeated. 'She didn't fall down the stairs.'

Everyone fell silent, and Penrose felt the shock ripple through the room. 'Mr Pendean, are you sure of what you're saying?' he asked. 'Please think very carefully before you continue.'

'Yes, I'm sure,' Tom replied, without hesitation. 'I killed her on the morning of Christmas Eve. We had an argument over something and nothing, and I lost my temper. Then I panicked, and tried to make it look like an accident.'

'But you were like a father to me,' Johnny objected, and the hurt in his voice was so much like Naylor's that Penrose could hardly bear to hear it. 'You cared more about me than my own father ever did. How could you do that?'

The two men stared at each other and Penrose was about to intervene when another voice beat him to it. 'Tom, what have you been saying?' Nora Pendean stood in the doorway, her face ashen with fear as she looked at her husband. 'What have you said, Tom?'

'I've told them what I did, love,' he said calmly. 'I couldn't go on hiding it. Johnny has a right to know what happened to his mum.'

'But you *didn't* do it!' She turned to Penrose. 'Don't believe a word of it. He's saying it to protect me, so please don't punish him. He's only lying because he loves me.'

'Listen to me, Penrose. I went in to see Emily yesterday morning, while Nora was up at the castle. She'd been mending one of the kings from the nativity and she had it on the counter in front of her, ready to be collected, so I offered to take it to save Nora the bother of coming down when she had so much else to do. We got talking, and Emily said something about our daughter that made me see red, so I just lashed out. I had the figure in my hands, and before I knew it, Emily was lying on the floor. I tried to help her, but there was nothing I could do . . .'

'Tom, please!' his wife screamed.

'. . . so I washed the figure and cleaned up after myself, and put Emily where we found her today.'

284

'And Mrs Pendean had nothing to do with this?'

He shook his head. 'No. I should never have told her, but she knew something was wrong. She wanted to help me, but all she did was put the figure back in the church last night. I swear that's the only part she played in any of this.'

'That's why you were in the church last night, Mrs Pendean?'

'No, don't listen to him. I went to the church to pray for forgiveness – for what *I* did, nothing to do with Tom.'

Penrose didn't know who to believe, but he could see that neither was about to stand down, and he knew that the only chance of getting to the truth was to question them separately once there was some forensic evidence to go on. There was certainly nothing to be gained from continuing such a public debate, particularly in front of the dead woman's son. 'I'd like you both to come with me,' he said quietly. 'You'll be taken to Penzance police station, and held there on suspicion of the murder of Emily Soper, and of conspiracy to pervert the course of justice.'

He took them outside, relieved that neither seemed inclined to object, and was just in time to see a couple of uniformed men from Penzance leading Gerald Lancaster over to the boats. He waved to attract their attention, and the detective inspector responsible for pursuing the case peeled off from the group. 'Busy day today, sir?' he said, looking curiously at the Pendeans.

'You could say that.' Penrose took him to one side and briefed him on what had happened. 'I'm hoping for some physical evidence to prove which one of them is telling the truth,' he said, 'but in the meantime, you'll have my full report first thing in the morning.'

'Thank you, sir.'

He watched as the Pendeans were escorted to the boat, then a thought struck him. 'Wait a moment,' he called. The policeman did as he asked and the couple turned back in surprise. 'Which of the three kings was the murder weapon?' he asked, looking quickly between them for their separate reactions.

Tom hesitated, baffled by the question, but Nora answered immediately. 'Melchior,' she said. 'I killed Emily with Melchior.'

'But I don't know their names,' her husband objected. 'That doesn't mean—'

'Gold, frankincense or myrrh, Mr Pendean?' Penrose interrupted. 'If you washed the figure, surely you noticed what he was carrying?'

'Myrrh,' Pendean said, looking nervously at Nora.

Penrose saw the relief on her face as her husband gave the wrong answer, and nodded to his colleagues to take them away. Deep in thought, he walked back along the harbour to the sail loft. Usually, it would have frustrated him to hand over a case before it was finished, but he was happy to let this one go. Perhaps it was because the island was so close to his heart, perhaps because he felt sorry for Hilaria, but the sadness of the day had affected him more than he would have cared to admit. 'So, Mr Penrose, will we all sleep safely in our beds tonight?'

He looked up and saw Marlene standing by the harbour wall, smoking a cigarette and looking out to sea. 'Some of us will,' he said, walking over to join her. 'Some of us might struggle a little.'

She passed him her cigarette case. 'I'm so glad you have come back. I didn't want to leave without saying goodbye.'

'You're going?'

'In the morning, yes. Miss St Aubyn has offered me a car to the airfield at Torquay. I'm going to Paris to be with Maria and her father. At times like this, you realise how important family is.'

Penrose nodded, suddenly longing more than anything to see his own daughter. 'Yes, you're right.'

'It has been such a pleasure to meet you, Archie. I wish the circumstances had been different – we might have had time to get to know each other better. You must come and see me when I'm next in London. Promise me you will.'

'I promise.'

They went back inside, where some of the islanders had begun to gather. Johnny was surrounded by well-wishers, and Penrose waited to speak to him. 'As soon as there's any news, you'll be the first to know,' he said, when he had explained what was happening.

'And you and Miss Carter must stay at the castle for as long as you need to,' Hilaria added. 'It goes without saying that we would love you both to make your home on the island. Your mother ran the museum for so many years, and I can't think of anyone better to take over the reins. Take some time to talk it through. You don't have to give me your answer until you're ready.'

Penrose saw the look of horror pass across Violet's face, but she needn't have worried. 'That's very kind, Miss, and I know how much the Mount meant to my mother, but we've got our own life now,' Johnny said. He squeezed Violet's hand. 'We're happy as we are, but thank you for the offer.'

Hilaria smiled. 'Well, if you change your mind, you'll always be welcome here.'

'Will *you* go away for a while now?' Penrose asked her, as she watched them walk off together.

'You must have read my mind. I'll spend a few days with my father when everything is settled here, then go abroad for a bit. Somewhere hot, I think, where they don't hold much with Christmas.' He smiled, but she didn't return it. 'Not for long, though. I'll have to leave permanently sooner or later, so I want to make the most of the time I've got left. There are still things to do.'

She left him to greet some new arrivals, and Penrose was grateful to slip quietly away for some time on his own. He lit another cigarette and stared up at the sky, which was remarkably clear and still after the violence of the storms, strewn with frosted white stars that offered all the light he needed. In the distance, he heard the chugging of a boat and watched as it approached the island, cutting its engine as it entered the harbour. The boatman jumped out and helped a woman with a suitcase to climb the steps, then set off back to the mainland, and Penrose watched as Josephine and Marta walked along the pier to welcome the house party's final guest. To his surprise, they obviously knew her, and as the three women hugged and turned towards the castle, he wondered why they hadn't mentioned that Mrs Carmichael was a friend.

He caught them up by the old dairy, halfway up the Mount. Josephine saw him first and gave him that smile again, then caught the stranger's arm. The woman turned round, unwinding the scarf from her face, and Archie stared at his daughter in astonishment and joy. 'Phyllis! What on earth are you doing here? And what's all this about Mrs Carmichael? Surely you haven't got married without telling me?'

Phyllis threw back her head and laughed, then put her case down and gave him a hug. 'Of course I haven't! And you'll have to ask Josephine and Marta about Mrs Carmichael. They made all her arrangements.'

'With a little help from fate,' Josephine said. 'Phyllis is our Christmas present to you. She was coming as a surprise to Loe House, but then the plans changed and we had to sort everything out with Hilaria. We didn't want to give the game away, though, so we invented the mysterious Mrs Carmichael for the sake of the guest list.'

'Except Mrs Carmichael got held up in the blizzards and missed her connection, so she had to spend the night at the hotel in Marazion.'

'You were at the Godolphin Hotel all the time I was there?' he asked, and Phyllis nodded. 'Why didn't you let me know?'

'Because you were obviously busy! I heard about what was going on from the staff, so I thought I'd better wait until things were more peaceful. Anyway, I wanted it to be special – we've never spent Christmas Day together before.' Phyllis had been born during the war, but Archie and her mother had drifted apart and Archie had been oblivious to her existence until very recently. Missing her childhood had angered and saddened him, but now, as Phyllis smiled at him and gave him another hug, he couldn't imagine loving his daughter more, even if he had been part of her life all along. 'Please tell me that Marlene Dietrich really is here?' she said. 'I've been dying to meet her.'

'You're just in time. She's leaving in the morning, but I'll introduce you later.'

'What's she like?'

'Fabulous,' Marta said, 'and she likes your father *very* much. In fact . . .'

They walked ahead, chatting about Marlene, while Josephine hung back with Archie. 'I'll never forget the look on your face just now,' she said, taking his arm. 'It made Christmas what it's supposed to be.'

'Thank you, Josephine,' he said. 'This would have been a wonderful surprise at any time, but after everything that's happened since we got here . . .'

'You couldn't have done more, Archie.' He was about to brush her concern away, but she had always been able to read his thoughts, and there was something precious in the fact that she cared enough to know him better than he knew himself. 'I'm sure you're looking back now, thinking that you could have asked different questions and Jack Naylor's life would miraculously have been a bed of roses from that day onwards, but you couldn't. Life doesn't work like that. If it did, Marta and I would have arrived early yesterday and been chatting to Emily Soper when Mrs Pendean came in to collect the nativity figure. These deaths aren't your fault.'

'Perhaps not, but—'

'Do you know the first thing that Phyllis said when she got here, after she'd asked how you were?'

'No.'

'She told us that she'd watched you from the window of the hotel while you were going about your work and getting ready to come back to the island. You spent a long time talking to a young man by the boats. I'm assuming it was Jonathan Soper?'

Archie nodded. 'That's right. I was explaining that Jack hadn't killed his mother, and promising to find out who did.'

'Phyllis said how kind you were to him. Obviously, she didn't know the circumstances, but she could see how much you cared and what a difference it made to him. She told us how proud she was that you were her father.'

'Did she?'

'Yes, she did. And when we explained what had happened, she said that she wished she'd known you better when *her* mother was killed, because you would have helped her like no one else could.' He felt again the tears that had been threatening all day, and this time he didn't fight them. 'Take a lesson from Dickens, Archie. You can't change the past, but the future doesn't have to be full of ghosts as well.'

They walked on in silence as the steep climb up to the castle took its toll. 'Talking of brighter futures, I thought we might move on to Loe House tomorrow,' Archie said. 'After lunch, when all the formalities here are dealt with. How does that sound?'

'Like all our Christmases have come at once,' Josephine said. 'We thought you'd never ask.'

ACKNOWLEDGEMENTS

When I sat down to write about a beautiful island, cut off by extreme circumstances, I could have had no idea that – within the space of a few months – St Michael's Mount would indeed be isolated from the mainland, its causeway eerily deserted in the wake of another international crisis. As I write these acknowledgements, the island has just reopened to the public, with the castle shortly to follow, and I wish everyone who lives and works there a safe and happy future. There really is nowhere quite like it. Today, St Michael's Mount is managed in a unique partnership by the St Aubyn family and the National Trust, and you can find out more at www.stmichaelsmount.co.uk.

I'm extremely grateful to Lord and Lady St Levan, James and Mary St Aubyn, for taking the time to talk to me about the Mount's history and their personal experiences of looking after such a special place, and for showing me parts of the castle normally closed to the public. I will never forget my climb to the top of the church tower to see St Michael's Chair, although not even a desire to make this book as authentic as possible could persuade me to sit on it.

This novel is also indebted to the time and generosity of Stephen Mathews, whose family has lived on St Michael's Mount for generations, and who gave me a wonderful insight into the unique life of an islander. Other accounts of the Mount by Sir John St Aubyn, Joan Wake, Diana Hartley, Jane Mason and Barbara Steer gave valuable additional information on the island's legends and history. *The Butler's Guide* by Fiona St Aubyn and former castle butler Stanley Ager contains wonderful memories of entertaining in the 1930s as well as a useful guide to the etiquette of house parties.

The Honourable Hilaria St Aubyn left her home at the Mount on her father's death in 1940, but is remembered there to this day with great respect and affection. An intrepid traveller, she was admired for her charitable work, and loved for her kindness. She died in 1983, aged eighty-eight.

The Mount was promised by Hitler to Joachim Von Ribbentrop, who often visited Cornwall during his time as German Ambassador to Britain. Andrew Lanyon's *Von Ribbentrop in St Ives* gives a fascinating account of those years. I'm sorry that the scope of this book didn't allow me to do full justice to Marlene Dietrich's courageous and spirited war work, but I hope it shows a woman who was perhaps even more remarkable off screen than she was on it. There are brilliant accounts of a long life, well lived, in Dietrich's autobiography, *My Life*, and in her daughter's book, *Marlene Dietrich: The Life* by Maria Riva.

Huge thanks to my editor, Walter Donohue; to my publicist, Sophie Portas; and to every single department at Faber, whose loyalty to these novels means the world to me, as does the continued support and friendship of my agent, Veronique Baxter, and the dedication of her colleagues at David Higham Associates, Nicky Lund and Sara Langham. I'm grateful to Gráinne Fox of Fletcher & Company and Matthew Martz and Jenny Chen at Crooked Lane Books for taking such good care of Josephine in the US. The longevity of any series is a collective effort, and I appreciate the efforts of everyone who works so hard to enable me to breathe life into the characters I love.

Love and thanks, as always, to my family and friends, whose enthusiasm and kindness never cease to amaze me. And to Mandy, who makes each book better than it would otherwise have been, and never more so than this one: thank you for the title and the real-life events that inspired the story, and thank you for making Christmas sparkle from September to the end of January.